THE EX
BOYFRIEND

BOOKS BY RONA HALSALL

THE EX BOYFRIEND

RONA HALSALL

bookouture

Published by Bookouture in 2020

An imprint of Storyfire Ltd.
Carmelite House
50 Victoria Embankment
London EC4Y 0DZ

www.bookouture.com

ISBN: 978-1-83888-816-9
eBook ISBN: 978-1-83888-815-2

For all my friends, in real life and online, for the love and support during lockdown. I have never procrastinated so hard in my life, but you guys made it possible.

PROLOGUE

Becca twisted the chocolate wrapper and tied it into a neat knot. Then another and another. Her eyes glanced at the double doors which led into the A & E department before checking the clock on the wall again. Almost forty minutes since her husband, Dean, had arrived and she'd been asked to wait outside. Their three-year-old daughter, Mia, was having tests, and the medical team had insisted that Becca stay in the waiting room to calm down, her agitation making her daughter more anxious than was necessary. To be fair, she had been screechy and loud when she thought she was being fobbed off again – but sometimes that sort of behaviour was needed for people to actually listen and take you seriously.

The waiting room was mercifully quiet, only a trickle of people coming in and going out. She watched them, her nurse's eye trying to gauge what their problem might be, as a way of distracting herself from what was happening to her daughter. Were they taking the blood tests she had requested so many times now? Doing toxicology to see if they could identify what was causing these acute bouts of illness?

Her leg bounced up and down, her whole body twitching with the not knowing. Okay, she understood why they'd chosen Dean to go with Mia instead of her. He was calm, always calm, and she was so thankful he'd finally arrived at the hospital. But Becca was Mia's mum, the one who looked after her most of the time, and she felt she should be there, making sure they were checking the right things, telling them the whole story. Dean hadn't been there half the time Mia had been ill – he'd been working away, as was the norm these days.

She stood and did a tour of the walls, reading the posters, willing her heart to beat at a more sensible rate. What if it was something serious, some underlying condition that hadn't occurred to her? She'd never forgive herself if it turned out to be an obvious disease. Something a district nurse should be aware of.

'Becca.' She turned at her name and saw Dean walking towards her, Mia holding his hand. His face was grim. 'They want to have a chat with you.' He nodded his head towards a doctor and nurse, who stood by the door of a little meeting room that opened off the waiting area.

'Is everything okay? Do they know what's wrong with her?'

A third person came bustling through the double doors. A woman with a stethoscope round her neck, but not in the white coat used by the A & E doctors. *A consultant*, Becca thought, her heart leaping up and down now, hands clammy.

Dean sat down and pulled Mia on to his knee. The three people were standing by the open door of the room, obviously waiting for her.

'Aren't you coming in?' Becca asked him.

He shook his head, an odd expression on his face that she couldn't quite interpret. 'It's just you they want to talk to.'

Mia snuggled into his chest, clearly exhausted.

Three of them? Oh God, no, this is serious.

She took a deep breath and steeled herself for bad news. *I'm a nurse. I've heard bad news before. I can handle this.* Giving them a tight smile, she walked into the room and sat in the chair they indicated. Waited while they introduced themselves, not really hearing anything as her pulse whooshed in her ears.

Silence.

'Have you found out what's wrong with my daughter?'

They glanced at each other and the woman with the stethoscope nodded. 'Yes, we think we have.'

Becca waited.

'We think someone has been deliberately poisoning her.'

Becca swallowed. Her skin prickled as she took in the stern faces, three pairs of eyes fixed on her.

Do they think it's me?

CHAPTER ONE

Two and a half weeks earlier

Connor. Becca's mind woke her up with his name, as if she'd just said it out loud. *Maybe I did?* Her heart gave a little skip of panic, eyes staring into the darkness, while she listened. Dean's steady breathing, slow and regular, the slight rumble of a snore, filled her ears. The sound of a sleeping person. *Even if I did say it, he didn't hear.* She breathed out, slow and quiet, worried that her rush of relief would be so loud it might wake her husband.

The digital clock, which sat on the bedside table next to her, clicked over to 3.08 a.m.

She turned away from the time, eyes closed as she snuggled against Dean's back, but her mind was being treacherous, filling with images of Connor as she remembered him from ten years ago, just before she'd left. Surfer hair, bleached blond, hanging past his shoulders, that glorious wide smile, dark blue eyes and a wonky nose, bent slightly to the right after he'd been hit in the face by his surfboard several years earlier.

Connor.

There it was again, his name in her head, right where it shouldn't be. Her eyes flicked open, not wanting to see his face in her mind but still wanting to revel in the warmth of the memory of him. *Why now?* she wondered, her nose full of the scent of her sleeping husband, her body clasped against his. *Not that he'd notice,* said a voice in her head, tinged with resentment. Her hand slipped from Dean's waist and she turned on to her back, gazing at the ceiling, the flower-shaped light shade just visible in the darkness.

She listened to the rhythm of Dean's breathing, noted his blissful lack of awareness and envied him his peace of mind. He could always sleep, was never awake at three in the morning, whereas this time of night was very familiar to her – a particular moment in time that her body seemed to want her to experience on a daily basis. Quietly, she slipped out of bed and pulled on her dressing gown before padding to the door. Not a conscious decision, but something she did out of habit. *I won't get back to sleep if I don't have a wander*, she told herself, a slave to her routines, which had started to multiply at an alarming rate.

She walked down the hallway and peeked into the next bedroom, smiling at the tangle of bedclothes on the floor, the little girl on the bed with her arms and legs flung wide, like a starfish. Mia. Strawberry-blonde curls formed a halo round her dainty face, freckles dotting her cheeks and the bridge of her nose. *Mini-me*, Becca thought, having looked identical at the age of three. Now her own curls had straightened into shoulder-length waves, her hair darkened to brown, and her hazel eyes were permanently clouded with a whole swarm of worries that wouldn't let her sleep.

Connor.

It was disconcerting, the way his name called to her, snapping her out of the present and taking her to the past. She'd lived in such a different world then, when he'd been part of her life, on a different continent, a different hemisphere. When she'd first met him, she'd been a carefree twenty-eight-year-old. Six months into her planned year-long sabbatical in Australia, she'd felt renewed and healed and invigorated, her head filled with such plans for the future. It felt surreal thinking about it now, as if it had happened in a parallel universe, and she wondered how she'd got here, to this place in her life where she felt like she was a chameleon,

colouring herself to fit in, her true self unseen by the people she
shared her life with.

She found herself in the kitchen, filling the kettle with water,
no recollection of coming down the stairs. It was strange how her
mind blanked like that, almost like sleepwalking. *So tired*, she
thought, rubbing her hands over her face, wiping at eyes sticky
with sleep. That was the irony: she was catatonic with weariness,
but the moment she lay down, her mind went hyperactive, whirring through the day, the future, the past. Fixating on things she'd
done that she wished she hadn't, and things she hadn't that she
wished she had. All the should haves and could haves and what
ifs banging together into a riot of voices shouting and crying and
whispering in her head. Phew, it was noisy in there, and the only
way to quieten everything down was to get up, have a cup of tea,
do a bit of meditation and then go back to bed. Sometimes it
worked. Recently, not so much.

It's Connor's fault.

She nodded to herself as she made her tea, still unfamiliar with
her surroundings, the newness of the house they'd moved into only
three months ago, everything sparkling and working properly,
smelling of fresh paint and new carpets. Connor was the grain of
sand in her shoe, his reappearance in her life something she had to
address whether she wanted to or not. She drifted through to the
lounge and pulled a large cushion on to the floor, the pattern the
right way up, edges flush against the front of the settee. When she
was satisfied that it was properly aligned, she got herself settled like
she'd been taught by her yoga teacher, legs crossed, back straight,
supported against the settee, her mug of tea on the coffee table
to her left, out of her line of sight so it wouldn't distract her. She
gazed at the fake fireplace in front of her, the screen projecting
flickering flames, and let her focus blur and her thoughts wander.

It had started a week ago. He'd popped up on her Twitter feed,
a new follower. Connor Cywinski. She'd stared at the name, her

heart skipping as she studied his avatar: a surfboard. The only thing written on his profile was 'surf's up…' and she knew immediately it was him. Not the usual random Twitter follower. This was Connor, her ex. Who'd bewitched her with his happy-go-lucky philosophy, his inability to worry about things he had no control over, his belief in 'tomorrow is another day' and handing his problems to the universe to sort out. This was the Connor she had loved. The Connor she had wronged. And here he was liking her cute cat pictures and her little witticisms about life and the funny things her daughter Mia had said and done.

Yesterday, though, she'd followed him back and he'd gone one step further, sending her a direct message.

G'day! How you doing?

That was it. Short and to the point, but a question so big she had no way of answering without writing an essay. How was she doing? To be honest, she really wasn't sure. She'd replied:

Fine.

Just one word, typed and sent before she could think to stop herself. To ask the question, *Is it wise to respond?* And now she was itching to see if she'd had a reply, or whether she'd sounded too terse and non-committal. Dismissive. Whether she'd let him go again. Because he couldn't go, not now. There were things she needed to say, things he needed to know. Then, maybe, a bundle of her worries, neatly tied with regrets, could be packed away for good. Was it possible that the piece of her conscience which burnt with shame at the thought of him could be soothed into silence?

She sighed, reached for her tea and took a big sip before carefully replacing it and refocusing on the flames, bringing her mind back to the meditation. The idea was to let her head empty itself of random thoughts of its own accord, like taking the plug out of the sink and watching the water drain away. *Just watch but don't engage*, she reminded herself, something she'd been taught but not yet mastered to any degree.

Shall I look? Check if he's replied?

Suddenly she was on her feet and walking to the kitchen and her handbag, where she'd left her phone. She'd taken to keeping it out of sight this last week – a way to stop herself from compulsively checking to see if he'd posted anything or left a comment. Her hand closed round the familiar cold oblong and she pulled it out, switched it on, her pulse speeding up a little as she waited for it to wake up. She flicked through to her Twitter app. *A message!* She stared at the little envelope icon for a moment before she opened it up.

Great to hook up with you again. Want to chat?

She read the message a couple of times, could detect no hidden agenda, but then Connor wasn't that type of guy. He was all for 'call a spade a friggin' spade, mate', no messing about with flowery language or diplomatic niceties. It was something she'd loved about him.

Loved. There was that word again, and with it came such a swirl of emotion that for a moment she was battling a hurricane. She steadied herself against the kitchen table while she took a deep breath and weathered the rush of longing, remembered the sound of his voice, the soft touch of his lips against hers. She swallowed and studied the screen, rereading the words.

Do I want to chat? Wow, talk about a loaded question. She wondered what he thought they might chat about. Her husband? Her child? The life she'd built without him? She flicked back to her profile, checking what he already knew:

Rebecca Thornton @beccanurse7

District nurse in Llandudno, North Wales. Happily married to Dean, mother of Mia (3). Loves mountains and beaches. Talks a lot.

He knew her situation. No need to hide anything. *But how does he feel about it?* A knot of guilt tightened in her stomach. She read his reply again and knew that she shouldn't chat, knew that she couldn't allow the past to invade her present, whatever unresolved feelings there might be. He was her ex and she was a married woman now.

Her fingers ignored her and flew over the screen, her conscience dictating the words that she'd been wanting to say for so long.

I'm so sorry I didn't come back. I know at the airport I said I would. Honestly, I meant to, but after Mum's funeral, Dad was a mess and I couldn't leave him. Life changed. Different priorities.

It was rushed, as apologies went, and only told half the truth, but at least she'd had a chance to say sorry now, and that felt better. Even if he didn't reply, he'd see her words, know that her choices had been limited by a tragic situation. She read her message on the screen, a lump of dissatisfaction sitting in her chest, hard and heavy. There was more she could have done at the time, more she could have said, but she'd been torn in two with grief, her emotions in tatters, and she couldn't explain her behaviour, not even to herself.

There was no rational line of logic that could sensibly explain how she'd come to be with Dean instead of Connor. Apart from the thousands of miles between them, of course, which made talking about things that mattered just a little bit too hard. And the fact that she didn't hear a peep from him after she'd returned to the UK.

In Australia, they'd been on a break from each other for a few weeks before she'd suddenly had to leave, her life ambitions seemingly incompatible with his. She'd grown tired of the constant travelling and wanted to settle somewhere, while he wasn't ready for that. But he was her best friend and they'd still chatted regularly. When she'd told him her mum had died, he'd insisted on driving her to the airport – he was that sort of guy. He was off on a road trip a couple of days later, and they'd left it that he would contact her when he was back – she'd assured him she would have returned to Australia by then.

On the day of her mum's funeral, the day when she'd really needed him to be there for her, he hadn't answered her message. That had hurt and suddenly all the negatives about him ate up the positives, until the only things left were the things she didn't like.

But really, did that add up to the answer? Was it that simple?

She looked at her message. It wasn't enough, there was something more she needed to say, so she tapped out the question she really wanted him to answer.

I hope you can forgive me?

If he said yes, would that make her feel lighter, or would it wrap another chain of doubt around her neck?

The past ten years had been emotional. First her mum dying, and her dad struggling to cope with the grief. Then, less than a year later, she and Dean had married. Four years ago, her dad had had a heart attack and needed more support, especially when he'd had to take early retirement and hadn't known what to do with himself. And then, three and a half years ago, after several miscarriages, Mia had been born. But Dean's business had suddenly taken off just when Becca had gone back to work, and life had been hectic ever since.

Every time she thought they'd reached a settled phase, something else would happen. The most recent upheaval was buying this house next to the golf course on the edge of Llandudno. It was more stressful than she could have imagined because it was a new build and Dean had wanted changes to the specification, so it fitted their needs perfectly. 'If it's going to be our forever home, we've got to get it right,' he'd said more than once.

Becca would be the first to admit that she and change were not good friends.

It took her a while to adjust to new ideas, and after the troubles of her past, her therapist had advised her not to take on too much change at once, to let one thing become part of her routine before introducing anything else that was new. Life had other ideas of course, pulling her this way and that, thrusting decisions and situations in her path at a speed she found overwhelming at times.

Too much change at once gave her a mental paralysis, a state of mind where she was incapable of knowing what it was she actually wanted. Unable to voice an opinion, she just let events happen. And that was how she'd ended up here, married to Dean with a three-year-old child, instead of in Australia with Connor and – who knew – possibly a different child. She couldn't pretend she hadn't thought about it a hundred times. Probably a lot more, if she was honest. Especially on those days when Dean wasn't there and she was alone, trying to entertain a hyperactive Mia. *Lonely.* Yes, that was the truth of it. She often felt lonely.

Dean's business was like a third person in their marriage, regularly taking him away for weekends and sometimes weeks at a time. In recent years, he'd specialised in running corporate events based on golf – his passion – using iconic courses all over the world. Companies would run team-building activities, strategy workshops or sales events in the mornings, followed by a round of golf in the afternoon or evening. Work and play. It was a win-win formula. He'd spotted a gap in the market and he'd been so right. Now he had so much work, he'd taken on a partner, an ex-professional golfer who had the industry contacts he needed;

together, they were dynamite. It didn't help that his partner was lithe and attractive and called Alice.

Becca didn't like Alice. Or was it that she didn't like Alice being Dean's business partner?

The fact that Dean and Alice spent so much time together was the problem, and she found her insufferable, all puffed up and full of her own importance. She had a tendency to ignore Becca because, really, what did they have in common? Alice was focused, driven, her life all about golf, to the exclusion of almost everything else. There was no overt animosity, just a tendency to avoid each other if at all possible, a strategy they all seemed happy with.

Becca sighed. Hand on heart, she couldn't say she was happy. Stressed: that was her overriding state of mind, a hamster on a wheel, running to keep up with everything life was throwing at her. It wasn't how she'd envisaged her life with Dean.

Did I make a mistake? she wondered now, looking at her message to Connor. *Did I pick the wrong man?*

CHAPTER TWO

Becca woke feeling groggy and unprepared for the new day, having stayed up longer than she usually would, waiting for Connor to answer. Eventually, when her eyes had kept closing, her chin nodding on to her chest, she'd understood there would be no reply and she'd crept back to bed.

In her first hazy moments of wakefulness, Becca thought back to when she and Dean started dating, and he would bring a cup of coffee for her to drink in bed in the mornings – workdays and weekends. It was a routine that had never faltered from the first night she'd stayed with him. He'd always done it for his mum, he'd explained, after his dad died and she was on her own. It was his way of showing her she was loved.

Once Mia had arrived in their lives, and Dean's business took off, their routines were transformed, and coffee in bed became a thing of the past. Not even on birthdays or Mother's Day. In fact, Dean was so distracted by the myriad tasks he always had to do that he hardly bothered to say good morning these days, his mind on work as soon as he hopped out of bed. Of course, she was happy for him that he found his business fulfilling, but it absorbed so much of his time and mental energy there was nothing left for her. Or Mia for that matter.

How strange, she pondered now, as she watched him getting dressed, that the man who had been absorbed by the idea of a family for all those years before Mia had arrived now spent so little time with his daughter. *Perhaps the reality doesn't match the dream?* Not for the first time, a cold emptiness filled her chest, a sense that somehow she wasn't shaping up to be the wife and mother he'd hoped she'd be. That home life wasn't as enjoyable as being at work.

She watched him slick back his short dark hair and gave herself a mental shake. *It's all for us*, she reminded herself. *He's building a secure future.* Wasn't that what he'd said the other night when she'd told him she missed him? 'It won't be forever. But we're in the middle of our expansion plans and I can't take my foot off the gas just yet.' He'd kissed her then. But even when he was kissing her, she wasn't sure his heart was in it.

Loneliness was the last emotion she'd expected from marriage. But there it was, chilling her heart, the moment she woke up and saw her husband eagerly preparing for his day. Was it any wonder she'd taken to daydreaming about her past? *No harm in daydreams*, she told herself, pushing Connor's face out of her mind and focusing instead on her husband.

Dean slapped aftershave on his face then stood in front of the wardrobe surveying his assortment of ties.

'Jon Snow,' she said as she watched. It was a little game she liked to play, each tie having a name, and this one was named after a newsreader who loved a splash of colour.

He reached for the tie, raised an eyebrow as he turned to her, holding it up under his chin, a riot of fluorescent patterned silk. 'This one?'

'Perfect.' She watched him deliberate then carefully put it back, pulling out a conservative navy and maroon one instead.

'Alice hates Jon Snow.' He grimaced in the wardrobe mirror as he slung the tie round his neck. 'Says it's juvenile and lacks class. I'll go for David Cameron instead, I think.'

Becca took a sip of water from the glass on her bedside table, swallowing her retort back down. *So, Alice has a say over how you dress now? Nice.* Of course, she wouldn't say it, wouldn't want to start the day with an argument, and she knew how petty it would sound.

Dean finished tying his tie and took his suit jacket from its hanger, shrugged it on. 'Presentable?' he asked as he turned to face her.

'Very smart.' It was her stock answer, the same one she gave every day because she wasn't even sure he was listening, his mind already somewhere else.

He walked over and bent to give her a kiss. A fleeting touch of his lips, the kiss gone before it had properly landed, another part of the routine. *That's me*, she thought as she watched him walk out of the bedroom. *Just part of the routine.*

'Bye, Alice,' he called as he left the room, and she froze as if he'd unwittingly fired an arrow into her heart. It wasn't the first time it had happened. It wasn't even the second, and she stared at the empty doorway, her breath hitching in her throat.

Just a mistake, she told herself. *His mind's on work, doesn't mean anything.* She thought back to her childhood, her mother always calling her and her sister Kate by the wrong names, distracted by whatever she was doing at the time. *Doesn't mean anything*, she reassured herself again, but decided that she'd mention it to him. Present it as evidence that he was spending too much of his time thinking about work and not enough thinking about his home life.

She sat staring into space, her thoughts sneaking back to what might have been. *Connor.* His name flowed into her mind, along with a flurry of images until they filled every little space. She lay back on her pillows and closed her eyes, inspecting each memory before putting it back and picking another. Sunshine and laughter. Lots of banter. The sea, surfing, cooking barbies on the beach, salty skin, road trips to the Blue Mountains, watching the sunrise, the sunset, boat trips. Snorkelling over the Great Barrier Reef. And talking. So much talking about everything and nothing. *Connor knows more about me than anyone else on the planet.* She knew this to be true, and she missed his friendship, the way he would always listen. And frankly, he'd had a lot to listen to when they'd first met, things that she'd never revealed to Dean lest she frighten him away.

Becca had been signed off work for four months before she'd been persuaded to take a sabbatical and had headed off to Australia. It was at the suggestion of her friend Tina, a fellow nurse who'd emigrated to Sydney five years earlier and had settled there with her Australian husband.

'Come and stay,' she'd said. 'We've loads of space. The weather's fantastic, you can just hang out, or find yourself a job, whatever works for you. I think getting away from the whole mess is going to be best. Fastest way to put it all behind you, don't you think?'

'Oh no, I couldn't,' had been Becca's first response, dismissing the idea before she'd even had time to think about it. Her go-to answer of the moment being 'no'. She'd been trying to catch herself doing it, as her therapist had suggested, making a conscious effort to turn 'no' into 'yes' at least some of the time, but it really was a struggle.

Her therapist had been delighted by the idea of a break. 'What a wonderful opportunity,' she'd said, beaming over the top of her bifocals, her blonde hair a curly nest sitting on top of her round moon of a face. 'I think some time away from home, putting some distance between you and your… troubles would be just the ticket. You wouldn't dwell quite so much on what happened, and if your friend is a nurse, well, you'll be in sympathetic company. Unlike your mother.' She'd cocked her head. 'With the best will in the world, being at home is not really working, is it?'

The next time Tina had repeated the offer, Becca had forced herself to accept. Spurred on by the fact her mother had been hinting that it was time for her to move back into her own apartment because, really, there was nothing wrong with her, was there? The tension had been mounting, and she'd noticed an increase in the hissed conversations between her parents, little digs at every opportunity. Eventually, it had become unbearable, and the challenge of flying halfway round the world by herself was more palatable than moving back into a place of her own, where she'd have nothing but her thoughts to keep her company.

Tina had lured her with talk of sunshine and heat and kangaroos and kookaburras and koalas, all out there in the countryside, common as rabbits. It was strange, she thought now, how random things could unblock your thinking. Once she'd been there a few weeks, Tina had helped her find a bar job, and Becca had been surprised to find that she loved it. Six months into her stay, with her mental health well on the way to recovery, she'd met Connor.

Their relationship was intense, spending every moment they possibly could with each other. They'd had a couple of weekends away, going up to Cairns so she could see the Great Barrier Reef. Then she'd given up her bar job to travel round the south coast with him, surfing and picking up casual work, living in his campervan. After five months, though, she was yearning for stability. Connor hadn't been ready to stay in one place. That's when they agreed to have a break, and she'd gone back to stay with Tina while he'd carried on his travels.

Her heart had ached for him, but her head had told her he wasn't long-term partner material. They'd continued talking every other day and she'd been completely conflicted, her head and heart at war with each other, and her biological clock ticking away in the background. Her dreams had children in them. Lots of children. But Connor was a free spirit, and parenting hadn't been in his plans for the foreseeable future.

When her mum had had a stroke and died, it had turned her thinking on its head.

She'd travelled home for the funeral but had bought a return ticket. 'I'll be back in a month,' she'd assured him at the airport. She hadn't understood how grief would hit her once she'd arrived back home. Or how diminished her father would appear, shaking and swaying, hardly able to walk on his own, let alone look after himself. She'd soon understood she couldn't leave him. A month at home was nowhere near enough to deal with the loss of her mother, or the unresolved issues which had been left hanging between them. With her mum gone, her dad became her priority, and Australia seemed as distant as another planet, completely out of her reach.

A little hand tugged at her hair and she blinked her eyes open, shocked out of her reverie. Big hazel eyes gazed back at her. 'Are you awake, Mummy?' Mia asked, earnestly, as if it wasn't obvious. Becca laughed.

'I am now,' she said, pulling her daughter into a hug, burying her nose in her tangle of curls, filling herself with the scent of the little person who ruled her heart. *Connor's in the past*, she told herself firmly. *This is my future.*

'I'm hungry,' Mia said, wriggling from Becca's grasp and tugging at her hand. 'Time for breakfast, Mummy.'

Becca allowed herself to be pulled out of bed and padded downstairs with her daughter's tiny hand wrapped in her own, a sensation that she never ceased to delight in. Because there was a time when she'd thought she'd never be able to trust herself to look after a child. A time when she hadn't trusted herself to know what was real.

CHAPTER THREE

It was never a good idea to let her mind go back to those dark days; it was like stepping in quicksand, which grabbed at her thoughts, pulling her down and refusing to let go. She focused on chopping up fruit for Mia's breakfast while she tried to keep the past at bay. Her phone pinged with a new message. *Connor?* She made herself finish what she was doing, settled Mia with her food and then checked her phone. Her shoulders slumped when she saw it was from her boss, Carol, asking her to call.

That was all it took to connect the dots in her mind and send her thoughts spinning back eleven years and four months to another message from another boss, asking her to come to her office.

*

Becca's ward manager, Jane Fielding, was a brisk middle-aged woman with hair dyed a shade darker than suited her lined and jowly face. They'd never had a harmonious relationship, Becca's sense of humour and her habit of being silly to cheer up her patients apparently unprofessional in her manager's eyes. Jane was always pulling her up on little things that didn't really matter. *Nitpicking*, Becca thought, putting it down to a controlling personality who liked things done her way. But this was something else.

She'd never been called into the office for a formal chat before, and the mood was sombre. Becca's hands felt clammy where they rested in her lap.

'I'm sorry to have to do this,' Jane said, her voice brusque and businesslike, 'but I'm afraid circumstances demand it.' Her mouth became a hard, scarlet line, a mean slash across her doughy face. 'I'm going to have to suspend you from duty pending an investigation. With immediate effect.'

Becca held on to her chair, shocked beyond words for a moment while Jane continued. 'These are very serious allegations.'

Her patronising tone unblocked the logjam of words that had been stuck in Becca's throat. 'You can't think I'm in any way involved in harming the patients?' she said, incredulous. Her heart was racing, revving like a jump-started engine. 'You can't think that. I treat everyone like they're family, and everything I do is to help make them better.' She glowered at her manager, fingers tightening round the seat of the chair as her mind scrabbled for a way to make Jane see that she'd got it wrong. 'Who made these accusations against me? Let me talk to them. Maybe it's a misunderstanding.'

Jane sat back in her seat, her eyebrows knotted into a continuous line. 'It's not one accusation; it's a number of incidents. Initial investigations show they appear to have started when you first joined us here on the ward.'

'What incidents?' Becca's mind immediately started reviewing recent events. There had been a crisis the previous day, a resuscitation. And one a couple of weeks earlier. *Is that what this is about?* She wiped her clammy hands on her uniform as if smoothing out the creases. 'Surely I've a right to know exactly what I'm being accused of?'

Jane nodded. 'Yes, you do, and you'll be given a formal letter detailing everything. It's being prepared as we speak, but the decision was made to suspend you immediately to safeguard the patients in our care.' She gave Becca a stony look. 'We're investigating incidents of patients being given the wrong medication and the wrong doses, leading to catastrophic outcomes in some cases.'

Becca shook her head, her heart racing so fast she felt light-headed. 'I'm always extremely careful with medication. Ask the other nurses.' There was desperation in her voice. 'Please just talk to them. They'll tell you. I'm always double-checking.'

Jane gave her a curt nod. 'We will be checking, don't you worry. And in the meantime, you are relieved of your duties. The police will be wanting to interview you, and I hope you will give them your full cooperation in this matter.'

The police? Becca thought she was going to faint and could only nod her response. She was being picked on, made a scapegoat by a woman who had her favourites amongst the nursing staff, and Becca wasn't one of them. Had a colleague pointed the finger? Was anyone else being suspended? She had no answers, only questions, as she was sent home.

From that moment on, Becca's life spiralled down into the worst hell she could have imagined.

Days at home, ostracised by her colleagues while the investigation was underway, made her start to doubt herself as she walked through her medication rounds in her mind, trying to remember every detail. But memory is a fickle creation at the best of times, and instead of reassuring herself that she was in the right, she became convinced that it was possible she'd made some terrible mistakes. That people had died because of her actions.

She found herself repeating mundane tasks, and the repetition turned into an obsession until she couldn't drink from a mug until she'd washed it three times. Couldn't empty the washing machine until she'd done another rinse and a spin. Had to check three times that she'd locked the door when she went out. Switching things on and off, washing her hands before meals, after meals, while she was cooking. Her hair started to fall out. She couldn't eat, and when her sister found her collapsed on the bathroom floor, she was admitted to the mental health unit, suffering from anxiety and depression.

The truth, when it eventually came out, that the ward manager had been behind the problems, was shocking. Although Becca was exonerated from any crime, she'd been broken by the experience, both mentally and physically, her confidence shattered.

She'd become incapable of caring for herself, and her mother suggested she come and stay in the family home for a couple of weeks so she could be discharged from hospital. It turned into a couple of months and became increasingly clear she'd outstayed her welcome.

Tina's invitation to go and stay with her in Australia was a major turning point in Becca's life. Their friendship had started at university, where Tina had trained as a mental health nurse, and although she specialised in caring for dementia patients these days, when Becca arrived at her house, she spent hours helping her to see that she'd done nothing wrong. Gradually, Becca started to get control over her obsessive behaviour, and one by one she managed to eliminate all her little tics. By the time she met Connor, she was feeling like her old self again, and the bar work was making her socialise and interact with people. She began to think that she could leave the whole traumatic incident behind and move on with her life.

Leave the past behind? How naive to imagine scars like that could ever properly heal. It only took a bit of pressure, a bit of stress, to pull the wounds apart, and all the old doubts and fears and obsessions came bursting out again, like the stuffing from a ripped cushion.

CHAPTER FOUR

The sound of her phone ringing roused Becca from her thoughts. It was Carol again. There was only one reason for her to call, but Becca answered, hoping she was wrong.

'Hi, Carol. I just picked up your message. Everything okay?'

'Hello, love. Yes, fine.' She gave a quick laugh. 'I always say that, don't I? To be honest, I'm under pressure today. There's two off ill and we've four new patients just out of hospital. I wondered if you could do an extra shift this week. You know I wouldn't ask unless we were desperate, but could you manage to come in tomorrow morning?'

Becca worked three mornings a week, which felt like a lot with Mia to look after and Dean away so much, but she had to work a certain number of hours to keep her nursing registration. It was such a long-winded process getting back into the profession if she were to let it lapse, and once Mia was at school, she'd want something to get her out of the house and fill her days.

Quite apart from that, nursing was a vocation for her, rather than a job, and something she really enjoyed – looking after other people was a fundamental part of who she was. Admittedly, it had been a struggle, an extra pressure going back to work when Mia was six months old, but she'd landed a position as a district nurse, based at the local medical centre in Llandudno. It used to be a short walk from the house they'd been renting at the time and gave her flexible hours, the staff covering for each other if ever there was a problem. They were like a little family, all getting along, and she loved being part of a team. She also enjoyed the variety of the job – being out and about in the community – much more than she'd ever enjoyed working on a ward.

'No problem,' she said without thinking, always ready to step in, just like the other nurses would do for her, and because Carol was a great boss. One of those quietly efficient women who mothered everyone and was generally unflappable. 'I'll ring the childminder and check and then get back to you, okay?'

Mia loved her childminder, Ruth, who took the three children in her care out for walks and to the playground whatever the weather. She was a real earth mother, a genuinely peaceful soul who kept her house free of anything artificial if she possibly could. She fed her charges fruit and chopped-up vegetables, made bread with them, did crafts, took them to the library and the beach. The whole day was a learning experience, and she'd been graded as outstanding by Ofsted. She'd been such a support to Becca now she had no mother to call on for advice, and she thought of her as a friend as much as someone she paid to look after her child.

Ruth answered on the first ring.

'Hi, Becca, funny you ringing. I was just about to call.' Her voice sounded different; weak and distant. 'I'm really sorry but I'm going to have to let you down this week.' She sighed down the phone. 'Well, it's not just this week actually. I've had some bad news.'

'Oh, dear, I'm sorry to hear that. Are you okay?'

Ruth gave a little laugh. Or was she actually crying? 'Apparently not. I had my first mammogram a couple of weeks ago, since I've just turned fifty, and they found… well…' Her voice turned into a whisper, as if she hardly dared say the words. 'It's cancer.'

'Oh, no,' Becca gasped, feeling like she'd just had a bucket of icy water thrown over her. Ruth was never ill – not even a seasonal cold managed to get past her immune system, so the idea she had something seriously wrong was almost unthinkable.

'Oh, yes, unfortunately. But they're rushing things through, so that's good.' She was trying to sound practical and positive, but there was a tremor in her voice. 'I've got to go and see the specialist and sort out what they're going to do with me. Chop off my boobs, I expect. Whip out a few lymph nodes and then…' Her voice cracked, and Becca could hear her sobbing down the phone.

'I'm coming round, Ruth. I'll be with you in twenty minutes.' She ended the call, her mind busy rearranging her life now she had no childcare. She knew the local nursery was full and there was a waiting list because one of her colleagues had been lamenting the shortage of places. Now she'd have to trawl round and see if any spaces had opened up with other childcare providers. She pushed all the practicalities to one side. *What matters is Ruth; everything else can wait.*

Once she'd gathered Mia and had her settled in the buggy, she rang her sister, Kate, talking as she started the walk to Ruth's house, which was only ten minutes away on foot. Kate was self-employed as a bookkeeper, her hours flexible as she worked from home. She used to work for a large accountancy firm in Manchester but had moved back to the family home to keep an eye on their dad three years ago. After he'd had his heart attack, Becca had popped in on a daily basis, but when she and Dean moved from their apartment in Bangor to a rented house in Llandudno, and she couldn't call in so often, it was clear he wasn't coping on his own. Kate had stepped up to take on caring duties. Maybe she'd look after Mia for a couple of days until Becca could get something else sorted out. It was only half-days after all, and Kate could work in the evenings to make up the time.

'Hi, Becs,' Kate said, sounding preoccupied. 'Can I call you back? I'm just in the middle of something.'

'This won't take a minute,' Becca said, glad to have caught her sister, who was in the habit of letting her phone go to voicemail. 'I just need to know if you could look after Mia for a couple of mornings this week. Ruth's not well.'

Silence. Becca stopped walking and listened, frowning. 'Kate? Are you there?'

'Yes, I bloody well am,' she snapped. 'Tell me, why is my job less important than yours?'

'It isn't… I wasn't…' Becca stuttered to a halt, thrown by the tone of Kate's voice. *Christ, she's in one of her moods*, she thought.

After a moment, Kate sighed, sending a crackle of white noise down the line. 'Sorry, I didn't mean to snap, I'm just trying to finish some accounts and they won't balance and I really can't stand this guy I'm doing the work for. He makes me so bloody angry the way he treats his staff and he's a creep and he won't listen, so…' She stopped her rant and was quiet for a few seconds. 'Anyway… I'm sorry to hear about Ruth.' Her voice softened. 'I hope it's nothing serious?'

'That's just it, she's been diagnosed with breast cancer.' Becca could feel her throat tighten, fully aware of the implications for Ruth and the struggle that lay ahead for her. Becca had nursed several breast cancer patients, and the outcomes had been a mixture of triumph and tragedy. She caught her train of thought, told herself to be positive. *You don't know all the facts. Maybe they've caught it early.* She took a deep breath, steadied herself.

Kate tutted. 'Oh my God, that's awful.'

'I know. I can't imagine how she's feeling. Such a shock, and she's got nobody close to her. No kids, no family. I'm just going over to see her now.'

Kate sighed. 'Okay, I can have Mia tomorrow if I get these accounts sorted today. Then maybe Dad would keep an eye on her the other day? I'm sure he could entertain her for a few hours while I get some work done, and I'll be in the house, so I can make sure they don't get up to any mischief. Honestly, he's like a kid himself when he's with Mia. Do you remember last time he decided to do some drawing with her, borrowed my marker pens and they drew a mural on the kitchen wall?'

Becca laughed. 'God, yeah, took us hours to get that off, didn't it?'

'It might be good for him to have something to keep him busy though. Stop him bothering me when I'm trying to work.'

'Hmm. I did wonder about asking Dad, but I worry about Mia wearing him out. She's just non-stop these days, and after his heart attack… well, I suppose I don't want him getting over-tired or too stressed. But if you're there as well, that'll be perfect. I'll pop over after I've seen Ruth and we can have a chat.'

'Right, I'll let Dad know you're coming. That should cheer him up. He's been on a downer recently. Feels like you've forgotten he exists.' The little dig didn't go unnoticed, Kate always keen to emphasise that she'd changed her whole life to care for their father, whereas Becca's efforts to share the responsibility were increasingly lame.

Becca was about to reply, say it hadn't been that long since they'd been over, when she stopped, remembering she'd cancelled both of her usual visits the week before and was ashamed to admit it had been at least a couple of weeks. She cringed and vowed to do better.

Her sister's voice broke into her thoughts. 'Amazing how you can manage to make it over here when you need something, isn't it?' Her words were dipped in a heavy coating of sarcasm and Becca rolled her eyes but didn't respond.

Kate and their father, Frank, were only half an hour's drive from Becca's home in Llandudno. It was an easy journey down the A55, but Becca struggled to organise visits because Mia had started to get carsick and always resisted getting in the car, let alone going any distance in it. Becca had a system of bribes in place for essential journeys, but on the whole she either walked or did the shopping and other chores while Mia was with Ruth or Dean. Still, it wasn't good enough, and Kate was right to say something. Her jaw tightened.

'I'm sorry if I've not been there as much as I should have been. I promise I'll make it up to you.'

'And how exactly are you going to do that?' Kate asked, her tone suggesting that it wasn't really possible.

'Shall we check diaries later, see if we can work out a new routine? Make sure you get more time for yourself.'

'Yep. Let's do that,' Kate said, still snippy, before saying her goodbyes and ending the call.

Becca started walking again, her mind darting this way and that, like a little bird trying to catch insects, as she wondered how she could fit everyone's needs into her tight schedule. Dropping Mia off with Kate and Frank was all well and good, but it added an hour to the beginning and end of her working day, and it wasn't like she could just roll up there, grab her daughter and drive off when she'd finished, either. There were always things to do, little chores that she got roped into helping with, and her day ended up gone before she knew it. Then she'd have to spend her evening catching up with her own household jobs.

A burst of anger flared in her chest. 'You did this, Mum,' she muttered to herself as she stomped down the pavement towards Ruth's house. 'You made Dad helpless.' She was immediately contrite, annoyed with herself for being mean to her poor dead mum. It wasn't her fault she was an enabler, treating Frank like he was some form of royalty and she was a servant there to do his bidding. It was the way her grandmother had brought her mum up, an old-fashioned woman who'd been 'in service', on the staff of the country home of Lord Lowther up in the Lake District. *Ingrained subservience.* That's what it was, and Becca had always been determined that she wouldn't end up in the same sort of relationship.

She thought about the big bags of washing Dean brought home after his trips. All the shirts that needed ironing. The golfing clothes – because if you were running corporate development events at a golf course, it would be daft not to fit in a few rounds, wouldn't it? And always a present to say thank you for 'looking

after him so well'. It had taken her a while to see the pattern that
had formed in their relationship.

I'm just like Mum. It was a truth she was loath to accept but
there was no easy way to change things, and now it seemed she
needed to commit to keeping more of an eye on her dad as well.
Her heart gave one of its palpitations, making her stop and clutch
at her chest for a moment. She knew it was stress. Just like the way
half her face kept going numb. That was stress as well. And all her
stupid little routines that meant it took twice as long as it should
for her to do anything. She took a few deep breaths and waited
for her heart to settle down before she set off again, walking more
slowly, trying to silence the mental chatter.

Her life was spinning out of control, she was being pulled
in too many different directions and her responsibilities were
multiplying at the same rate as her nervous tics. This wasn't the
life she'd wanted. *How on earth do I change things, though?* Instead
of making things better, all she seemed to do was take on more
work for herself as she tried to keep everyone happy. It would be
nice to have someone to talk things through with, someone who
knew her history, her vulnerabilities, who wouldn't judge. Someone
who could help her get things clear in her mind.

Connor.

His name filled her head again, familiar and comforting.
He was, without doubt, the best friend she'd ever had, and she
wondered why he'd gone silent after she'd arrived home all those
years ago.

Has he replied to my message now? He'd asked her if she wanted
to chat. Well, she did. And she would. As soon as she got home,
and had a moment to herself, she'd start the conversation, tell him
what was going on. He'd always been a good listener. Always balanced in his views with a knack for finding solutions to problems,
seeing things from a different perspective. A people person through

and through. If anyone could help her see a way out of this mess without letting anyone down, it was Connor.

She opened Ruth's gate and pushed the buggy to the front door, her fingers itching to check her phone. Before she could reach into her bag, the door opened and there was Ruth, with her tear-stained face, and all thoughts of Connor were firmly pushed away.

CHAPTER FIVE

By the time Becca had comforted Ruth and answered her questions about her treatment and what to expect as best as she could, she was emotionally drained and dreading the drive to her dad's house. She wondered, for a fleeting moment, if she could postpone but knew that Kate's patience was at breaking point and there was no excuse for not going.

Mia was tired now after Becca and Ruth had taken her for a long walk along the West Shore, stopping at the playground so she could have a run around while they chatted. It was so much easier to talk about emotional things outside, rather than inside, where you were trapped with the problem, no distractions to remind you that life was bigger than just you, and that whatever happened, you'd get through it. *One day at a time.* That was always her advice to patients who were struggling. *Just get through today, and who knows what tomorrow might bring?*

If only she could listen to her own advice sometimes.

Mia fell asleep in her buggy, and Becca was able to get her home and transfer her into the car seat without waking her up, which made the next part of her day much easier than she'd anticipated.

Half an hour later, she pulled up outside the three-bedroom, semi-detached house which overlooked Bangor's harbour, with views out over the Menai Strait. She'd grown up here and it held a lot of memories.

To Becca, this was where she felt closest to her mum, surrounded by all the little knickknacks she'd loved. Her collection of china animals in a glass case in the front room. All her cross-stitch samplers lovingly framed and hung in the hallway. And above the fireplace, there was the montage of photos that Becca, Kate and their dad had put together. A memorial to the person who'd been the beating heart of their family and whose loss they still felt every day.

She pulled into the drive and Frank, who'd obviously been waiting for them, was out of the front door before she'd even turned off the engine.

'Becca!' he called as she got out of the car, delight shining in his eyes, and she felt a new twinge of guilt for leaving it too long between visits. 'Kate did mention you might come, but I didn't want to get my hopes up.' He bent to peer through the car window, no doubt looking for his granddaughter. 'I know it's tricky with Mia in the car.'

Becca gave him a hug, the familiar smell of Old Spice filling her nostrils. Without warning, her eyes prickled, tears springing from nowhere, and she tensed, pushing away from him before she started crying. That wouldn't do at all. Then there'd be all sorts of questions to answer, and her dad was not a fan of Dean. She'd never got a straight answer as to why exactly but thought it was probably to do with the fact that Dean had been keen to get married and find a place of their own, taking her away from Frank when he was quite dependent on her for emotional support. Things could get out of hand very quickly and turn into a situation where she was defending Dean; her dad would get all offended that she wasn't listening to him, and then... She checked her thoughts, told herself to get a grip and opened the back door to coax a sleepy Mia out of the car.

'Hello, poppet,' Frank said, holding out his arms for a hug.

Mia's face lit up. 'Dandad!' she squealed, squirming out of Becca's arms and reaching for Frank, who picked her up and clasped her to him. 'How did you get here?'

He laughed. 'I've always been here. You're at my house.'

Mia looked surprised, then squinted at Becca. 'How did that happen, Mummy?'

'You fell asleep and we came in the car, and you didn't feel even a little bit sick.' Becca hoped this experience might help Mia to feel less nervous about travelling in the car in future, which would be a huge bonus given they'd be doing this journey for a little while until she could sort out alternative childcare.

Frank was jigging Mia up and down in his arms, clicking his tongue, pretending to be a pony as he trotted towards the house.

Kate had been right – Frank was delighted to see Mia, and Becca felt a new flush of guilt that she'd missed their visits the week before. *Got to do better*, she told herself as she grabbed her bag and followed them inside.

She found them in the lounge, a large, oblong room at the front of the house, still decorated to her mum's taste: a neutral palette for the walls, floors and seating, with bright flashes of colour in the cushions and the rug in front of the fire. An excited Mia was already emptying a plastic tub of cuddly toys which had been set in the middle of the floor. 'Mummy, there's unicorns!' she squealed. 'And doggies and pussycats and—' she turned towards Becca, her arms full of the little creatures '—there's dinosaurs!'

'Oh my God, I remember these.' Becca laughed and glanced at Frank, who was sitting in his armchair next to the fireplace, watching Mia with a satisfied smile on his face. 'Beanie Babies. These were mine, weren't they?'

'That's right. Quite a collection.' Frank perched on the edge of his seat while Mia carried on emptying the box, sorting the animals into different piles that only she knew the relevance of. 'I remember when you were young, we used to go into town, and you'd have your pocket money, and the only shop you wanted to go in was the one that sold these little things. Took you ages to decide which one you wanted next, and they kept bringing out new collections.' He beamed at her. 'I wish I could have bottled the joy in your heart when you came out of that shop clutching your latest baby.' His eyes glistened. 'Priceless.'

'Happy days, Dad.' Becca bent to pick up a cat, which was battered and misshapen but had been her favourite and the hero of many a game of make-believe. 'I thought these had been thrown out years ago.'

Frank looked at her, appalled. 'God, no. I'd never throw anything of yours out. Not without asking.' His expression changed. 'Talking of throwing things out… We've been having a reorganise. Me and Kate. Or should that be Kate and me?' He winked at Becca. 'She likes to give me little jobs to keep me busy. Anyway, she got fed up of working in the dining room because I'm always disturbing her with the telly or playing my guitar, and her bedroom's not big enough to get a desk in there as well as the bed and the wardrobe and whatnot.' He sighed. 'We had a bit of a set-to about it, to be honest, and she was all worked up because you hadn't been over, and she felt everything was her responsibility.' He pressed his lips together, frowning. 'Anyway, long story short, she said it wasn't working and she couldn't stay here unless she had her own office, so I finally gave in and we've cleared out your old bedroom so she can use that. There's a sofa bed in there for visitors, and like Kate says, it's a waste just having it as a spare bedroom when she needs a proper office, and nobody comes to stay anyway.'

Was that a little dig? It felt like it.

Becca nodded, a little sad that she no longer had her own room in the house – the end of an era – but she could see that it made sense. Kate was doing her best to have a career and keep an eye on Frank, and Becca was grateful to her for her efforts. While Becca and Dean had still lived nearby, she popped in every day to help him sort out shopping and meals and laundry, practicalities he had no clue about. The problems had started when Dean suggested they move to Llandudno, to make things easier for his work. Once

Becca wasn't checking on Frank so often, it became obvious he wasn't looking after himself properly.

At the time, Becca had thought that it suited Kate to move back from Manchester.

'It's only a temporary thing,' Kate had said when she'd rung to tell Becca of her plans. 'To be honest, I'm not enjoying work at the moment. It's time for a change, and I owe it to Mum to make sure Dad's okay.'

'Oh, Kate, that's so good of you. As you say, it's just till he finds his feet again, and I'll help as much as I can.' Becca had made the promise in good faith, completely unaware of the exhaustion that would come from going back to work while caring for a baby. Needless to say, her input had been minimal, and Kate had been left with the lion's share of the responsibility. Once she'd moved in, Frank hadn't wanted her to go again, getting upset at the very mention of being left on his own. After declining three excellent job offers over the years, Kate's temporary solution had turned into a permanent fixture. As had the edge of resentment in her voice whenever she and Becca spoke.

It's only right she has a proper office, Becca told herself now, trying to remember what might be left in her old bedroom. If her cuddly toys had still been there, were there other things she'd forgotten about?

Frank stood and stretched his back. Mia was now sitting in the box, happily chattering away to an audience of new friends, oblivious to what was going on around her. 'She'll be fine for a minute, won't she?' He walked to the door and beckoned for Becca to follow. 'Come on up, see what we've done.'

She followed Frank up the stairs and peered round the door of her old bedroom, a room she no longer recognised. Gone were all her posters and trophies from school, her nursing certificates and awards. Nothing of her remained on the blank white walls, or the swish new window blinds which had replaced her flowery curtains. Even the carpet was new – a corporate beige instead of the rusty red she'd once chosen herself.

'Wow, a complete makeover,' she said, the ghosts of her old furnishings still clear in her mind. 'You got rid of my desk, then?'

'It was too small. Kate said she needs to be able to spread out lots of paperwork. You know, receipts and invoices and the like. The dining room floor used to be covered with stuff, and I was always getting into trouble for messing it up. Opening the door too fast and creating a draught, then all these little scraps of paper would go flying everywhere.'

Becca could see the rationale. The room was a good size for an office, and the sofa bed sat unobtrusively against the side wall, a coffee table and lamp next to it. Kate's large desk fitted along the far wall under the window, flanked by a couple of filing cabinets to the left. 'It looks very…' She pressed her lips together, trying to find a word that wouldn't offend.

'Sterile,' Frank said, hands in his pockets, jingling his loose change. 'Wouldn't be my choice but I've had no say in the matter, and it's Kate who'll be working in here.' He cleared his throat. 'A bit of colour would be good, don't you think?'

Becca laughed and nudged her dad with her elbow. 'I was thinking the same thing myself but didn't want to say in case it was your choice.'

'Give over,' he scoffed. 'White's never been my favourite, has it? Not practical if you ask me.' He scanned the room. 'We only finished a couple of days ago. Got a few pictures to put up – you know those motivational sayings that Kate likes. And then we're done.' He turned to Becca. 'In fact, while I think about it, I've some boxes of your stuff in my bedroom if you want to take them home and have a sort through?' He turned and walked down the hallway, Becca following. 'Just stuff from that little desk of yours and a few bits and pieces you'd left in the wardrobe.'

He led her into the large double bedroom at the front of the house, and Becca noticed nothing had changed. Her mother's embroidered pictures still hung in a group above the bed, her collection of wooden boxes that contained her craft materials sat on the dressing table. Her family of ornamental ducks still swam along the windowsill. There was even a little posy of fresh flowers in a vase on the bedside cabinet on the side where her mother used to sleep.

A lump formed in Becca's throat and she swallowed it down. It was weird how grief had a habit of hitting you out of nowhere. But seeing her mum's things brought home to Becca how much she wanted her mother to still be around. She could feel herself being torn apart by her responsibilities, her emotions fighting each other for dominance. Each day her life was slipping further out of control to the point where it was starting to scare her. She sat on the bed, picked up the teddy that her mother had always kept on her pillow and put it to her nose. It smelt of lavender, her mum's favourite.

'I still miss her too,' Frank said with a heavy sigh, sitting next to her. 'But then, I don't suppose you ever stop missing people you love.'

Becca sniffed. 'I'm sorry I've not been over more, Dad. But at least you've got Kate here for company.'

Frank didn't reply, just stared into space, one hand rasping over the stubble on his chin. Becca laid her head on his shoulder, and he put an arm round her, pulling her close. They sat like that for a little while until his voice broke the silence. 'I'm grateful that she's here,' he said eventually. 'But she can be snappy and it's not always easy when—'

'Mummy! Dandad! I need a wee.' Mia's voice cut into the conversation and Becca jumped up, rushing down the stairs. Mia was only just potty-trained, and the gap between her realising she needed the toilet and being unable to hold it in any longer was a couple of minutes at best. Becca ran into the lounge, swept her daughter into her arms and dashed to the little cloakroom under the stairs just in time.

Mia gazed at her while she sat on the toilet. 'Are you crying, Mummy?'

Becca smiled and wiped the dampness from her cheeks. 'No, love. Just having a laugh with Grandad.' She couldn't tell her daughter she was sad because Mia was such a sensitive child, it would make her sad too. She didn't need to feel Becca's pain, didn't need to be involved in her emotional storm. And anyway, how could she ever explain?

As she waited for Mia to finish, she wondered what Frank had been about to say. *Is there still a problem between him and Kate that the new office hasn't resolved?* She knew they bickered – that was part and parcel of their relationship – but a serious falling out between her dad and Kate was the last thing she needed.

There was no chance to go back to the conversation, ask her father what he meant, as Kate arrived home, full of news about a friend from school who'd just got the most amazing job offer. Then Becca was caught up in helping her make something to eat and the opportunity drifted away. *Another time*, she promised herself. Because she loved Frank with all her heart, and if he needed her support, then she wanted to be there for him. Like he'd been for her over the years.

She was just about to leave when Kate put a hand on her shoulder and pulled her back into the kitchen while Frank and Mia sorted out which of the Beanie Babies was going to go with her for a sleepover.

'I just need to ask you a favour,' Kate whispered, obviously not wanting Frank to hear. 'But this might sort out your childcare problem as well. I have some business to attend to in London, and with the trains and everything, I'm going to have to stay over. I was thinking Dad could come to you Friday and stay the night.

What do you think? Might be a good experiment in relation to childcare, because I think he'd be all right keeping an eye on Mia for a morning if it was at your house, with all her toys and everything. And it would be a change for him. I'm sure he'd love it.'

Becca had never had anyone to stay at their house in the three years they'd lived in Llandudno. It hadn't been practical in their rental property as they hadn't a spare room, but now she couldn't offer that as an excuse. There was plenty of space in their new house, and if Frank stayed over, not only would it save her a lot of driving time, it would mean she wouldn't have a battle to get Mia in the car.

'You'll have to invite him,' Kate continued. 'Otherwise he'll think I'm shipping him off, trying to get rid of him.' She sighed. 'He's so clingy sometimes. Honestly, it's a job to get any time to myself without a full interrogation about where I'm going and why.'

'Well, we can give it a try,' Becca said, hoping Kate didn't hear the note of panic in her voice. 'He'll be doing me a favour and it'll be lovely having him to stay.'

Having someone to stay was actually her worst nightmare. Another person to look after being one too many for her frazzled state of mind.

It's Dad, she told herself. *He won't mind the mess.* Then another voice piped up in her head, the voice of her real fear. *Will he notice the other stuff? Will he know that it's happening again?*

CHAPTER SIX

Mia was sleepy after her busy day, and Becca took the opportunity to get her to bed before Dean returned, in the hope that they could at last have some time together. She'd just got back downstairs when her phone rang. It was Dean.

'Hey, sweetheart. I forgot to mention I'm going to meet the committee of the golf club tonight. They've invited me to talk about that new competition I've been wanting to launch for the local business community.'

Her heart sank. It had been an emotional day, and she'd been looking forward to snuggling up on the sofa with a glass of wine, telling him about Ruth being ill and her dad coming to stay. Once again, she was home alone, nobody to share her news with.

'Fine,' she said and ended the call, wanting to throw the phone across the room while a silent scream filled her head.

Connor. His name came out of nowhere, the events of the day having pushed him to the back of her mind.

She tapped and swiped at her screen, opened Twitter and there it was, a message.

Good news or bad? Has he forgiven me?

The not knowing gave her a delicious little thrill, but given the sort of man Connor was, she thought she already knew the answer. She opened the fridge, took out a bottle of wine and poured herself a glass before walking into the lounge and getting herself settled on the sofa. The place where she always sat – curled up like a cat, feet underneath her, body tucked into the corner.

She made herself wait, took a long sip of wine, then opened the message.

Nothing to forgive ☺ Family had to come first.
I couldn't afford to come over there, you couldn't get back here.
I went on a trip after you left, lost my phone and all my contacts.
Basically… shit happens ☹

So that's why he'd suddenly gone quiet. He'd lost her contact details. *Hmm.* That sounded a little lame. He knew her email address. He also knew Tina and could have asked her. But he would have been in seriously remote terrain. Just him and nature. He'd told her before about some of his trips, how it could be weeks before he saw anyone. She checked her thoughts – who was she to question when she hadn't told him the truth? Did it really matter now?

She took another sip of her wine and studied the mantelpiece, the row of family pictures staring back at her from their frames. *My family. My future.* Connor was her past. As a lover, anyway. *But he can still be a friend, can't he?* Her fingers tapped out a reply.

What are you up to? Married? Family?

She watched the screen, waiting for an answer, but given the time difference, she knew it was unlikely to come. She drained her glass, put her phone down and went into the kitchen to get a refill. That's when she saw the boxes she'd brought back from her dad's house: three of them, stacked against the kitchen wall, where they were going to be in the way.

Unsettled after Connor's message, she put her glass down and opened the top box, finding it full of fashion accessories: belts and handbags, a couple of old purses, hair bands, a collection of baseball caps and a boxful of costume jewellery that she'd never wear again. All the detritus that had been left behind in her wardrobe when she'd moved out. Mia might like some of it for her dressing-up box, she decided, keeping a few bits and pieces that would be safe for a young child before putting the rest back in the box and taking it through to the utility room, ready to go to the tip.

The next box was full of footwear: shoes and wellies, a pair of flippers, trainers and a couple of pairs of high heels that she wouldn't be able to walk in now. She kept the flippers and wellies and put the box with the other one in the utility room.

The last box was quite heavy, full of paper and picture frames, stuff she'd had on her walls. She recognised the contents of her desk and knew this would need careful sorting – there were memories in here, together with records of achievements and official paperwork that she'd want to keep. She yawned and stared at the box, wondering if she should leave it for another day and take the opportunity to have an early night.

Her curiosity had been piqued, though, as she couldn't remember exactly what might be in there. Old school reports, photos from university when she was doing her nursing degree. Yes, she was pretty sure there'd be a few laughs amongst the paperwork. After topping up her wine, she lifted the box on to the kitchen table and started sorting the contents into piles.

Halfway down she found an A5 notebook, fat and well used with a picture of a kangaroo on the front. Her heart gave a little skip. This was one of the journals she'd kept while she was on sabbatical in Australia. Something her therapist had suggested, so she could record her thoughts, note down the positives, address her worries and work through the issues which had been weighing on her mind for so long. She'd got into a routine with it and knew if she searched through the box, there would be others. She smoothed the front cover, relishing the familiar feel of it, stirring memories like silt from the bottom of a pond. This was the journal she'd been keeping just before she came home. This one was full of Connor.

A fizz of anticipation bubbled through her as she opened the book. On the very first page, there was a picture of her and Connor on the beach – her in a hot-pink bikini, him in faded black bathing shorts, both leaning on surfboards, hair still wet, matching grins. She stared at her image, a slimline version of herself, tanned and glowing with good health. *Look at that smile!* Happiness shone from her. She appeared light and carefree. Quite the opposite of how she felt now.

She glanced at the date and worked out the figures in her mind. Maybe two months after she and Connor had met. This was a picture of those early, heady days of their relationship, when friendship had blossomed into love, but nothing was serious. When their focus was on having fun. What a perfect playmate he'd been, lighting up her life with his silly jokes and gentle nature. She started reading her scrawled thoughts, and she was taken back to some of the happiest days of her life.

As she flicked through the pages, her eyes were drawn to the pictures of Connor. She studied his face, remembering his touch and how it felt to lie in his arms and feel the fuzz of his chest hair against her cheek. 'G'day mate,' she whispered, a smile in her voice, delighted by her find – a whole book of escapism. It was like finding treasure.

It was only when the front door banged closed that she realised Dean was home, and she quickly threw the journal back in the box, hiding it under a couple of framed certificates. She fumbled the lid closed as if it was some terrible secret. Her cheeks were burning and she jumped up, took her glass to the sink and let the cold water run over her hands in an attempt to cool the heat that flushed through her body.

He knows about Connor, she reminded herself, only to be castigated by her conscience. *Doesn't mean he'd be happy with you mooning over his picture, though, does it?* She picked up the box just as Dean came into the kitchen. He gave her a tired, preoccupied sort of a smile that hardly had the energy to turn his mouth up at the corners.

'What you got there?' he said, studying the box she had clasped to her chest.

'Oh, Dad's been having a clear-out. It's just stuff from my old bedroom that I need to sort out.' She grasped the box a little tighter. 'I'll stick it in the spare room for now, I think. Out of the way. Then I can sort through as and when I've got a moment.'

He moved to one side to let her get past him into the hall.

She hurried up the stairs and into the bedroom at the end of the landing, which had become a storeroom for belongings yet to be unpacked and find a permanent place in their home. It had been furnished as a spare bedroom, though, with a double bed, a chest of drawers and a built-in wardrobe along one entire wall. She opened this now and pushed the box into a corner on the floor, shut the door and glanced around the room.

I'll have to have a tidy up if Dad's coming to stay. Dean had a bag of golf clubs stacked in a corner, along with a number of golfing umbrellas adorned with his company logo. There were a couple of large cardboard boxes filled with company merchandise – jumpers and jackets and gilets, all branded. Her heart sank. In truth, the room was a mess.

I'll have to get Dean to help, she mused, frowning as she opened drawers and found them full of golfing paraphernalia. It seemed he'd commandeered the room without her really noticing. *No time like the present*, she decided, hurrying back downstairs. Her dad would be coming the day after tomorrow, and she'd need to have the room ready for him.

Dean was sitting in the kitchen, sipping a cup of tea, lost in his thoughts. She noticed the grooves on either side of his mouth, the deep furrow between his eyebrows. He worked hard, she'd have to give him that, and she was grateful for the financial security – and the lovely new home – his efforts had given them. She went over to him, bent to give him a hug and a kiss, but he hardly responded.

'Long day?' she asked, the sting of rejection making her pull away. 'Is everything all right? How did your meeting go?'

He blinked. Sighed. Took a sip of tea, his eyes focused on the table. 'Fine. It's all fine.'

'I've had quite a day myself,' she said, and sat across the table from him, reaching for his hand. 'Ruth can't look after Mia any more. She's just been diagnosed with breast cancer.'

He blinked, awakened from his trance. 'Oh, no. Poor Ruth.'

Becca thought he might have more to say but he went back to sipping his tea. 'It's put me in a bit of a tight spot with work.' She studied his face, watched him chewing the inside of his lip, clearly distracted by something.

'Hmmm.' He nodded, but she was sure he wasn't listening.

She bristled, her words getting a little snippy round the edges. 'Anyway, I've sorted out a plan B. Dad's coming over to keep an eye on Mia. Day after tomorrow. It was Kate's idea. She's got a meeting in London and has to go away for a night.'

Dean took another sip of tea. 'Right.'

Becca's jaw hardened. 'I'm glad you're so interested. Anyway, I need your crap out of the spare room so Dad can sleep in there.'

His eyes met hers then. 'Sorry, what was that?'

'Honestly, Dean, I hardly see you these days, and when you *are* here, you're just not bloody present.' She pressed her lips together to stop more words from tumbling out, giving voice to her true feelings.

They glared at each other. Then he finished his tea, put his mug on the table and stood, hands clasping the back of his chair as he leant towards her. 'I'm doing my best to provide a lifestyle and home that you and our daughter can enjoy. I don't work twelve-hour days for the pleasure of it, Becca.' His voice hardened, his tone patronising. 'But, hey, I know your job is more important than mine, so of course I'll go up there right now and sort it out. Because I've got a busy day tomorrow and then I'll be organising everything for the event at the weekend. Now is all the time I have spare because, you know, I don't even need any time off for relaxation, do I?'

She swallowed. 'You don't have to be like that about it. I just want the room to be nice for Dad when he comes. It's the first time he will have stayed, and it might have to be a regular thing if I can't find another childminder.'

Dean glared at her again before leaving the room without another word. She listened to him clumping up the stairs, then a little while later he came back down with one of the boxes in his arms. 'You don't have to work. I've always said that.'

Becca bit back her reply, not having the energy for the circular argument that spun around them whenever she asked him to help a bit more. It was a battle of wills that she wasn't prepared to lose. He could never understand why her job was so important to her, why she was determined to keep nursing. But then she hadn't told him about Rosie. He didn't need to know that she was responsible for the death of her best friend.

CHAPTER SEVEN

Once she'd calmed down, Becca relented and went to give Dean a hand clearing his stuff out of the spare bedroom. She'd just managed to empty a drawer when a sudden wail sent her running to Mia's room. The smell hit her as soon as she walked through the door, and she gagged as the aroma of vomit and diarrhoea filled her nostrils, so pungent she could practically taste it.

She flicked on the light. Poor Mia was sitting up in bed, the front of her pyjamas covered with vomit, a puddle of it on the duvet in front of her. She was holding up her Beanie Baby unicorn, which had obviously been in the firing line and was dripping chunks of regurgitated food on to the floor. Becca stood for a moment, wondering where to start.

'Oh, sweetie!'

'Mummy,' Mia sobbed, 'unicorn's all icky.'

'You're both a bit icky. Let's get you to the bathroom, shall we? See if we can clean up the mess.'

Mia slid gingerly off the bed and Becca noticed the stain on the back of her pyjamas. Thankfully she still wore a nappy at night, so the leakage wasn't as bad as it could have been, but the stench was horrendous, and despite her years of nursing, Becca's stomach heaved. Although she'd been a very healthy baby, Mia did seem prone to stomach upsets. But then, like most young children, a lot of her toys seemed to gravitate to her mouth.

Probably some sort of twenty-four-hour bug. That's what these symptoms usually meant. Maybe something she'd picked up at the playground, from the children she'd been playing with.

Dean poked his head round the door and pulled a face when the smell hit him. 'Oh my God! Shall I run a bath for her?'

'Good idea. Can you get the changing mat and the baby wipes into the bathroom, and we'll get the worst off with that first, I think?' She held out her arms and picked up her smelly, puke-covered daughter, trying not to breathe as she carried her out of the bedroom.

She was thankful for the floral scent of the bubble bath as she wiped Mia down as best she could, then popped her in the foamy water.

Dean came back up with a bucket for Mia's clothes before heading off to strip her bed.

'Mummy, unicorn needs a bath as well,' Mia said, big hazel eyes so mournful that Becca gave the toy a good rinse in the sink before handing it to her daughter, who started splashing it in the water.

'How are you feeling now, sweetie?'

Mia's mouth turned down. 'My tummy hurts.'

'Do you still feel sick?'

Mia looked at her, silent, pouting, and Becca realised that she wouldn't know what feeling sick meant. Dean stopped in the bathroom door, a bundle of bedding in his arms. 'Shall I put this lot in the washing machine?'

Teamwork. She gave him a grateful smile. 'Could you put it in the sink in the utility room? It'll need a rinse before it goes in the machine.' She got to her feet. 'Tell you what. You keep an eye on Mia and I'll sort out the washing.' She took the bundle from Dean's arms, picked up the bucket and made her way downstairs, forcing the thought that she was too tired to cope with this out of her mind. She locked into nursing mode, reminding herself that she'd seen worse on the wards.

Twenty minutes later, she'd rinsed off the worst of the mess, got the wash on and was back upstairs, sorting out clean bedding. Dean came back into the bedroom, Mia in his arms, wrapped in a towel. She was still clinging on to the unicorn, and Becca sensed there was going to be trouble parting them from each other. She checked Mia over, tested her temperature, asked if her tummy still hurt, and when everything seemed okay, she got her settled back in bed. After a couple of stories Mia was asleep and Becca stumbled into the shower, dead on her feet now but feeling so dirty and germ-ridden that she knew there was no chance of getting to sleep until she felt clean again.

Dean was sitting in bed, scrolling through his phone, when she walked in from the bathroom.

'I hope she's okay,' she said to him as she pulled on her pyjamas.

'Just a bug, I suppose,' Dean said, still busy with his phone.

Becca frowned as she sorted out her pillows. 'I suppose so. I can't remember her being this bad before, though, can you?' She could hear the worry in her voice, told herself not to panic. Mia was such a precious child to her and the only one she was likely to have.

'A few months ago, you were worried, don't you remember? I think it was a rash as well that time. Then she had a high temperature and went pale as a ghost.' Dean pulled a face. 'I know it's normal for a mum to be concerned but I honestly think this is just one of those things. If we sit it out, it'll go away. Just like all the other times you've ever worried about her health.'

Becca got into bed and pulled the covers up to her chin. 'I just hope you're right. Some of these vomiting bugs—'

'Mummy!' Mia's plaintive cry rang down the hallway and through their open bedroom door.

Becca and Dean looked at each other.

'Christ! I can't be up all night,' Dean said, clearly horrified by the thought. 'I've got a really important meeting tomorrow, prepping for the weekend.'

Becca clambered out of bed. She was the nurse in the family, the one who should be keeping a close eye on their daughter. 'It's okay. I'm off tomorrow. You go to sleep; I'll get her sorted.' She was halfway down the landing when she remembered she'd promised she'd go into work the following day, and a lead weight landed on her chest, a heaviness pulling at her shoulders. *You've done back-to-back twelve-hour shifts in the past*, she reminded herself and took a deep breath of clean air before entering her daughter's room.

They were up most of the night in a cycle of clean up and sleep. By dawn, poor Mia was exhausted and crying, and Becca felt like joining in. She now had a great pile of washing to do, and was worried that Mia would be dehydrated – she'd refused to drink anything because she couldn't seem to keep it down. Thankfully, Mia finally drifted off to sleep, and Becca hoped that the worst had passed.

'I think I'll take her to the doctor's,' she said to Dean at breakfast, having already broken the news to Carol that she couldn't work because Mia was ill.

'She's asleep now, though, isn't she, so why don't we leave her? Let nature do its thing.'

Becca poured herself a coffee and hugged the mug to her chest. Her eyes felt scratchy and sore with tiredness, her body longing to lie down, but she couldn't take any risks. Not with her daughter's health. She'd taken risks before with Rosie, and look what had happened. She shuddered. In her heart, she could see the sense in letting Mia sleep, but in her mind, where her fears prowled like hungry wolves, she couldn't trust her instincts. What if Dean was wrong? What if it happened all over again and she'd be to blame?

She took a sip of coffee, her mind taking her back to the worst day of her life.

*

She was eleven and playing with her best friend Rosie, on their way to the field just up the road, where the houses ended and the countryside began. Sometimes there were a few ponies in there, and they would gather handfuls of grass and giggle as the ponies' hairy lips tickled their hands. This day, the field was empty. They had a den in the hedgerow, underneath the hawthorn bushes, and they had to crawl to get inside. It was their special place and they enjoyed many happy hours there, hidden from the world in a space where they could be anything they wanted to be.

Rosie was a little pale today and her mother didn't really want her to go out, but they sneaked away when she wasn't looking.

'Mum's so fussy,' Rosie said as they walked up the road. 'She worries way too much.'

'She just cares about you. And it is a bit worrying having epilepsy, isn't it?'

Rosie had only recently been diagnosed with the condition after having had a couple of episodes when the family were away on holiday. Now she was on medication, which she hated.

Rosie shrugged. 'I don't remember anything about it.'

Becca frowned and stopped, pulling Rosie to a halt alongside her. She studied her friend's face, noticed the clammy sheen on her brow. 'Are you sure you're feeling okay? If your mum's worried about you, then maybe we shouldn't go to the field today.' She turned to go back the way they'd come, tugging on Rosie's arm. 'We could watch a film or something instead.'

Rosie pulled her arm out of Becca's grasp, anger crumpling her forehead. 'There's nothing wrong with me. Don't you start fussing as well. Honestly, it's like I can't go anywhere or do anything any more.' Her voice cracked. 'I just want everything to be normal.'

Becca relented then and gave her friend a quick hug before they set off again up the road. 'Let's not be too long, though.'

Rosie sighed and linked her arm with Becca's. 'Let's just do what we usually do. I just need to be... I want to forget about all that stuff.' She glanced at Becca. 'Please?'

Becca pushed her concerns away. It was impossible to comprehend what it must be like to suddenly be told you've got this serious
illness. Poor Rosie. She decided she wouldn't mention it again but
would try and cheer her up, pretend nothing had changed.

They crawled into their den and were creating a bigger space to
play in when Rosie stopped talking, eyes wide and staring before
she started shaking. Then she fell forwards, limbs twitching, her
face in the soil.

Oh my God! She's having a fit!

Becca had never seen anyone having an epileptic fit before and
she was paralysed by fear, not knowing what to do. She tried to turn
her friend over, but her arms flailed, and her body was going into
spasms. There was no way she could manhandle her in the awkward
space, not when there was hardly room to kneel let alone stand.

I'll go and get help, she thought, starting to crawl out of the den.
But then she stopped, unwilling to leave Rosie on her own. She
started crying, frightened by her friend's twitching body, wanting
to do something to help but not knowing what to do for the best.

Finally, after dithering for ten minutes, she ran for help.

When she got back to the den, with Rosie's mum running
behind her, Rosie was dead.

                              *

If Becca had got help sooner, Rosie would still be alive. At least
that's what Rosie's mum had said at the time. Becca knew that
a lot of people on their estate and many kids at their school had
thought the same.

She'd lived with the guilt ever since. It had spurred her on to
train as a nurse because then, she reasoned, she'd always know what
to do. Then she would never again be in a position where, because
of something she did, somebody died who should have lived.

Now, she didn't listen to her training, her years of experience;
she listened to her regrets, and she picked up the phone and rang

the doctor's surgery. Small children were so vulnerable, there was no sense in taking chances, whatever Dean might think. *It can't hurt to have a second opinion*, she told herself as she waited for the phone to be answered. At least the doctor would listen to her. They'd pay attention.

CHAPTER EIGHT

A virus, Dr Graham thought. Mia was tired after a bad night's sleep, but she'd surprised Becca by eating her breakfast, and by the time they were seen by the doctor, she was bright and chatty. Still, Dr Graham had taken her concerns seriously and given Mia a thorough examination, asking Becca to bring samples if it happened again so they could do further checks. Becca left the doctor's surgery, which was also the base for the district nurses' team, feeling relieved.

Her boss, Carol, caught up with her when she was on her way out. 'Everything okay?' she asked, flicking a glance at Mia, who was tugging at Becca's hand, trying to pull her out of the door and to the playground – the promised treat for being a good girl for the doctor.

'Yes, yes, just me double-checking. Dr Graham thinks it's a virus, nothing to worry about.' She laughed and rolled her eyes. 'As you can see, there appears to be nothing wrong with her now. And I'm so sorry to let you down after promising I'd work today.'

'Oh, don't worry about that – you've got to put your family first.' She gave her a smile and Becca knew she'd been forgiven. Carol was very fair like that. 'Lisa said she'd do an extra shift if you'd swap with her on Saturday so she can go and do wedding shopping with her sister. Would that be okay?' Carol put her hands together, praying for the right answer.

Becca thought for a moment. It would mean leaving her dad in charge of Mia for four hours. Five at the most if there were any complications. Two days in a row. She'd done it without a second thought when Mia had been a baby, her dad so gentle and patient, she'd had no qualms about trusting him. It was the fact that Mia was such a busy child these days, exhausting to entertain at times and she didn't want him to get over-tired. The memory of his heart attack was always there, sitting at the back of her mind – a reminder that she'd nearly lost him. But that was four years ago now and his doctor was delighted with his recovery. In fact, you'd never know he'd been so ill. She remembered how well Mia and Frank had been playing the evening before, how much they obviously enjoyed each other's company, and she knew she was worrying too much again.

'Yes, I'm sure I can do that. But remind me, or I'll forget. Memory like a sieve at the moment.' She glanced at Mia, who was still tugging at her hand, impatient to get outside. 'Look at her. I feel like a bit of an idiot bringing her in, to be honest.'

'Best to be sure, though, isn't it?' Carol gave her shoulder a reassuring pat. 'Trust your instincts, love. Must have been something that got you worried.'

Becca thought for a moment. 'It was just so sudden, you know? She'd been happily playing, eaten her tea fine. No hint of anything, no temperature or complaining that her tummy hurt.' She frowned. 'I got her to bed at a reasonable time for once and then, wham, it all started. No build-up, no warning signs or anything.'

Carol gave a sympathetic tut. 'You know when they're not right, don't you? Especially with your nursing experience. At least the doctor's put your mind at rest, but if you're not happy, be sure to bring her back.'

'I did try and be rational about it, but something didn't sit right with me. And you know what it's like when it's your own kids. You sort of doubt yourself.'

Carol cocked her head and studied Becca's face. 'You're looking shattered, love. Are you sure you'll be all right for your shift tomorrow? You're not going down with anything, are you?' She grimaced. 'If you think it might be norovirus, or anything like that, it would be better not to come in. You know how frail some of our patients are, and we'll manage somehow.' She gave a little laugh. 'We always do, don't we?'

Becca nodded. 'I did think about that, but honestly, I'm feeling absolutely fine. I just need a good night's sleep. Dad's coming over to keep an eye on Mia, so I don't have to worry about childcare tomorrow, even if she's not so well in the morning. Anyway, if things change and I do go down with it, I'll ring straight away.'

Carol held up her hands, fingers crossed. 'Let's hope you're right.'

They said their goodbyes and Becca put Mia in her buggy, even though she wanted to walk, because they were by the busy main road and she was always worried about her running out into the traffic. At least if Mia was fastened in her seat, she was safe.

Becca thought about her conversation with Carol as she pushed Mia down the road, singing songs to keep her from fussing about being in the buggy. It was odd that Becca hadn't come down with the illness too, given that she couldn't have avoided coming into contact with a virus. But what else could it be? *Maybe it was those old toys.* Becca's eyes widened. *Yes, that's it.* They could be crawling with bacteria if they'd been stuffed away for years.

It seemed a more likely explanation. At least the unicorn had been through the wash now, but she'd make sure that the other animal Mia had brought home was washed as well. Then she'd have done everything she reasonably could.

Feeling better now she'd got her thoughts properly organised, she sped up and they were soon at the playground, which she was glad to see was empty. Mia ran off with her unicorn to play in the little house under the slide, and Becca flopped onto the nearby seat.

Her phone pinged in her bag and she fished it out.

Her heart gave a little flip. Connor had replied to her message.

No wife and no children. But you have a daughter? How lovely. Does she look like you?

Becca glanced up to see what Mia was doing. Once she saw that she was engrossed in some imaginary game, she quickly sent a reply.

She does. A proper mini-me! Dean jokes that there's nothing of him in her.

She found a recent picture of Mia and attached it before she could stop and work out if that was a bad idea. A reply pinged back almost straight away, and she realised with a jolt of excitement that Connor was online now. She thought about the time differences. It was probably the only time of day when they were both likely to be awake.

Oh, she's a cutie. Just like her mum ☺ Same lovely eyes as you. She suits pink. I remember you in that pink bikini. My favourite ☺

She smiled to herself, his cheeky response wrapping her in a momentary glow that felt like a hug. She could almost picture his face as he'd typed his reply, a little smirk twitching at his lips.

And I will never forget those budgie smugglers you used to wear sometimes! ☺

She was blushing as she typed, remembering his athletic body clothed only in a tiny pair of Speedos, all long limbs and bronzed skin. He'd been a champion swimmer in his youth, and it had still showed in his broad shoulders and muscular physique when she'd met him.

Yeah. At least I've seen sense now. Those were the days, hanging out on the beach, golden sunsets. I loved the way you used to put flowers in your hair. Beautiful.

The warm glow spread until it filled her heart, which started to beat a little faster. She glanced up to check on Mia, before sending her reply.

Long time ago.

His next message came quickly.

Feels like yesterday. In fact, I think about you every day, Becca. Such special times. We had some conversations, didn't we? And you've got such a lovely voice. I used to say you should be on the radio, didn't I?

The glow expanded round her entire body. He had said that. He'd said her voice was so sexy he'd even listen to the news if she was reading it. Being with Connor had been such a tonic for her confidence because he'd so obviously adored her and hadn't been afraid to say so.

You also said I could talk the hind leg off a donkey.

She waited, her eyes glued to the screen for his response, a laugh caught in her throat.

Ha ha! The donkey wouldn't mind, though. Seriously, Becca, I would have happily listened to you talking all day. No worries. In fact, I did most days ☺

Her fingers flew over her screen as she typed her reply, giggling to herself.

Cheeky! I do remember we had a lot to talk about. It wasn't just me, was it?

She glanced up, relieved to see Mia still enjoying herself playing house under the slide, chattering away to the unicorn. Connor had pulled open the door to hidden feelings, ones that she'd thought had vanished into the past, and she didn't want to shut them back inside just yet. She was having fun. Harmless fun. And what was wrong with that?

I always thought you were my soulmate, Becca. We thought the same, didn't we? I miss being able to talk about things without worrying I'm going to be laughed at.

Becca closed her eyes for a moment, his words echoing exactly how she'd felt about being with him. It had been effortless. Until she'd decided she'd had enough of travelling and wanted to be settled. She'd understood that their adventures were a moment in time, not real life, just a step off the hamster wheel. At some point they'd have to get back on, but he'd been in denial. That's when they'd started to argue. That's when she'd ruined things, wanting to rush their relationship to the next stage, asking for commitment.

She was wondering what to say next when Mia came running over.

'Can I go on the swings, Mummy?' She grabbed Becca's hand and started tugging. 'Come on. Will you push me?'

Hiding her disappointment at having to curtail her chat with Connor, Becca shoved her phone in her pocket and allowed Mia to lead her to the swings, her mind travelling back in time to the day that changed her fate. The day that took her away from Connor, to a different future altogether.

CHAPTER NINE

Just over ten years ago, it was the day of her mother's funeral – an emotional day for any child, even when the child had become an adult. But it was especially difficult given the unresolved issues that had formed a barrier between Becca and her mum. After Becca's suspension from work and her subsequent mental health problems, a lot of things had gone unsaid – consequently, her mum's sudden death was not only shocking but left a mountain of regrets about not clearing the air, not knowing how their relationship actually stood at the end. Becca had practically run off to Australia without a backwards glance, hurt by her mother's reluctance to try and understand her situation and how she was feeling. Her mum was one of the 'keep calm and carry on' brigade who kept her feelings to herself most of the time and took whatever problems life threw at her in her stride. She hadn't understood why Becca couldn't do the same.

Communication between them while Becca had been away was sporadic at best. Then the news had come that her mum had died, a sudden stroke when she was alone in the house. Frank had found her when he'd arrived home from work, slumped on the sofa where she'd obviously been watching something on TV. He'd thought she was asleep, had tiptoed around for a little while, even made her a cup of tea and only found out something was wrong when he'd felt the chill of her skin.

The wake was held in a hotel in Llandudno, which stood on the corner of a long row of Victorian properties that ran along the promenade. Her mother had loved to go there for afternoon tea, and it was the venue for many a family celebration. Birthdays, wedding anniversaries, coming of age, Kate's ill-fated engagement party. And now her mother's funeral tea. It felt terribly fitting and unbearably sad, and Becca availed herself of far too many glasses of wine from the waiter's tray.

Feeling nauseous and unable to cope with the sympathies of all those people her sociable mother had known, she fled outside to get some fresh air, heading for the promenade. She checked her messages, upset that there was still no word from Connor.

It was one of those calm sunny days, no waves on the surface of the sea, which reflected the deep blue of the sky. It shimmered, so inviting she thought she'd go and have a paddle. It was one of her mum's favourite things to do, and she wanted to go back in time to when she was a child, a time when they'd let the waves lap around their ankles, caressing and tickling their skin, making them scream at the coldness of the water. She wanted to remember her mum from the time before Becca's troubles came between them.

In her haste to get to the sea – and unsteady on her feet after too much wine on an empty stomach – she managed to trip over and took a tumble down the short flight of steps that led to the beach.

A man in running gear rushed over to help. That man was Dean. After making sure she wasn't injured, he pulled her to her feet and led her to the steps to sit for a moment. Flustered and embarrassed, she felt a need to explain, and he said he understood because his dad had recently died, and they'd been estranged for a couple of years. Becca and Dean bonded over their regrets and they stayed on the steps for hours, talking about their relationships with their parents and death and how life was shaped by random moments. It was easier, somehow, to talk to a stranger about her deepest feelings than it was to share with her family.

As evening fell and the air chilled, they grabbed fish and chips, and later, desperate to stay a little longer with someone who understood how conflicted she was feeling, she went home with him. An impulsive decision which caused a whole new set of problems.

'So, where've you been, then?' her dad asked when she arrived home the following morning, still in her funeral clothes. He'd opened the door before she'd had a chance to use her key, and it felt like he'd been waiting for her. Perhaps he had. His shoulders were tense, his jaw set, the muscles in his cheeks moving as if he was chewing something. Anger sparked in his eyes and she felt like her teenage self, arriving home after curfew. Frank had been strict like that. Protective.

'Oh, I just… I um… I stayed with a friend.' She squeezed past him into the hallway and noticed Kate then, halfway down the stairs. Her face was puffy, eyes red from crying, and although she didn't say anything, her glare was enough to communicate that she was just as angry with Becca as her dad was.

The sinews in Frank's neck pulled tight as he leant towards her, one hand still grasping the open door, the other pointing at her as he spoke.

'You walked out of your mother's funeral, not a word to anyone about where you were going, and then you stay out all night with a "friend"?' His sarcasm sliced her excuse into shreds, his eyes popping out of his face.

She recoiled and inched backwards until she collided with the wall behind her.

'We didn't know where you were,' Kate said, coming down the stairs. She leant against the bannister at the bottom, arms folded across her chest. Becca was pinned now between the two of them, heart racing. 'Poor Dad was frantic.'

Becca understood then how selfish she'd been, wrapped up in her own grief with no thought for the rest of her family. Not understanding they might be worried about her. Or how it would look when she didn't return to the wake. Like she didn't care.

'Oh, Dad, I'm so sorry. I just couldn't cope with all those people. I know they were Mum's friends, but I don't know any of them and they were all over me.' She bit her lip, knew it sounded feeble. Her eyes flicked between the stony stares of Kate and her dad. 'I'm just…' Her voice thickened with tears. 'I'm really struggling.'

Frank slammed the front door shut, making her jump. Her heart raced even faster. 'And you think we're not struggling as well?' His face crumpled then, chin quivering, eyes brimming as he fought his emotions. 'I've just lost my wife of thirty-two years.' He covered his face with his hands, shoulders shaking as sobs wracked his body.

Kate gave Becca a look that said it was all her fault before going to Frank and trying to comfort him.

Becca escaped to her room, aware there was nothing she could say to make things better because it would just sound like excuses. The only way to make amends was to offer practical support, and she threw herself into taking on all the household jobs that had been left since her mum had died.

A week later, when Kate had to go back to work in Manchester, Becca readily agreed to stay with Frank. She changed her plane ticket back to Australia, delaying it by a couple of months. Then she sent a message to Connor to explain the situation. When she didn't receive a reply, she assumed he was out of reach on his trip. Or perhaps his continued silence meant he'd decided that their relationship was over. She waited but didn't hear from him again.

In the meantime, she met up with Dean quite regularly. Not dates, as such, she told herself, just socialising with a friend, drawn to him, to their bond of loss and his comfortable friendship. She felt guilty about sleeping with him on the day of her mum's funeral, and even though she and Connor had agreed a break to their relationship, it felt too soon to be moving on. She remembered his kindness taking her to the airport, the spark between them still there. It felt like unfinished business, a lingering connection not properly severed.

A few weeks later, when she discovered she was pregnant, she knew that her life had taken a sudden turn that couldn't be reversed. Those dreams of settling in Australia had evaporated like a puddle on a sunny day.

Becca was keeping the baby, of that she was sure, because having a child of her own to love and nurture was something she desperately wanted.

'It's my fault,' she told Dean as they walked along the beach after she'd broken the news. 'I'm on the pill but it's been a bit hit and miss since I've been home, what with everything…' She looked away, feeling foolish, a woman of twenty-eight – and a nurse, at that – making such a stupid mistake.

'It can't just be your fault, can it?' Dean said, pulling her to a halt. He wrapped her in his arms. 'I could have taken precautions. Should have taken precautions.' He kissed the top of her head, laid his cheek on her hair, and she could feel his warm breath against her scalp, his strong arms encircling her, holding her tight. She sank into his embrace.

'It's okay, though,' she mumbled into his chest. 'I don't expect you to get involved. This is my choice.' She bit her lip, emotions filling her throat, and it was a moment before she could trust herself to speak. 'It's something I've wanted for a while.'

'Well, let's not be hasty,' Dean urged. 'Let's see how it goes, shall we? And whatever happens, I will support you and the baby however you want that to be, okay?'

She burst into tears then because he was being so kind and reasonable, and she'd thought he'd be horrified. At least she knew she didn't have to face the challenge alone, but she couldn't bring herself to tell Connor what was happening. Anyway, perhaps she didn't have to, she reassured herself. He wasn't communicating with her, so presumably, from his point of view, their relationship had ended.

Over the weeks, nothing went according to plan.

She focused on her unborn baby and caring for her dad, wondering how she was going to tell him that she'd conceived a child on the night of her mother's funeral. Did she need to tell him? The very thought of it brought her out in a cold sweat. She put it off, waiting for the right moment.

The one thing that she hadn't anticipated was for Dean to be so excited about being a dad. Apparently, since childhood he'd always loved babies. He bought her books, discussed everything about pregnancy with her and never seemed to get bored of the subject. And because she couldn't tell anyone else what was happening, she spent more and more time with him. Instead of breaking their budding relationship, her pregnancy encouraged it to blossom. She loved his enthusiasm, but did she love him? She allowed herself to believe that she might and pushed all thoughts of Connor out of her mind.

Dean spoiled her, buying her all sorts of healthcare products. He'd surprise her with baby clothes. He decorated the spare bedroom in his flat as a nursery. Bought a cot so he could have the baby to stay, determined to play an active part in their child's life. He didn't need asking; he was always one step ahead, and she loved the way it allowed her to feel excited about having a child, rather than ashamed about how the baby had been conceived. She felt treasured and special and not a burden at all. He even made lists of baby names. He was everything any prospective mother could ask for in a partner.

When she was four months pregnant, she finally summoned the courage to tell her dad and Kate about the baby. Frank threw an almighty fit, told her she had to go; he couldn't have her in his house after she'd been so disrespectful to her mother's memory. Imagine conceiving on the day of the funeral! Kate was just as incensed. Becca realised she could have kept some of the facts to herself, but she was an inherently honest person and it had all come out before she'd really thought about editing the truth a little.

In tears, she called Dean, who came and helped her pack up her belongings, and, having no job or money to rent a place of her own, she moved in with him. Once it was done, it felt so right for them to be together, in their little bubble of baby anticipation. It seemed like the obvious thing to do. Two weeks later, she had a miscarriage.

*

Was moving in with Dean the right decision? she asked herself now as she pushed Mia on the swings. Had they stayed together because they both desperately wanted a child? They'd certainly been focused on trying again. And again. And again. She'd had a whole series of tests, to make sure there weren't underlying problems, but it seemed it was just bad luck and never once did Dean suggest they should stop trying.

He'd supported her all the way, his desire for a family as strong as hers, and their bond had been strengthened by adversity. When she'd been pregnant with Mia, she'd suffered nine months of fear rather than joyful anticipation, wondering if her body was going to reject this baby as well. That was why Mia was so precious to her – to both of them. It had been the focus of their whole relationship.

A moment of clarity made her stop pushing Mia. *Was marrying Dean more about having a baby than love?*

She gave herself a mental shake. *Don't be ridiculous!* She reminded herself of a truth she had never before questioned. *I love Dean.* She summoned his image, made it blot out Connor's face in her mind, tracing the features that she knew so well. Yet, there was a distance between them that had seemed to grow since Mia was born. The end of the struggle to have a baby had opened into a new chapter that was completely different. Mia was undoubtedly the centre of Becca's world, but was Mia the centre of Dean's? It seemed that the excitement of growing his business was more important than spending time with his daughter, and that bothered her. *Perhaps family life isn't shaping up quite the way he'd imagined in his dreams.* Then the big question reared its monstrous head. *Does he still love me?*

CHAPTER TEN

'Becca! Becca!'

The call of her name made Becca turn to see Ruth hurrying towards them, her long limbs striding across the playground. She was a gangly woman, with a prominent beak of a nose, and she reminded Becca of a wading bird, her movements measured, her demeanour observant, always watching, alert to her surroundings.

'Hi, Ruth, we were just about to head off. Last go on the swings for madam here. She wasn't well last night, so I want her to take it easy today.'

Ruth tutted. 'Oh, dear, poor mite.'

'I don't suppose either of the other two children you look after have been poorly, have they? The doctor thinks it's probably just a virus, but I'm not sure.'

Ruth shook her head. 'No. Not that I know of.' She studied Mia, who was swinging backwards and forwards, legs kicking. 'Still, seems like she's got over it if she wants to play.'

Becca looked at her daughter's grinning face as she swung up in the air and back again. She'd stay on the swings for hours if Becca was willing to push, and it usually took an element of bribery to get her to come off the thing without a fight. She didn't want to do that with Ruth there, though; didn't want her to see that she seemed to have a discipline problem with Mia where Ruth appeared to have none.

She carried on pushing. Ruth shifted her weight from one foot to the other, pulling her fleece jacket tighter around her thin frame. There was always a breeze by the beach, and today it was blowing from the north, bringing an unseasonal freshness to the first day of June.

'I had my emergency appointment with the consultant this morning. Thought I'd have a walk, clear my head, you know, and then I saw you in the playground. And... God, I just need to talk to someone.' Ruth's eyes were shining.

Becca readied herself for bad news as their eyes met.

'They made a mistake. Can you believe it? Got my mammogram mixed up with somebody else's. I haven't got breast cancer at all!'

Becca stopped pushing the swing, her mouth agape. 'Oh my God, Ruth, that's fantastic news.'

Tears were rolling down Ruth's face now, and she wiped them away with her fingers, gave an embarrassed laugh. 'Oh, don't mind me, I'm being stupid, but I just can't tell you... the relief!'

Instinctively, Becca gave Ruth a hug, delighted to hear her good news. 'How awful that you've been put through that, though.'

Ruth laughed while the tears kept coming. 'Oh, they couldn't have been more apologetic. It's fine, I know these things happen. But I honestly thought I was going to die.' She pulled back and a shadow crossed her face, the smile falling from her lips. She was silent for a moment, her eyes on Mia. 'I was planning how I'd wind up everything, you know. I even wrote a will.' She turned to Becca. 'I should probably tell you about that, actually. I have no family, as you know. And Mia is very special to me.' She beamed at Mia, who had her face turned to the sky, her blonde curls flying in the breeze. 'There have been a few children over the years that I've really bonded with. Quite a list, actually. I've loved them like my own, and I was going to leave them all a little bit of money. Just to help with university fees, or whatever else they might need a nest egg for. I mean, I don't have much, and I wanted to give some to Friends of the Earth and World Wildlife Fund and Save the Children. But I very much want Mia to have a little something from me when I'm gone.' Ruth's eyes met Becca's. 'You don't mind, do you?'

Becca took a moment to digest what Ruth had said, wondering why she felt uncomfortable. *Is that weird?*

'Oh no, Ruth, I couldn't let you do that,' she gabbled after an awkward silence. 'Surely you have some relatives, somewhere?'

Ruth shook her head. 'Unfortunately not. I'm an only child of only children. Neither of my parents had siblings. It was always just us.' She watched the restless sea for a moment. 'I would have liked brothers and sisters. It was a very quiet childhood. That's why I became a childminder. I love to hear them and play with them.' She gave a little laugh. 'I suppose I'm catching up on all the noise I would have liked as a child. It's a great sadness I couldn't have my own. That's why my marriage didn't last, you know.'

Becca didn't know but had always wondered why someone who was so good with children didn't have a family. She'd guessed, but if there was anything she'd learnt from nursing, it was that you never knew what was happening in other people's lives.

Ruth's words latched on to her previous train of thought, dragging it back into focus. *Would our marriage have survived another miscarriage?* She shooed the question away, appalled that she'd even considered it.

'Siblings can be overrated,' Becca said, ushering her thoughts in a new direction, remembering the way she and Kate used to fight when they were growing up. Right up until a few years ago, if she was honest. Thankfully, it was different now and their relationship had become much more supportive once Kate had suffered a few knockbacks and the hard edges had softened slightly. She wasn't quite so black-and-white about everything these days.

Mia had changed the family dynamic, giving them something new to focus on, a distraction from their grief at her mum dying and recriminations about disrespectful behaviour. She'd helped them to put all the nastiness behind them and move on, and for that Becca was grateful. Kate was adamant that she didn't want her own children, preferring the role of aunt, and although she was happy to babysit Mia every now and again, Frank was Mia's favourite. He was playful and patient, qualities that weren't so visible in Kate.

Imagine having nobody in your life. Becca wanted to think that Mia wasn't missing out by not having a brother or sister, because having another child seemed very unlikely after the trouble she'd had conceiving Mia. She hoped Mia wouldn't end up lonely and on her own like Ruth.

With a start, Becca recognised that her comment about siblings was insensitive. 'Shall we go and get a coffee? I know someone who'd enjoy a hot chocolate.'

Her daughter heard and swung her head round, staring at Becca before trying to wriggle out of the swing.

Ruth beamed at Mia and went to lift her from the seat. 'That's a lovely idea,' she said, giving Mia a kiss on the cheek.

Becca hadn't noticed before how Ruth looked at Mia, the genuine love in her eyes, but she could see it now and there was something about it that made her uneasy.

Ruth held on to Mia's hand as she put her on the ground, and Becca went to pick up her bag from the seat, following behind the two of them, Ruth's words still rubbing like sandpaper on her mind. Was Ruth too attached to Mia? Or was it a good thing she felt such a strong bond if she was responsible for looking after her three mornings a week?

Becca filed the thought away with all her other uncertainties and made herself focus on the positive: her childcare problem had been resolved. Now she wondered about her dad coming to stay. *Surely that's no longer necessary?* And she'd feel a lot less tense if he didn't come.

Ever since their big fallout, after the truth had come out about where she'd disappeared to on the day of her mum's funeral, Frank had kept his distance from Dean. Relations between them had been prickly. Dean thought Frank was jealous and – still, a decade later – struggling to let his daughter go, especially now his wife was dead. Becca thought he might be right, but the truth was the two men could hardly be left in the same room together without bickering about something. She'd only accepted Kate's suggestion of Frank coming to stay because she knew Dean would be away, and she had felt guilty about not going over to see him often enough. She'd thought it might be a chance for her and Frank to have a proper chat.

Frank was the one who'd understood what she'd gone through when the hospital had suspended her. He was the one who'd sought treatment for her mental health problems, whereas her mum had gone with a tough love approach. A 'snap out of it' sort of tactic.

Becca decided to stick with plan A. Frank coming over was a positive thing, and anyway, it was all organised. Plus Kate would feel more relaxed at her meeting if she knew Frank was with Becca and not on his own, and she really did owe her sister that.

Flipping her thoughts back to the present, Becca shivered in the cool breeze, wishing she'd thought to put on an extra layer. The coffee shop was a short walk into town, five minutes if she was on her own, but double that if Mia wanted to walk. 'I'll get her in her buggy,' she said to Ruth when she caught up with them at the entrance to the playground. 'Then we can make a dash for it, get out of the cold. What's up with this weather?'

Ruth bent down to speak to Mia. 'What do you think? Are you tired or do you want to walk?'

Of course she wanted to walk. She always did, which was why Becca usually made the choice for her rather than asking, with some diversionary tactic in place to halt any protests. Becca was about to say something then decided it wasn't worth an argument. Mia was clearly delighted to see Ruth and was merrily chattering away to her, telling her about all the new toys she'd found at Grandad's house. Her unicorn was her new prized possession and she was telling Ruth how it had been sick the night before and had to go in the bath.

'Dad found all my old Beanie Babies in a box. Remember them?'

Ruth rolled her eyes. 'Oh my goodness, yes. They were all the rage, weren't they? Collectors' items if I remember rightly.'

They walked along at Mia's speed, a tricky pace to maintain and another reason why Becca liked to have her in the buggy. 'Not mine.' Becca laughed. 'They're all battered. Had adventurous lives, those little creatures. I remember having picnics with them outside. Rosie and I used to—' A sudden rush of emotion blocked her throat, and it was a moment before she could carry on, eyes on the pavement. 'Let's just say they're well played with.'

'All the best toys are. And that's a very lovely unicorn, Mia. What's it called, and is it a boy or a girl?'

'It's called Peppa. Like Peppa Pig. But it's not a pig. And it's a girl, like me.'

Ruth nodded, a smile tugging at her lips. She gave Becca a wink. 'Good name.'

Finally, they arrived at the coffee shop, which was on the main road that led from West Shore right across town to the beach on the northern side of Llandudno. It was a wide avenue with trees in the middle and broad pavements, the houses petering out to be replaced with hotels and ornate Victorian shopping arcades.

Becca made sure she kept to the outside of the pavement and Mia stayed between her and Ruth, so she could grab her if she slipped from Ruth's grasp. *Stop being so paranoid*, she admonished herself, her body jerking in a reflex response, ready to grab her daughter every time she thought she might be about to run off. She was so on edge these days, her pulse racing at the slightest thing, and she seemed to exist in a permanent adrenaline rush.

Her phone pinged with a message. *Connor?* Her hand instinctively went to her pocket and she stopped for a moment, pulled out her phone while Ruth walked ahead. She took a quick peek, heart racing with a delicious thrill of expectation. But it wasn't Connor; it was Dean.

Forgot to mention, Wi-Fi might be a bit hit and miss this weekend, so could be hard to chat. That's the Highlands for you! You can always call hotel reception in an emergency. See you Monday x

She frowned, didn't bother with a reply and stuffed her phone back in her pocket. What if Mia was ill again and she couldn't reach him? But then, in reality, what use would he be hundreds of miles away? At least she'd have Frank with her, and that made her feel better about him coming to stay.

'Problem?' Ruth asked when Becca caught up with her a few moments later.

'Typical Dean.' She sighed. 'He's off to Scotland for the weekend and he's just messaged me to say it might be hard to get hold of him.' *Handy*, she thought to herself, *that he doesn't have to think about us for a few days. Is he thinking about somebody else maybe?*

'He called me Alice this morning.' She spoke her thoughts and instantly regretted it when she saw the expression on Ruth's face. There were going to be questions now, and she gave what she hoped was a dismissive laugh, like she didn't care. 'He's so busy, he thinks I'm his business partner half the time.'

'Oh, dear, he does seem to be away a lot, doesn't he? Perhaps I could have Mia for a sleepover when he's back and give you two a chance for a proper night out?'

They'd arrived at the coffee shop and Becca started collapsing the buggy, ready to take it inside. 'That's very kind of you,' she said, perhaps a little too quickly. 'But I wouldn't want to put you to any trouble. We can always get a babysitter.'

Ruth nodded, thoughtful. 'A couple of hours isn't the same as having a whole night together, though, is it? Without having to worry about this little one. You'd be able to relax then. Have a proper chat about everything that's worrying you.'

'Nothing's worrying me, Ruth. Honestly. I think you might have misunderstood.' She pushed open the door, eager to end the conversation, thinking that Ruth was way too observant for her liking.

CHAPTER ELEVEN

The next morning, Becca was up early as she had to go and fetch Frank, bring him back to her house for babysitting duties, and then get to work. She felt exhausted just thinking about it. A knock on the door startled her. Nobody ever knocked on their door – they didn't even know the neighbours yet. *Maybe a delivery?* she wondered as she went to answer it.

Ruth stood on the doorstep, a big grin on her face.

'I hope you don't mind me coming round. It's just I was thinking I've put you in a sticky situation today, saying I couldn't have Mia because I thought I was going in for treatment.' Her words rushed out and she seemed a little out of breath. 'I cancelled everyone, so I'm just going to be hanging around while you're dashing about. Anyway, I thought maybe I could make things easier for you by keeping an eye on Mia while you go and pick up your dad. I know what Mia's like in the car and… well…' She faltered, hands wrapping themselves round each other, like she was giving them a wash.

Becca stared at her for a moment while her brain tried to catch up. Mia had already been making a fuss about going to Frank's, even with the lure of all the Beanie Babies. *Why not?* Becca opened the door wide. 'That would be a big help, Ruth.' She smiled at her. 'Come on in.'

The day was going to be complicated enough for the sake of a four-hour shift, and her reservations were put to the back of her mind as she made Ruth a coffee. Whatever Ruth's reasoning,

Becca had to admit it had saved her a tussle with Mia and made her day less stressy – and for that she was thankful.

Frank was ready and waiting and out of the front door, his over-night bag clasped in his hand, before Becca could even get out of the car. He opened the passenger door and climbed in, beaming at her. 'This is such a treat, Becca. I can't tell you how much I've been looking forward to coming over to your new house.' A flash of anxiety clouded his face for a moment. 'I'm right in thinking Dean's away, aren't I?'

Becca patted his leg before she started the car and reversed out of the drive. 'It'll be fun, Dad. And yes, Dean's away until Monday.'

'I could stay a couple of nights, then?'

Becca blinked, surprised by his request. 'Um… yes… yes, if you want. I'm sure Mia will love to have you as her plaything for a while.' *It'll be fine, absolutely fine*, she told herself, concentrating on her manoeuvre.

Frank laughed. 'She's such a funny little thing. Never stops talking, does she? Reminds me of you when you were little. Talk about a chatterbox. You used to drive your mum mad, but I loved to hear your stories. Such a vivid imagination.' He chuckled to himself. 'I remember the games you used to play with those stuffed animals – they all had names and different characters. Honestly, you were hilarious!'

Becca smiled as she drove, memories flashing through her mind. Frank had been such a big part of her childhood, the one who'd take her on little trips to get her out of the house and give her mum a break. Looking back, she could see that her constant chattering, her endless questions had tested her mum's patience. She'd been a quiet woman herself, hadn't liked noise and had preferred the company of Kate. Her sister had been a self-contained child who loved to read, quite happy in her own company and much more like their mother.

Before he retired, Frank had been Head Warden for the National Trust in Northern Snowdonia, responsible for a great swathe of land along with his team. He used to take her out on the hills, teach her about birds and wildlife, plants and flowers, the names of all the mountains. Since his heart attack and subsequent retirement, he'd lost the motivation to go out walking and had become a bit of a hermit. She wondered whether she could help him to rekindle his love of the outdoors – revive his interest in birdwatching maybe, and give him something to fill his days. Now Mia was getting older, it was something they could do together, and she made a promise to herself that she'd start putting more time aside for her dad, give him the attention he used to give her. With Dean being away so much, there really was nothing stopping her.

'I've brought some more of those little animals for Mia,' Frank said. 'I picked out her favourites.'

'Ah, well, I might just pop them in the wash first, if you don't mind. Mia had a bad stomach upset when we got home the other day. Doctor said it was a virus, but it came on so suddenly and I didn't get it, so I'm not so sure. Then I realised it could be the Beanie Babies. If they've been festering in a box for years, there could be all sorts of bacteria on them, and she does like to put things in her mouth.' She glanced over at Frank, caught the frown on his face.

'I'm sorry to hear she was poorly. But it can't have been the toys. I put them in the wash before I gave them to her. I remembered last time I tried to give her a toy and I got a right ticking off because I hadn't washed it. You went and sterilised the thing before you'd let her have it.'

Becca ran her tongue round dry lips, concentrating on driving. 'I don't remember that.'

'Yes, well, I do. You're a shocker when you get a bee in your bonnet.'

Am I that bad? She hoped not but was aware she could flare up if she was feeling stressed. Perhaps she'd been having a bad day.

'Sorry, Dad,' she murmured, wishing she could be more relaxed, like other mums.

'It's okay, love. I know what it's like being a parent, remember?' He chuckled. 'When you were little you ate all sorts and it never harmed you. I remember taking you out in the baby carrier when you were just crawling and I found this lovely place to stop for a rest, put you on the grass and let you have a nosy around. Then I spotted this bird you don't normally see in the valley, and when I checked to see what you were up to, you were eating bits of sheep poo, like they were chocolate drops.'

Becca gasped. 'Oh my God, Dad! You never told me that.'

'Yeah, well, not my best parenting moment. But it didn't do you any harm.' He winked at her. 'I think if you could just learn to chill out with Mia, you'd enjoy her childhood a whole lot more.'

She snorted. 'That easy?'

'I know parenting has its challenges, love, but you're supposed to enjoy your kids. A stomach upset is par for the course, especially at Mia's age. I mean, it's not the first time she's had something like this, is it?' He turned to her. 'She's all right now, though?'

Becca nodded. 'Oh, yeah.'

'Come to think of it, where is she?' He glanced in the back seat as if he might have overlooked her.

'Ruth popped round to keep an eye on her while I came to pick you up. She's my childminder. You know, the one who had a cancer diagnosis. Anyway, they gave her the wrong results, so she's actually fine, and I think she felt guilty that she'd cancelled on me without warning.'

Becca puffed out her cheeks, her mind filling with everything that had happened in the past few days, turning her world upside down. 'What a weird week I'm having, Dad. You wouldn't believe who—' She stopped herself before she mentioned Connor. This was not the time to open that particular can of worms, not when she had to concentrate on driving.

She hadn't received any more messages from him. *Maybe that's the last I'll hear of him.* A flash of alarm ran through her, the idea that she wouldn't speak to him again unthinkable. *He wanted to chat,* she reassured herself. *Be patient. Or maybe I should start a conversation?*

His reappearance had made her think about a lot of things, made her understand that she needed to address the past so she could pack it away properly, instead of bits flopping out at random moments and taking her by surprise. At the very least, she needed to understand the creeping dissatisfaction which had begun to invade her psyche, making her question the nature of her relationship with Dean.

Perhaps it wasn't Connor she needed to speak to. Maybe the thing would be to talk everything through with Frank once Mia was asleep and they had the evening ahead of them. There was so much that hadn't been said over the years, it was time to get it all out in the open. Life was incredibly awkward when her dad and her husband couldn't get on, and it needed sorting out. She'd missed spending time with Frank and there was no reason why he couldn't come and stay more often, if only she could resolve this bad feeling between the two men. Then Kate would have a bit more freedom and everyone would be happier.

They arrived back at the house to find Ruth and Mia in the kitchen, making French toast for breakfast. 'I'll make some for you, Dandad,' Mia announced, dunking a fresh piece of bread in the egg mix.

'Dad, this is Ruth. Ruth this is Frank.' Becca glanced at her watch, and knew she was going to be late if she didn't get a move on. 'Look, I've got to dash. I'll see you just after one, Dad, okay? And thanks for coming round, Ruth.'

'Not a problem,' Ruth said, helping Mia lift the bread into the pan.

Frank shooed her out of the kitchen. 'Off you go. We'll be fine, won't we, Mia?'

But Mia didn't answer, too busy patting the piece of bread with a spatula under Ruth's watchful gaze.

Becca left feeling like she was missing out on something, but soon she was too busy with her patients to think about anything else, and the notion of being on the outside was stuffed to the back of her mind.

She stopped for a mid-morning coffee break, getting a takeout to drink in her car. The promenade on the north shore was a favourite place between calls, where she could watch the sea and have a bit of space to collect her thoughts. Today, her phone was practically burning a hole in her pocket, even though she'd been checking regularly all morning and no messages had arrived. She pulled it out, not expecting there to be anything, but there it was, on Twitter, a message.

She opened it up and laughed. It was a picture. Her and Connor in costumes for a fancy-dress party. New Year's Eve. A night that was firmly lodged in her memory. She'd been Groucho Marx and he'd been Liza Minelli. She chuckled to herself as she remembered what a fantastic night it had been. The night, in fact, when he'd first told her he loved her.

Another message arrived.

Remember this?

She replied:

How could I forget? You make a great woman. And you sang, if I remember rightly.

A moment later, a laughing emoji filled the screen, followed by:

One of the best nights of my life.

She replied before she'd properly considered it:

Mine too.

Her eyes widened as she read the words on the screen, knowing it was true. She clicked on the picture, enlarging it.

Look at my face, she thought. *Proper happy. When have I had fun like that with Dean?* A rhetorical question because Dean didn't do fun like Connor, who was a natural clown and really didn't mind making an idiot of himself. Dean was the opposite, and that, in a way, had been the attraction. He was a man she could rely on – steady and kind, and he put providing for his family at the top of his agenda. *Unexciting.* Unable to stir the passion that had been there with Connor.

She blinked, shrank the picture and put her phone away, horrified at the route her thoughts were taking. But it was true. *Passion is not the most important part of a marriage*, she told herself. Maybe she yearned for it, but that didn't mean she should ignore all the great things about her relationship with Dean, or the things that had worried her about Connor. She made herself list them in her mind, to balance out the bias of her thought processes. Connor was unpredictable, a free spirit who didn't want to be tied down. A loveable idiot who made rash decisions and didn't have a mean bone in his body and made her laugh. He'd adored her, of that she was sure. However, would he ever have been able to give her the stability she had with Dean?

Stop it. Just stop it. But this connection with Connor was an itch she had to scratch.

The picture reminded her of the journal and the box of stuff from her desk, and she decided she'd have a look later, when her dad was in bed, because with Dean being away, she'd have the perfect opportunity. Perhaps she'd find a photo she could send to Connor. She finished her coffee and made her way to her next patient, warmed by her memories and excited by the thought of revisiting a time in her life when she'd been a different person. A person she'd like to be again.

She arrived home to the smell of cooking and tracked the delicious aroma to the kitchen, surprised to find Ruth still there, sitting at the table with Frank, engrossed in conversation. Mia was colouring in, her cuddly animals lined up on the table in front of her as if they were watching.

Frank noticed her in the doorway. 'Ah, Becca. Ruth and I have realised that we've met before.'

'Oh, wow. How's that?' Becca couldn't imagine two such different people ever moving in the same circles.

'I used to volunteer with the National Trust a while ago,' Ruth said. 'Then I was poorly for a while and got out of the habit of going. We've just been chatting about it now and figured out we worked on a couple of tree-planting projects together.'

Becca smiled, thinking that it might be nice for Frank to make friends with Ruth. And it could be good for Ruth as well, because she was clearly at a loose end when she wasn't childminding. 'Small world,' she said, putting her bag down before hanging her coat in the cupboard under the stairs. Her stomach rumbled. 'Something smells good.'

'Oh, we made some soup, didn't we, Mia?'

Mia spotted her then. 'Mummy!' She slid off her chair and ran to Becca, who picked her up and held her tight. She kissed her soft cheek and Mia gave her a sloppy kiss back. 'We cooked,' she said, seriously. 'I stirred. Dandad chopped and Ruth told us what to do.'

'That's amazing,' Becca said, thinking she'd be worried about her daughter stirring a pot of boiling liquid and glad she hadn't been there to see it.

'It'll be ready now. I'll dish up, shall I?' Ruth stood. 'Frank, do you want to get the cutlery?'

Becca watched, a little bemused, as someone else took charge in her kitchen. *Leave it*, she warned herself. *She's just trying to help.* She put Mia back in her chair and cleared her colouring stuff to the end of the table, then busied herself getting drinks, refusing to be a bystander in her own space.

Mia, who was generally a fussy eater, behaved perfectly, especially when Ruth reminded her what a clever girl she'd been making them all lunch. Becca squirmed in her seat, joining in the conversation but hoping that Ruth would go home after lunch.

She didn't.

'How about a walk to the playground and then go for afternoon tea?' Frank suggested, looking at Ruth, making Becca feel like a spare part. 'My treat.' Becca was about to say Mia could probably do with a nap, when he turned to her. 'It'll give you a break, love, let you get your head down, maybe get some sleep.'

And she realised she wasn't invited.

Enjoy the peace, she told herself ten minutes later as she waved goodbye and closed the door. The quiet was disconcerting. It was strange – when her life was usually hurtling along at a hundred miles an hour – to be given a chance to just stop and do nothing.

Suddenly drowsy, she climbed the stairs and lay on the bed, but she couldn't get comfortable, the chatter of her thoughts keeping her awake. After a while she gave up and decided she'd go and sit in the garden with her book and a cup of tea instead. She checked her phone. No new messages. Her fingers flew over the screen.

We had a lot of fun, didn't we?

She didn't expect a reply, and stuffed her phone back in her pocket, but the ping signalling a response came almost immediately.

Best times of my life. You made me laugh. Didn't judge, just let me be myself. That's what real love is all about. I don't know how it all went so wrong. Well, I do, if I'm honest. I was scared of commitment. I wasn't ready. Thing is, I miss you.

She stared at the screen, her heart thumping as she read and reread his words. *He misses me.*

She typed and pressed send:

You too.

Her mouth dropped open. *What am I doing? I'm married to Dean.*

She could feel Connor's grip tightening on her heart, the love she'd felt for him rushing back, filling the hole that Dean's absences had created. She yearned to be the centre of someone's world again. And she knew she'd been that to Connor.

Perhaps I could be again?

The thought was so shocking, she put her phone away as though it was responsible for the wayward path her mind was taking. The hooks of obsession had got her; thoughts of Connor were taking over. And instead of fighting it, she wanted to surrender, wanted to enjoy the thrill of flirting, of knowing that they still had a bond, and to revel in the feeling that she was loved.

CHAPTER TWELVE

Mia was ill again that night. The same symptoms, and just as violent as the last time. At least Frank was there to help with the messy, stinky awfulness, even if Dean wasn't present to accept his share of parental responsibilities. Frank couldn't brush away her worries as being insignificant now. He couldn't deny the situation was pretty scary, and Becca could tell by his wild eyes and the pallor of his skin that he'd been shocked by the whole experience.

'I think she's settled now,' Becca said with a heavy sigh as she walked into the kitchen to see Frank making them a cup of tea. 'It's just like the other night.'

Frank glanced up as he poured milk into their mugs and brought them over to the table, where Becca had slumped into a chair, hands rubbing her tired eyes. 'These bugs can come back, though, can't they?' He sat in the chair opposite. 'Maybe there were still some of the germs about on one of her toys or something. It's impossible to sterilise the place, I would imagine.'

'Hmm.' Becca put her mug on a coaster, something Frank never thought to do, straightening it up so it was in line with the edge of the table. 'Well, I definitely didn't do a deep clean of the whole house. I haven't had time to even think about that.' She chewed her lip. 'It's something I probably should have done though.'

'Let's hope we don't pick it up.' Frank sipped his tea. 'I'm sure it's nothing to worry about. She bounced back last time, didn't she?'

'I should probably take her to the doctor's again.' Becca was in two minds whether to take her now, go to the out-of-hours doctor at the cottage hospital round the corner. It wasn't far.

'There's nothing a doctor can do if it's a virus. There's no point taking an emergency appointment when somebody else might need it. Why don't you just see how she is in the morning?'

She glanced at Frank, her fingers knotting together as if they were seeking comfort from each other. 'I don't think it is a virus, though. The symptoms don't seem right to me.' She sighed. 'It could be all sorts of things. A whole range of illnesses present like this.' She caught Frank's eye. 'What if it's something serious and I just ignore it?'

Frank frowned, his voice stern. 'Now you're catastrophising, Becca. Don't start down that road again.'

Her jaw clamped shut, annoyed that her dad was wafting her concerns away. This was her only child, the centre of her world. Nothing and nobody was more important, and Mia was dependent on Becca to look out for her.

'Anyway, you've got work tomorrow, haven't you?' Frank slurped his tea, put his mug down. 'I'll be here to mind her, so you don't need to worry, and if there's any signs of illness, I'll let you know.' He reached over and patted her hand. 'You worry too much, love. Kids that age are always getting tummy bugs. That's just how it is. No need to rush off to the doctor's every time. It's always the same with you – no confidence in yourself when it comes to Mia, always thinking the worst. Remember last year when she had that rash and you were sure it was meningitis? Then before that, when she had an ear infection and you were convinced she had some neurological problem?' He took another sip of tea. 'Anyway, whatever's upset her seems to have passed now, and hopefully that's the end of it.'

They sat in silence as they finished their drinks, Becca expecting to hear a wail of distress from Mia at any moment. Thankfully,

the house stayed quiet, and Frank went up to bed. Becca found
the soiled nappy and scraped a sample into a Perspex tube, ready
to drop off at the surgery in the morning, to be sent away for
analysis. Better to be safe than sorry. If she had tests results, she
was more likely to get a clear diagnosis.

Feeling jittery and anxious, her ears still straining for Mia's cries,
she got ready for bed and was just climbing in when she spotted
the box that she'd retrieved from the spare bedroom. She'd put
it next to her side of the bed, ready to sort through before Dean
got home on Monday. *That might relax me*, she thought, *looking
through old photos.* Her heart skipped at the thought. She checked
her phone. No message from Connor. Or Dean for that matter.

She scowled as she typed out a quick message to her husband,
telling him Mia had been ill again, still angry with him for calling
her Alice. *I've got to pull him up about it, let him know how much it
hurts that he's got another woman on his mind.* Even if she was his
business partner. That's what he'd tell her – all to do with business,
his mind already full of what he had to do that day as soon as
he got up. *Is that the truth?* she wondered now, very aware of the
empty space beside her. *Or is there something going on between them?*

There was no arguing the fact that even when he was physically at
home, his mind was on other things, constantly distracted with messages and conversations with people in different parts of the world.
She pictured Dean's face, the deep frown lines that had developed
on his forehead, his tetchy demeanour. *Is it all to do with work?*

He used to come home with flowers. Or other little gifts that
he'd picked up on his travels. That didn't happen any more. He
used to burst into the house and rush to find her as soon as he got
home, wrap her in a big hug and kiss her like he hadn't seen her
for a month. It used to make her laugh, make her feel so warm
and loved. But that didn't happen any more either.

She loosened her jaw, rubbing at the muscles on either side of her face. *Dean wouldn't be unfaithful.* He was loyal and kind and had stood by her when he really didn't need to. He'd seen her at her worst, when they'd been to hell and back through three miscarriages and then the tense wait to see if the fourth pregnancy would finally result in the baby they both so desperately wanted. He'd left her in no doubt that he truly wanted to be with her in sickness and in health. For better and for worse.

It's just a blip, she told herself, deciding that she should initiate a date night, like Ruth had suggested. In fact, now she thought about it, a date night was a great idea.

A whole night together, with no fear of interruptions, would give her time to explain how she was feeling – because, when she thought about it, communication between them had been on a surface level for quite some time now. Conversations about household chores and arrangements, what Mia had said and done. Nothing about feelings. What they needed was a proper heart-to-heart, then she could explain that she felt like a single parent. Remind him how much he was missing out on with Mia.

Hopefully, he'd come to see that things had to change. It wasn't as though they were short of money. He didn't need to work so hard any more. Perhaps she could persuade him to lighten his schedule, employ another assistant and let Alice take more control of some aspects of the business.

With a clear plan of action in her mind, she filed away that particular bundle of worries and opened the box, pulling out the three journals from her time in Australia.

Slowly, she turned the pages, reliving her journey from mental hell – when she'd been accused of crimes against patients at the hospital – to mental health, when she'd been cared for by Tina in Australia, and then when she'd met Connor. She'd written the last entry in the third journal just after she'd heard news of her mum's death and was getting ready to go back to England. She'd laid out how she felt about going home, the funeral, her heart-wrenching grief. Underneath, she'd stuck a picture of her with Connor, their last one together, and beside it she'd written, 'Au revoir, my love. See you soon.'

Although they'd been on a break for a few weeks before he'd given her a lift to the airport, as soon as she'd seen him, she'd known she still loved him. Not that it had ever been in doubt. The question had been about them having a future together, wanting the same things. At the time, she hadn't told him how she felt because by then the grief had hit, and she couldn't really speak.

Now, a lump clogged her throat and tears welled in her eyes as she remembered the impossible dilemma she'd found herself faced with, the squall of emotions that had battered her at the time. Connor still didn't know what had happened when she'd come home and met Dean. She picked up her phone, took a picture of the photo and sent it to him. Then she wrote him a long message explaining everything.

By the time she'd finished, her eyes were sore with staring at the little screen, but her heart felt lighter, her conscience clearer for at last being honest with him. She pressed send. Would it scare him away? Or would it help to repair the bond of friendship that had been so strong between them?

With that thought in her mind, she finally settled herself in bed, falling asleep almost immediately.

CHAPTER THIRTEEN

The next morning, the alarm woke her from a deep sleep, and she was still feeling groggy after she'd showered and got herself dressed. She peeked in on Mia, who was fast asleep, clearly exhausted by her illness the night before.

The sound of whistling from the kitchen made her smile. Frank had a whole repertoire of tunes he could whistle, a skill which had eluded her, making her even more impressed by her dad's abilities.

'Morning, love,' he said when he looked up from the newspaper he was reading, a cup of coffee in front of him and a plate with nothing but crumbs on it by his side.

'You're a bit chipper, aren't you? I can't believe you've already been to get a paper.'

'I'm always up early, you know that. Can't help it after all those years at work. My body won't lie in even if I want to. Anyway, it's a lovely day out there.'

'Mia's still asleep, so I won't wake her.' Becca made herself a coffee, stifling a yawn. 'Are you okay to get her breakfast?'

'I think she'll be wanting to make her own after yesterday.' Frank grinned. 'She was very taken with Ruth's French toast.'

Becca went to sit opposite him at the table, cradling her mug in her hands, happy to see him so cheerful. 'And I think you were very taken with Ruth.' She thought she detected a blush working its way up his neck and into his cheeks.

He cleared his throat and stood up, pushing his chair back, the legs scraping on the tiled floor. 'I'm going to make some more toast – you want some?'

He was definitely avoiding her eye and she couldn't tell if he was just embarrassed or whether she'd offended him. Ten years after her mum's death, he still hadn't found a rhythm to his existence. His life had become so much smaller and less sociable since retirement, with no reason to leave the house. She understood how claustrophobic it must be for Kate and resolved to work on her plan to get him out more, and maybe invite Ruth along as well.

'Toast would be lovely, thanks, Dad.' She sipped her coffee while her brain tried to organise her to-do list for the day ahead. *Should I take Mia to the doctor's?* It seemed a shame to wake her, and as Frank had said, she'd bounced back last time. Still there was a niggling feeling in the pit of her stomach. 'I think I'll have a chat to the practice nurse about Mia. Maybe she'll run some blood tests, just to make sure.'

Frank put the bread in the toaster, clicked it in place. 'Your call, if it's bothering you.'

Becca nodded, her mind made up. She'd talk to Carol when she went into the surgery to sort out her round for the day, see what she thought before she made a formal appointment for blood tests. She didn't want them thinking she was making a fuss about nothing again.

Her phone pinged, a message. She snatched it up. *Connor?* Her heart did a little skip, but it was from Dean.

She tapped out a quick response as Frank slid a plate of toast in front of her. 'Just Dean, checking everything's okay,' she said, aware that the disappointment was obvious in her voice. She put her phone down and took a bite of her toast, eyes on her plate.

'When's he home again? That absent bloke of yours?'

'Monday,' she reminded him. She chewed and swallowed, thinking about all the household chores to do while trying to entertain Mia.

'I could always stay Sunday night as well if that would help, you know?'

Becca glanced over at Frank, saw the hopeful expression on his face and stopped herself from automatically knocking him back. She'd thought she'd hate him in the house, watching her for signs that things weren't right with her again. But that had been her paranoia speaking, and it hadn't been like that at all. He was more interested in Mia. And Ruth. On top of that, they still hadn't had time for the chat she'd hoped for. To be honest, it was nice having him around.

'I'm not sure when Kate's coming home,' he continued. 'It was supposed to be today, but she rang when you were at work yesterday to say she was going to look up some friends while she was in London, so she might stay the weekend. She was keeping it "fluid", she said, whatever that means.'

He sighed, forlorn. 'It's a nuisance cooking for one, and that house feels so big with just me rattling round in it. I get to feeling all maudlin.' He swallowed. 'I miss your mum, love. I know it's been a while, but I still miss her so much.'

Becca's heart squeezed. 'I do too, Dad. Never a day that I don't think about her and wish we'd had time to clear the air after everything that happened when I was suspended from work.' She pressed her lips together, hardly able to carry on. 'We seemed to get our wires crossed for some reason, and there was so much tension between us, and I never knew why.' Her voice cracked. 'It's hard that we never got to sort it out. That I'll never understand what she really thought.'

Frank gazed over her head, his tongue licking crumbs from the corners of his mouth. 'I think she was scared, for all sorts of reasons that had nothing to do with you. And you're right, it's a shame you never got to sort things out between you. But all you need to know is she never stopped loving you, whatever misunderstandings there might have been.'

Becca could feel the tears welling up inside, couldn't speak for fear that she'd start crying. She cleared her throat, sensing now was the opportunity she'd been waiting for – a quiet moment, just her and Frank, discussing things that really mattered.

'Talking about bad feeling and misunderstandings, Dad. There's something I've been meaning to ask you about. Something I really don't understand. Why is it that you and Dean can't get along?'

Frank took a minute to collect his thoughts, and when he finally spoke his words were measured. 'He upset your mother. They had a hell of a row.' He took a deep breath. 'It was the same day she had her stroke, and I can't help thinking he got her so worked up it had to have something to do with it. You know she had high blood pressure, and an upset like that, well…'

Her brain froze as she understood the implications of her father's words. This must have happened before Becca had even met Dean. 'What? Wait a minute…' She stumbled over her words as she tried to get things straight in her mind. 'Dean and Mum knew each other… and nobody has ever mentioned this to me?' Her voice was getting louder as the deception became clear, her heart flipping in a peculiar rhythm. Frank studied his fingernails. She banged a hand on the table, determined she wouldn't be fobbed off by silence. 'How? How did they know each other?'

Frank reached for his tea, still not looking at her, as he put his mug on his plate, folded his newspaper. 'It's a small world round here, Becca. You know that. And being a dinner lady, your mum knew a lot of the kids and their siblings and cousins, even if they didn't all go to the same school. She had that sort of brain. Knew how everyone fitted together locally.' He glanced at her then, before his eyes slid away, his gaze fixed on the window and the garden beyond.

Her jaw clenched to stop more angry words from spewing out while she let his explanation settle between them, like leaves falling from a tree. It was true that her mum had known an awful lot of people, but Frank wasn't telling the whole story, of that she was sure. Another, more important question rushed into her mind and out of her mouth. 'What the hell were they arguing about?'

Her eyes narrowed as she tried to visualise the scene but found she couldn't. Dean wasn't an argumentative person and it took quite a lot to get him worked up to the point of a full-blown row.

Silence.

'Come on, Dad,' she snapped. 'Don't you think this has gone on long enough? It's time for the truth.'

He looked at her then. 'As far as I know… Dean did something she didn't agree with. You know what she was like… she tried to put him right and they had a row.' He shook his head, lips pursed. 'I wasn't there. I didn't hear exactly what was said. She rang me at work and was ever so upset, but I couldn't make a lot of sense of what she was saying. Then I came home and…' His face crumpled, and Becca's anger evaporated, horrified that she'd reduced her Dad to tears. Her voice softened and she reached over the table to squeeze his hand.

'Oh, Dad, why on earth didn't you tell me this before? We could have sorted things out years ago.'

'I didn't say anything because he's your husband and you were determined to be with him. And you were expecting a baby. Me and Kate agreed it wasn't our place to tell you. I've tried to see things from a different perspective, but in all honesty, I can't forgive him. If they hadn't been arguing, then…'

Frank didn't move, didn't finish his sentence, his chin wobbling, eyes squeezed shut. Now was not the time to push things, but at least she was getting closer to the truth. She'd have to make Dean tell her the rest of the story.

'You know… whatever they were rowing about, I don't think you can blame Dean for Mum dying.' She gave his hand another squeeze. 'Look, it would be lovely if you want to stay another night. And you could come and stay more often if you could see your way to getting along with Dean. Make peace with him. Could you think about that, Dad?'

Frank was staring into the garden again, and she wasn't sure he was listening.

'Dad?'

He blinked and took his hand from her grasp, wiping his eyes. 'I'll try, love. But he'll have to make an effort as well.'

'I'll have a word with him. See if we can negotiate a truce, eh?'

Frank sighed, like he had the weight of the world on his shoulders. 'I promise I'll try harder.'

'Forgive and forget, isn't that what you used to tell me and Kate when we were squabbling?'

He gave a little snort. 'You're right. Doesn't really do to hold grudges.' Although he was saying the right thing, his tone suggested his heart wasn't in it. He glanced at the clock on the wall. 'Isn't it time you were going to work?'

'Christ, you're right. I'm going to be late.' She jumped up, stuffing the rest of her toast in her mouth and swilling it down with a big gulp of coffee.

'Ruth said Mia loves to go for walks. A little bundle of energy who needs tiring out. I think those were her words. Anyway, there's the nature reserve further down the estuary, so I thought we could walk there and get the bus back.'

Becca checked her watch, flustered now. 'Oh, Dad, that would be lovely on a normal day, but after last night, I'm not sure she'll be up to it. Why don't we save that for tomorrow, when she's had a good rest? Then I can come as well?'

The cheeriness faded from his face and she felt bad for ruining his plans.

'How about something a little less ambitious today? Take the buggy so she can ride in that if she's tired.'

He nodded, looking wistful and not a little disappointed, his mouth drooping at the corners. He gathered the dirty plates and mugs together. 'I suppose you're right.'

'We'll do it tomorrow, Dad. Promise we will.' She picked up her phone, checked the time again. 'Okay, I've really got to go.'

She arrived ten minutes late. 'Oh, thank God. I thought you weren't coming,' Carol said as soon as Becca came through the door.

'I'm so sorry. Mia was poorly again last night. You know the sickness and diarrhoea thing? And I've got Dad staying while my sister's away. He hates being on his own, and to be honest, I don't think Kate trusts him by himself. Thinks he'll do something daft. He does tend to dip into these depressions. And Dean's working away.' She put her bag down, aware that she'd just been making excuses that had nothing to do with being late. 'Anyway, you don't want to hear about that.'

Carol gave her a motherly hug. 'I'm just relieved you're here.' She stepped back and studied her. 'You're looking tired, though. Bit peaky actually. You don't think you're coming down with this thing, do you?'

Becca frowned. 'I don't think it's a virus. There's no temperature. Just this vomiting and then her body seems to be expelling everything from both ends as fast as it bloody can.' She rolled her eyes. 'Horrendous.'

Carol frowned and pulled a face. 'Ewww. Sounds horrible.'

'Poor Dad. I had to rope him in to help. You should have seen his face. Anyway, I was glad to have him there. But it's got me puzzled. I thought it might be these old toys of mine that Dad dug out, but he says he washed them all before he gave them to her, so I don't think it's that.'

'Something she ate? Perhaps she's got an intolerance that you're not aware of?'

Becca nodded. 'Hmm. Yes, that's a thought. Ruth has her eating all sorts of healthy things, but perhaps there's something in the mix that disagrees with her.' She paused, thinking it through. 'She has had tummy upsets before but she wasn't at Ruth's when it happened this time. Mind you, Ruth did come round to our house yesterday. Perhaps she brought something with her?' She threw up her hands. 'Who knows? But that's a good call, Carol. I'll do a food diary for the last week and see if I can spot something I might have given her, see if Ruth can think of anything.' She rummaged in her handbag. 'I've brought a sample in for testing, and I was thinking of getting the practice nurse to take bloods too, just to make sure there's nothing more serious going on – what do you think?'

Carol pursed her lips. 'Well, if it's going to put your mind at rest, it can't do any harm, can it? I know what it's like when it's your own kids that are ill. Especially when you've got medical training. It's hard not to get carried away and think the worst, isn't it?' She gave Becca's shoulder a rub. 'You start to doubt yourself, then you're second-guessing everything. But you're an excellent nurse. I trust your judgement, so maybe you should too.'

Becca sighed, frustrated. 'But that's the problem – my judgement says it's not a virus. Which means she's eaten something she's intolerant to or put something else in her mouth that's poisoned her.'

'Poisoned?' Carol pounced on the word. 'If you think her symptoms fit with poisoning, you need to check at home, make sure there's nothing she's had access to that she shouldn't. Medication that looks like sweets. Cleaning fluids. Could there be anything?'

Becca's mind sorted through the contents of the cupboards, but nothing obvious came to mind. She was always very careful about that sort of thing, to the point where Dean took the mickey out of her for putting everything on the top shelf, out of her own reach let alone Mia's.

It was a puzzle. If her daughter was ingesting a poison of some sort, the question was what and where was she getting it from? Becca was absolutely sure that her house was child-safe. After everything she'd been through at the hospital, she always checked and doubled-checked and triple-checked that medication was out of reach.

Medication! Suddenly she knew that was the answer.

As far as she was aware, Dean wasn't taking any medication, but her dad was another matter. She remembered Kate telling her that he was on quite a few tablets and kept forgetting to take them, so she had to put them out for him in one of those trays marked with days of the week. *What if he left them out and Mia took them?* It was a strong possibility.

Relieved that she'd found something to explain Mia's symptoms, she got on with her morning, determined to ask him as soon as she got back to the house.

CHAPTER FOURTEEN

Becca arrived home to find no sign of Frank or Mia. With medication on her mind, she took the opportunity to go and check his room. The bed was all neat and tidy, his bag zipped shut. His clothes folded in the drawer she'd emptied for him. No medication anywhere. She went into the bathroom and found his toiletries bag stashed on top of the bathroom cabinet. No medication in there either. *Perhaps he forgot to bring it?* But if he had forgotten, she'd have to rule that out as the cause of Mia's illness.

Puzzled, she went to her en suite bathroom, checked her own tablets were still where they should be. Satisfied that everything was there, she went and sat on the bed. Dean's side. She hesitated, then pulled open the drawer of his bedside cabinet. It felt like a violation of his privacy for some reason, but a quick rummage found no tablets of any sort.

In one way, it was a relief to know that medication wasn't the cause of the problem, but it didn't solve the mystery. She checked her watch, wondered when her dad would be back with Mia. She made herself a sandwich and a cup of tea, still feeling jittery, wanting to make sure that Mia was okay but keen not to appear like she was fussing. She wolfed her food down then couldn't wait any longer and called her dad.

'Hi, love,' Frank's cheery voice answered, and she could tell he was outside, the sound of seagulls in the background. And voices. 'How was work?'

'Fine. It was fine. I was wondering… I thought you'd be back by now. Where are you?'

'Oh, we're having a lovely day. We got all the way to Conwy.'

'Conwy?' Her voice rose to a squeak. 'You walked four miles with Mia?'

'Well, she had to ride the last bit. Poor love was dragging her feet, but she'd been running round like a puppy up till then.'

Becca tried to keep her voice even, but there was no mistaking her annoyance. 'Dad! I told you not to go far today after her being poorly. I thought we agreed to let her have a rest and do a walk tomorrow. All of us together.'

She heard him tutting, and when he spoke, his voice had that 'calm down' tone to it that she knew so well. 'She's been fine. Honestly, love. Right as rain. And anyway, I met up with Ruth, so she came along to help. I did ask her opinion, to see if she thought Mia would be okay, and she said she walks miles with her. And Mia was totally up for it. In fact, she's had a lovely time. We're just having fish and chips by the harbour, then we'll be coming back.'

The idea of her dad and Ruth both ignoring her wishes regarding the care of her child added fuel to her anger. 'I'm coming to get you. You're not going to make her walk all the way back.'

'I didn't make her do anything.' His voice hardened. 'She wanted to do the walk. Insisted on walking, in fact. And she's been tucking into fish and chips, no sign of any tummy problems at all.'

Becca's jaw tightened. 'I'm still coming to get you.'

With that, Becca hung up, grabbed her car keys and set off, quietly steaming about Frank's behaviour. And Ruth's for that matter. She was still simmering when she pulled into a parking space in Conwy. At least she could ask Ruth about food now and work out if she might have given Mia something that had caused the illness. It was funny that up to this point she had trusted Ruth completely with Mia's care, but over the last couple of days her view of Ruth had shifted. As soon as Ruth had thought she would no longer be looking after Mia, she'd become a little clingy, obviously panicked at the idea that she wouldn't be in her life. *Is that normal for a childminder?*

She started jogging when she saw them at a table by the edge of the harbour, Mia running round, chasing seagulls. She grabbed Mia's hand and picked her up.

'Christ, she could go falling in the water. That wall's only low. Were you even watching her?'

Ruth looked shocked at her outburst. Frank scowled and said, 'I had my eyes on her, no need to worry. Honestly, what is wrong with you, Becca?'

She took a deep breath, realising how unhinged she sounded. 'Sorry, I'm just… I'm feeling a bit flustered.'

'Shall we go for a coffee?' Frank suggested, looking between her and Ruth before glancing up at the sky and the grey folds of clouds that were gathering, blocking out the sun. 'Might be in for a shower.'

'That's a lovely idea,' Ruth said before Becca could reply. 'I'm sure this young lady might enjoy a babyccino. What do you say, Mia?'

Mia jumped up and down, clapping her hands. Ruth glanced at Becca, who wasn't sure what to do now. She'd come barging in like a lunatic and accused them of not looking after Mia when, in reality, there wasn't a problem. Even though she just wanted to get home, she didn't feel she had a choice.

She forced a smile. 'Lovely, I think that's just what I need.'

Becca made sure she sat next to Ruth, and while Frank and Mia were having a conversation about the pigeons, which were pecking about on the pavement in front of the coffee shop, she saw the perfect opportunity to quiz her.

'I was talking to my boss today and she had an idea about Mia's sickness. She wondered about food intolerances.'

She had Ruth's full attention now. 'Oh, yes, that's an idea, isn't it? Mind you, I suffer from a number of food intolerances myself, you know.' She frowned, pensive. 'It's hard to avoid everything, to be honest, but if I eat something I'm intolerant to, it's not a violent reaction. It's more bloating and stomach pains. Lethargy, low mood, that sort of thing.'

'I don't suppose there's anything Mia had to eat when she was last with you that might have triggered a violent reaction, is there? If it was an allergy, rather than an intolerance, then the reaction would be more extreme.'

Ruth seemed horrified, her jaw dropping, a hand clasped to her chest. 'Oh, gosh no. I wouldn't have thought so.' Her voice became shrill, drawing curious glances from neighbouring tables. 'I'm so careful about what I give the children. She only eats natural foods with me. No nuts, if that's what you're thinking. Nothing allergenic whatsoever. It's all part of my risk assessments, which have been passed as excellent.' She shook her head. 'No, honestly, Becca, it really isn't a possibility. Not at all.'

Becca felt the force of Frank's stare. 'You're not fussing about this sickness thing again, are you, Becs?'

'She thinks I've given Mia something that's... made her ill.'

Becca was appalled to see tears shining in Ruth's eyes, and she reached out, put a hand on her arm, feeling terrible to have upset her.

'No, I wasn't suggesting anything... I just thought maybe... she had a nut allergy or something.' It sounded feeble and she wasn't sure what she had, in fact, been thinking. 'I'd forgotten you'd have all that covered with procedures. I'm sorry, Ruth. I didn't mean to suggest you'd been negligent in any way, I just...'

Ruth was blinking furiously. 'I'm so careful, Becca. Really, I am. I'm sure there's nothing in my house that a child would have a reaction to, and she's not eaten anything recently that she hasn't had dozens of times before. But maybe I'm wrong. I'll have to check when I get home.' She covered her mouth with her hands. 'Perhaps it *was* me?'

Frank glanced at Ruth and leant towards his daughter. 'Now, let's just drop it. Ruth has the healthiest diet on the planet. We were talking about it earlier. How age alters your body as you get older, how it tells you what it doesn't want any more.'

Ruth wouldn't look at Becca, who felt a creeping heat work its way into her cheeks.

Frank patted Ruth's hand. 'Becca didn't mean anything by it. She has this problem, you see. When she's stressed. Gets all OCD about everything. It's happened before and I think—'

'Dad, stop it!' Becca snapped, afraid that he was going to dredge up her whole medical history. 'I'm fine now. There's nothing wrong with me. It's Mia I'm worried about.' She took a deep breath, aware of the sharpness in her voice. 'I know you think I'm fussing, but I'm going through all the possibilities, that's all I was doing. I'm sorry if it came out as an accusation – I really didn't mean it like that.'

'I would never do anything to harm Mia.' Ruth's chin was trembling. 'You must know she's the most precious little person in my life?'

There was a hardness in Frank's eyes that warned of trouble. Mia became silent, sensing the tense atmosphere around the table. Becca averted her eyes, wanting the floor to open and swallow her up. Panic bloomed in her chest, like an inflating balloon, until it filled all the space. She started to hyperventilate, felt dizzy and stood, desperate to be outside.

'Sorry, I'm not feeling too great.' She grabbed the back of a chair as her body swayed. 'I always get anxious when I'm under the weather.'

'Maybe it's the same bug Mia's had,' Frank said, pointedly. 'Why don't you get off home and have a lie down. We'll see you later.' He glanced over at Ruth, gave her a reassuring nod.

Mia shuffled on to his lap, snuggling against his chest, thumb in her mouth.

Becca gave a tight smile, unable to do anything but agree. They didn't need her. She'd only managed to upset everyone and make a fool of herself. *What is wrong with me?* she thought as she hurried down the pavement to her car.

Even though it looked like rain, Frank and Ruth had been adamant they were happy to walk home, having come prepared with waterproofs and the cover for the buggy. She didn't blame them – who'd want to be in a car with someone who behaved all kinds of crazy?

She sat for a few moments until she'd calmed down and the dizziness had passed. *Everyone thinks I'm overreacting.* But she knew in her heart that she wasn't and came back to the only thing that made sense: Mia was ingesting poison of some sort. *If it's not medication, or food, then what the hell is it and where is it coming from?*

CHAPTER FIFTEEN

Becca arrived back at the house, too agitated to rest. She scoured the place for anything that Mia might have swallowed by accident but found nothing. She lay on her bed, trying to make herself relax, going through the process her therapist had taught her, and finally she was able to feel a little calmer, her eyelids heavy.

Her phone pinged. A message. Immediately she was alert. Perhaps it was Frank, wanting a lift after all. But it wasn't. It was Dean.

How's it going, love? Event's going great here. Back Monday night, not sure what time. Don't wait up. Love you xxx

She read it again, disheartened. She'd been hoping he'd be back at a reasonable time and she'd be able to talk to him about her concerns, but it was apparent that wasn't going to happen now. He hadn't even asked how Mia was. She started typing a reply then quickly deleted it and let the phone rest on her chest as she turned on her back, eyes fluttering closed. There was no way she could fit everything she wanted to say into a message, and she'd sound like a lunatic if she started accusing a mystery person of poisoning their daughter.

If that's what is happening. Perhaps Frank was right, and this was her old troubles coming back again. The fears in her head manifesting themselves in reality.

A horrible thought struck her.

Is it me? Could I have given her something different to eat and not remembered? Or given her something that was past its use-by date? Or forgotten to put something away?

There'd been a time before she went to Australia when she'd done things and had no memory of doing them. It had been brought on by the anxiety of fighting the accusations at work, which smashed her confidence, making her disassociate from reality. It had felt like she was watching life as an observer rather than a participant, her thinking fuddled and sluggish, as if she was operating in slow motion with big blanks where her memory should be.

Am I overdoing it? Tears welled at the thought of how terrifying life had been for her in the middle of her mental health crisis and how hard it had been to get herself back to normality. The thought that it might be happening all over again was quite overwhelming.

She sniffed back her tears, got up and went into the bathroom, pulling her tablets from the top shelf of the cabinet and counting each one. *Is that how many there should be?* She rubbed at her forehead, not quite sure if there were a couple missing. But would that give Mia sickness and diarrhoea? She didn't think so – it was more likely they'd knock her out, make her really sleepy, and there was no sign of that.

It's not me. It's not. I'm just tired.

She hurried downstairs and made herself a coffee, got a couple of chocolate biscuits out of the tin to boost her energy levels and sat at the table with her laptop, ready to do some research on Mia's symptoms. Perhaps there was another possibility that she hadn't thought of.

After half an hour, she kept coming back to the same conclusion.

She rang the doctor's surgery and spoke to Carol.

'I've ruled out everything except poisoning of some sort. I'd like blood tests to see if we can narrow it down. I wonder if you could book me in on Monday to have that done.'

'So… can I just ask, is she still ill?' Carol sounded a little hesitant.

'No, she's fine today. It's amazing after last night, but she walked to Conwy with my dad this morning.'

Carol laughed. 'Well, that's a relief. But Becca… you need to listen to yourself. Your daughter is fine, and if she can walk all that way, I'd say there's nothing to worry about. Kids that age put all sorts in their mouths.'

Becca sighed. 'That's what Dad said.'

'Maybe you should listen to him. He helped bring you and your sister up no problem, didn't he?' She laughed. 'But I think we need to put your mind at rest – I know what it's like when you get a worry stuck in your brain, I've been like that myself. I'll pop you in first thing on Monday, before the rest of the morning appointments. Okay? But if it is some sort of poison, it'll probably be out of her system by then, won't it?'

'Thanks, Carol. You're probably right, but I'd never forgive myself if anything happened to Mia.'

'No problem, love. You enjoy the rest of your weekend and I'll see you Monday.' And with that she was gone.

Becca sat for a moment, unsure what to do. Carol was right – a blood test on Monday wouldn't be much use. Still, it wouldn't do any harm either. *Not a pleasant experience for Mia*, said a little voice in her head. And then she was in two minds again whether it was a good idea or not.

To distract herself, she went on to Twitter, her eye drawn to a new message in her inbox. *Connor.* Her heart skipped as she clicked on the icon.

Thanks for being honest with me. I always wondered exactly what happened, and I feel better for knowing the truth. I never stopped loving you, Becca x

She sat staring at his words, too dumbstruck to formulate a sensible response. The truth was, she didn't know how she felt about anything any more.

She closed her eyes and could see his face, that cheeky grin, his eyes so full of love. She allowed herself to imagine his arms encircling her, pulling her to his chest while she wrapped her own arms round his waist. They'd stood like that for ages on the beach, listening to the waves, just enjoying the moment, the being together.

She'd thought it would never end. Had built a whole future in her head. At first, she hadn't minded that he was a free spirit, moving around, picking up casual jobs to fund his surfer lifestyle. Hadn't minded that he lived in a campervan. It had all seemed so romantic, so different to how she'd lived her life up to then.

At the time, she'd accepted that with Connor she'd never be rich, but she'd liked the idea of a minimalist lifestyle without the burden of possessions, a house and everything that went with it. She'd felt liberated from the rat race, and with that had come the freedom to be herself. Connor hadn't been bothered what job she did. All he'd been interested in was her as a person. They'd talked a lot about dreams.

Then she'd realised she couldn't live like that forever. Her biological clock was ticking towards thirty and she wanted a family. Not just one child, but a little gang of them, and once she'd shared this with Connor, said she was ready to settle somewhere, there was a tension between them, a pulling in different directions.

It wasn't real, she told herself now. *How could you live like that with a child?* It wasn't practical. *I made the right choice*, she reassured herself, opening her eyes and scanning her lovely house. *I wouldn't have this if I was with Connor.* Then another little voice piped up. *But you'd have a husband who wanted to spend time with you.*

Her jaw clamped tight. That wasn't fair. Dean was working for their future. It's what you had to do when you had a family and were running a business. *But still*, she thought, *ambition is overrated. Think of all the time he's missing with Mia. And with me.*

She read Connor's message again, typed a reply.

What are you doing now? Still chasing the waves in a campervan?

She was surprised when a response came a few moments later.

Lol! Those were the days, weren't they? No, I have a job now and a salary and a house in Sydney. Respectable citizen at last. Just need you to come back and life would be perfect. Xxx

She slammed her laptop shut, not able to think about his words because there was no denying the pull of the past, the yearning to turn back the clock and make a different choice.

CHAPTER SIXTEEN

The sound of the door opening stopped her thoughts from going down the treacherous road, and she got up to see Frank trying to manoeuvre the buggy inside. Mia was fast asleep, and Becca held the door open while he pushed it into the hallway. Once she'd checked that her daughter was warm enough, she wheeled the buggy into the kitchen, where she would let Mia come round at her own speed. She checked her watch. Half past four. If she left her too long, she'd never get her to sleep at bedtime.

'I'll give her half an hour,' she said to Frank, voice lowered. 'Let's have a cup of tea, shall we? You must be tired after all that walking.'

Frank grinned at her and she could see that he had a hint of colour in his cheeks, a spark of life in his eyes that had been absent before. 'It was perfect. Made me realise how much I've missed walks like that. Ruth said the same. She's often on her own so we've agreed we'll do a walk once a week. Maybe on a day when she has Mia.' His grin broadened. 'Oh, she reminds me of you at that age. So much energy. And curious as a cat. Never stopped chattering and asking questions.'

Becca waited for the kettle to boil and poured water into the two mugs. 'Sounds like you had a lovely time.'

'I did that.' He gave a happy sigh. 'It was wonderful. Haven't enjoyed myself so much since… well, for a very long time.'

She handed Frank his mug of tea and walked through to the lounge, feeling his eyes on her back, a shimmer of awkwardness in the air.

'I'm sorry about earlier. I feel so bad about upsetting Ruth,' she said when she sat in the corner of the sofa, legs curled beneath her, mug hugged to her chest.

Frank sat on the armchair to the other side of her and blew on his tea before taking a sip. 'It's all right. I explained everything to her. She's a very understanding woman. And wonderful with Mia. You've found a gem of a childminder there, I'd say.'

Becca nodded, still distracted by Connor's message, her mind taking her to places she didn't want to be.

'Are you listening?' Frank said, his voice louder than before, and she jolted upright, realising she'd been staring into space.

'Sorry, Dad. I've got a lot on my mind.'

He nodded, his lips a thin line. 'Too much if you ask me. You worry about things that really don't need worrying about.' He looked her straight in the eye. 'Now I know you won't listen to your old dad, but have you thought… that maybe it's a bit too much for you? The responsibility of nursing and having a little one running you ragged? Especially with your husband not here to support you and…' He tailed off, took another sip of tea, his eyes never leaving hers.

She clasped her mug a little tighter. 'I'm fine, Dad. Absolutely fine. It's just with Mia being ill and having a few nights without sleep… it catches up with you.'

Frank sat back in his chair, his gaze on the rug in front of the fire.

She wondered how to change the subject, fed up with always being the focus, like some creature being dissected under a microscope. 'Anyway, have you heard from Kate? Has she said when she'll be back?'

He gave a little laugh. 'Do you know, I haven't even looked at my phone today. It's been lovely.' He pulled it out of his pocket, his brow furrowed as he stabbed at the screen to access his messages. 'Ah, here we go. She's got a meeting on Monday, won't be back until Tuesday.' He smiled at her. 'Tell you the truth, it's been good to have a break from that sister of yours. She can be… Now this is going to sound mean, but she's a bit of a bully on the sly.'

Becca was about to laugh, because the idea of her big, gruff dad being bullied by her sliver of a sister was funny, but then she caught the expression on his face, and she knew he was being serious.

She frowned. 'Are you two not getting on?'

Frank shrugged, his body language telling her he maybe wished he hadn't said anything. 'It's not that. Most of the time it's fine, but she has an idea of how things need to be, and if…' He sighed, sadness in his eyes. 'Don't take any notice of me, love. Everyone gets narky sometimes, don't they? But I just feel like I'm in the way, you know?'

His voice cracked and Becca's heart felt like it was about to snap in two. *Poor Dad.* It was obvious that he was still struggling, and she knew what he meant about Kate. She was one of those people who was usually sunny, but when the clouds came in it was a big old thunderstorm that you just had to sit out and hope there was no damage done at the end of it.

Does she bully him? It wasn't impossible to imagine – Becca knew Kate was frustrated with having to keep an eye out for Frank. But then, what did she really know about her sister's life? Very little was the answer, and she resolved to be in touch with her more.

Dad's just as much my responsibility as he is hers.

'You know you can come and stay whenever you want, Dad? It's been lovely having you, and we've got the space now. I'm not that keen on being here on my own when Dean's away, and Mia's loved having you to play with.'

If he came over to keep an eye on Mia while she caught up with the housework, it would be a blessing. Perhaps that was the extra help she needed to tip everything back into balance.

He beamed at her. 'I'd love that.' Then his face fell. 'Have you decided what to do about Ruth and childminding? She felt awful letting you down at short notice and then finding out it was all a big mistake and she can carry on. What do you think?'

Becca cringed. 'It feels slightly awkward after today. I made a right fool of myself, didn't I?'

'I'll have a word with her, shall I? I know she'd love to look after Mia again.'

'How about she comes round Monday morning and you both do it? Mia loved that last time.' Becca noticed how Frank's face had lit up when he'd mentioned Ruth, and she'd feel more comfortable with Frank there as well. There was something about Ruth that wasn't sitting right with her, but she couldn't put her finger on it. Still, Becca had been more than happy with her up to now, and she was the best-rated childminder in the area. 'I think you'd like that as well, Dad.'

She thought he might be blushing. It was the perfect solution: Ruth doing some childminding and covert elderminding at the same time. *She won't think of it like that*, Becca thought, hoping she was right. They seemed to have hit it off, though, Frank and Ruth, and she hoped their friendship would develop as that would take the pressure off both her and Kate.

Mia's wails rang out through the kitchen door, signalling the end of naptime, and Becca gulped down the rest of her tea. 'Give her a ring, Dad.'

CHAPTER SEVENTEEN

Becca had a lovely day with Frank on Sunday, and she felt that her world had started to spin in the right direction again. He took them out for lunch and then they had a wander down the pier, Mia having a go on a couple of the rides, excited to be walking 'on top of the sea'. They even spotted a seal. The sun shone, the weather was kind and Mia was her normal, bubbly self, making them both laugh. It was the nicest day Becca had had for a very long time. She didn't allow herself to consider what that said about her marriage.

She even managed to push Connor to the back of her mind, where he belonged.

On Monday, Frank came to the surgery with her to take Mia for her blood test, distracting her while the sample was taken and promising a treat for being such a brave girl. There were only a few tears and Becca told herself it was the right thing to do as she waved goodbye to them and focused on her work for the morning.

Her phone rang when she was on her way back home after her shift, the ringtone telling her it was Kate. She pulled over to answer.

'Hey, sis,' Kate said. 'Just checking in on the old fella. I tried his phone but he's not answering, and I was getting worried because he always answers straight away, like he's sat there, looking at the damned thing, willing it to ring. Is he back at home?'

'Oh, he's fine. Nothing to worry about. He stayed the weekend because Dean's not going to be back until late today.' Becca laughed. 'It's been great actually. Nice to have some company, and Mia loves having him around.'

Kate's breath rattled down the phone. 'That's such a relief. Didn't want to think of what might have happened. It's such a worry when he's on his own. I always think it just takes one mad moment and then...' Becca was glad Kate didn't finish her sentence.

'Nothing to worry about. It's all good. I'm just on my way back home now, actually. He can stay for tea, then I'll drop him off this evening. He said you're back tomorrow.'

'Slight change of plan, I'll be back tonight. I've got a meeting this afternoon, so it depends how long that goes on for, but I'm going to come home after that. Might be quite late. I'll give you a call when I'm on the train, then you can wait till I'm back before you drop him off. He won't want to go back to an empty house if he's had company for a few days.'

'Okay, no worries. Did you have a good weekend?'

'Bloody marvellous.' There was laughter in Kate's voice. 'I feel like I've been let out of prison.'

Becca cringed. 'Oh God, it's not that bad living with Dad, is it?'

Kate snorted. 'We have our moments, I can tell you. He's a stubborn man, that father of ours. And he's so messy – drives me nuts. Anyway, I feel refreshed and ready to be caged in again for a little while.'

Guilt grabbed Becca by the scruff of the neck. It wasn't fair that Kate felt her life was so limited. 'Look, I've been thinking he should come over here more. Dean's away just about every other week at the moment, so that'll give you more time to yourself.'

'Well, that would be fantastic. Honestly, Becs, I'd really appreciate it.'

'It's the least I can do, and I'm sorry I've been so rubbish at helping since we moved to Llandudno.'

'Oh, it's okay.' There was warmth to Kate's voice. 'I know it's tricky with Mia hating to be in the car. But if we can sort out some time at your house for him, then that really would ease the pressure a little. I think we're getting on each other's nerves at the moment.'

They said their goodbyes and Becca hurried home, feeling better about a lot of things, having now cleared the air with Kate. A turning point had been reached and her focus was back where it should be, with her family. *Just a little dip*, she told herself. *Back on track now.* And she allowed herself to imagine days out with Frank and Mia, thinking how much she'd enjoyed adventures with her dad as a child. How lovely it would be to build those memories with her daughter.

She was humming when she opened the door.

But stopped when she heard the shouting, accompanied by Mia's wails. She dashed into the lounge to find Dean and Frank squaring up to each other like they were in a boxing ring and Mia curled in a corner with her hands over her ears, sobbing her heart out.

'What the hell is going on?' Becca demanded, looking at the men's angry faces.

They glared at each other, silenced by her sudden appearance.

'I was telling him he should support you more rather than gadding about all over the place,' Frank said, a vein throbbing in his neck, his complexion an unhealthy shade of red.

'What's he doing in my house?' Dean demanded, frustration in his eyes. 'I told you I didn't want him here until he could be civil. Soon as I walked in the door, he started on at me for leaving you on your own. I mean, how the hell am I supposed to run an events business without going to bloody events?' His sentence ended much louder than it had started, making her jump and Mia launch into a fresh bout of wailing.

Becca's first thought was her daughter, and she went to pick her up, the child clinging to her, wet cheeks rubbing against Becca's neck as she held her close, Mia's little fingers curling into her hair.

A knock on the door made them all turn.

'That'll be Ruth,' Frank said. 'She just went out to get some milk.'

Becca hurried to the door, Mia clasped to her chest, her little body still shuddering with sobs. She smoothed her daughter's hair, shushing her gently, and instead of letting Ruth in, she stepped outside, closing the door behind her.

'I'm so glad you're here,' she whispered to Ruth as she pulled her down the driveway a little. 'Dean and Dad are having a bit of a barney, and Mia's beside herself. I just walked in on it. Will you take her while I see if I can calm things down? They look like they're going to belt each other any minute.'

Ruth's face paled. 'Dean wasn't here when I nipped to the shops. I know you said they don't get on, but I didn't think things were that bad between them.'

'They're not usually. It tends to be sniping at each other, you know, little digs.' She glanced back at the house, heard muffled shouts. Her heart raced faster. 'Christ! I better get back inside.'

Ruth held out her arms and Becca untangled Mia's fingers from her hair, passing her over, shushing her plaintive cries of protest. 'I'll just be a minute, sweetie, promise.' She kissed Mia's cheek and hurried back inside, leaving Ruth with a shell-shocked expression on her face.

Becca dashed into the lounge to find it empty, the house ominously quiet.

Dean was in the kitchen, arms braced against the worktop, staring into the back garden, his jaw hard.

'Where's Dad?'

'Upstairs. Packing.' He sounded weary, and held out his arms for her, obviously needing a hug as much as she did. She could feel his heart hammering away in his chest as he held her close, and she supposed he was entitled to defend himself in his own house. *Why did Dad go on the attack?* Especially after their recent conversation when she'd pleaded with him to try harder. But Frank's anger hadn't been to do with the past and the death of her mother. He'd been sticking up for his daughter, something he'd always done. Now was the time to stand up for herself, instead of her dad doing it for her.

She pulled away and looked Dean in the eye, conscious that she had his undivided attention for once. *Now's the time for that conversation.* 'I'm sorry if he had a go at you.' She grimaced. 'To be honest, I have been bending his ear this weekend about how lonely I get sometimes and how tricky it can be juggling everything with you away.'

'Oh, Becca.' He gave a heavy sigh and pulled her to him again, kissing the top of her head, his hand stroking her hair.

She closed her eyes and laid her head on his chest, relishing his touch, the tickle of his breath on her skin.

'Expanding the business has been way more stressful than I ever imagined. It's got a life of its own and I feel like I grabbed a tiger by the tail and I daren't let go.' He held her tighter, swaying from side to side. 'I love you, sweetheart. And sometimes it breaks my heart to go away. But I don't really have a choice.'

'Can't you delegate to Alice more? Can't she go away instead?'

'It's not that simple unfortunately. It takes the two of us to manage the events. You can't do it with just one. Believe me, I tried. That's why I recruited Alice in the first place.' He released her then, his eyes finding hers. 'But we have started talking about finding some part-time staff to give extra support. We're both knackered, to be honest.'

A flood of relief tumbled through her, and she beamed at him, thinking again that today was the day when the tide had turned. 'That's great news. You're missing so much of Mia growing up, and I want you to myself a bit more.' She grabbed his hand and linked her fingers with his. 'The only thing is… I just promised Kate that we'd have Dad to stay sometimes, just to give her the occasional break.'

Dean's face fell and he extricated his hand from hers. 'Well, that's going to be awkward. He's always had it in for me. I don't understand why he can't accept I'm your husband and we're a family. Thing is, Becca, I'm not going to let him hurl abuse at me in my own house and just take it.'

Becca cringed, knowing that he had a point. 'I'm so sorry he had a go at you. I'll talk to him, tell him it's not on. But he's my dad and he needs company. You know what he's been like since he had his heart attack and had to retire. He doesn't know what to do with himself, and he's never got over Mum dying, has he? I would never forgive myself if something happened when Kate was away, and he was left on his own.' Becca put a hand on her chest as if that alone could steady her racing heart. 'I told you Kate was going away this weekend, didn't I?'

'You did, but I didn't expect him to still be here.'

'You said you wouldn't be back until later. I was going to take him home after tea.'

She listened to herself justifying her reasons for allowing her own father to come and stay for a few days. A surge of anger brought her hands to her hips, chin jutting forwards as she prepared to defend herself, the whole atmosphere now soured.

'Mia was sick again on Friday night, so I was really glad Dad was here to help. And we had a lovely weekend while you were away, thank you very much. Have you any idea how much energy it takes to look after a three-year-old? Hmm?' She waited a beat before carrying on. 'No, you don't, do you, because you never bloody do it!' Becca was shouting now, all her frustrations bursting out. 'You just swan around at your events, leaving me to mop up after a poorly child. Because that's my place, isn't it? Skivvy. You don't care what my life's like. In fact, I don't think you care about me at all these days. It's all bloody work.' She looked daggers at him.

Dean stared at her, hands out in front of him as if he was trying to magic the genie of her rage back in the bottle. There was a glimmer of fear in his eyes. 'Whoa, where did that come from? Just cool it, Becca.'

She slapped the worktop, making Dean flinch. 'Why the hell should I? We don't talk about things properly, Dean. Let's start with why you and Dad can't be civil with each other, shall we?

He said you had a row with Mum on the day she died.' She threw up her hands. 'I didn't even know you knew her! How could you have kept that from me? He thinks you upset her so much that she had a stroke. Only you can tell me what…'

She felt a hand on her shoulder and jumped, startled by the unexpected touch.

Frank stood behind her, his face still red. 'I think it's best if I just go home, love. Don't want to be where I'm not wanted.'

'Oh, we're playing that game, are we?' Dean snapped.

Becca looked between the two of them, her own anger with Dean snuffed out by the concern she felt for her dad. He was so upset, she could just imagine him having another heart attack, with his blood pressure problems. Or a stroke. Or a seizure. The possibilities flooded into her mind, her eyes scanning his face for warning signs. She grabbed her car keys, lips pressed together in an angry line.

'Come on, Dad. Let's go.'

Outside, Ruth was sitting on the garden wall, Mia in her lap listening intently as Ruth told her a story. Her eyes caught Becca's as she strode down the driveway, Frank tagging along behind, his overnight bag in his hand.

'Let's go and get some lunch, shall we?' she said, her voice over bright, keeping the mood upbeat for Mia's benefit. 'There's a pub with a soft-play area that Mia adores. I thought we could all go there. What do you say, Ruth? You fancy a trip out?'

Ruth hesitated before she replied. 'Well, it's very kind of you to invite me, but I don't want to get in the way. It seems like you have… family business to sort out.'

Becca knew she was right. She had to have a proper chat with Frank. She'd only just promised Kate he could come over more often, and now Dean had banned him from the house. The idea of going back on her word to Kate made her shudder. *Imagine having to tell her?*

Becca unlocked the car and Frank slid his bag into the boot. Mia was clearly apprehensive, clinging to Ruth, and Becca knew she was going to have to use all her persuasion skills to get her daughter in the car without a major tantrum. She crouched in front of her using her best cajoling voice. 'We're going to the soft-play. You like it there, don't you?' Mia's eyes widened, her face pink from crying. Becca wiped her tears and managed to pry her from Ruth's grasp. 'Everything's fine, sweetie, nothing to worry about.' She gave her the unicorn and fastened her in the car seat while Frank shuffled into the back seat next to her, getting his phone out of his pocket.

'Shall we see if we can find any games?' he said, glancing at Becca. As a distraction technique it would probably work, and she gave a little nod.

'I'll get off home,' Ruth said, handing Becca the carton of milk that had been sitting on the wall beside her.

'Let me pay you for that.'

Ruth waved a hand, dismissing the suggestion. 'Frank'll need some at home, won't he, if he's been away.'

'I'm so sorry about all this,' Becca said with a flicker of a smile, eager to get going before Mia had a change of heart. 'But I'll see you soon.'

There was an air of awkwardness between them, Becca's outburst from Saturday still fresh in her mind. Ruth turned and walked away before Becca could apologise again and she watched her for a moment, wondering if she should run after her. *Leave it for now. Concentrate on getting Frank home and Mia settled.*

She started the car, thinking that her day had been flipped on its head, her positivity ground into the dirt. Now she knew she'd be going back to an angry Dean, she wasn't in a hurry to return and decided she'd wait at Frank's house for Kate to get back first. At least then she could brief Kate on the day's events.

For both men, this behaviour was out of character. Dean was generally laid back and very forgiving. Her dad was more cut and dried in his views but was not one for conflict, tending to seethe and avoid rather than argue. Neither of them was being completely honest with her – there was something more to the animosity between them, that neither of them wanted to tell her.

What on earth had Dean been arguing with Mum about?

CHAPTER EIGHTEEN

Frank remained subdued, lost in his thoughts, and over lunch at the pub, Becca couldn't get him to respond to any of her questions about Dean's argument with her mum.

'I've told you everything I know,' was all he'd say.

Becca had no desire to push him while Mia was close by and listening, so she put it to one side and vowed to talk to Dean later. She unwrapped herself from the past and told herself to enjoy the moment and play with her daughter. Gradually, Frank became more animated, the atmosphere less strained, and they had a nice couple of hours at the soft-play barn, which was attached to the pub.

They picked up some groceries on the way back to Frank's to re-stock his fridge and make something for their evening meal, but the argument resurfaced in her mind when they pulled up to Frank's house. The promise she'd made to Kate and her dad now seemed impossible to keep if Dean wouldn't allow Frank through the door. It was another thing to worry about, another plate to spin, another problem to solve.

Now he was back at home, Frank became quiet, his body hunched as he trudged up the path to the front door.

'Are you okay, Dad?' she said a little while later when she'd put all the shopping away and came through to the lounge.

Mia was asleep on the sofa and he was sitting in his armchair, staring at the wall. When he turned to her there were tears in his eyes, and he sniffed and wiped them away. Then she noticed he'd been looking at a picture of him and her mother on their wedding day.

'I'll put the kettle on,' Frank said, getting up. 'I've a bit of cake somewhere if you fancy it.'

'Lovely, Dad, thanks.'

Mia stirred. 'Cake,' she said, the words having burrowed into her sleeping brain and woken her up. She slid off the sofa and staggered after Frank towards the kitchen, her hair all messy, eyes only just open.

Becca could hear the murmur of Frank's voice as he talked to her, the excited tone he reserved for his granddaughter, and Becca wanted, with all her heart, for them to have a close relationship. There were no grandparents on Dean's side of the family. His father had had a seizure while driving and died at the wheel. His mother had died a couple of years later of breast cancer, and there were no aunties or uncles or cousins. To Becca, that made the bond between Mia and Frank all the more important. Becca let out an enormous sigh at the very moment Frank walked into the room.

'You're sounding a bit fed up, love,' he said as he handed her a mug of tea and a plate with a fat slice of cake on it. 'Lemon drizzle. Your mum's favourite.' He gave a little laugh as he sat back down in his chair. 'Thing is, I don't really like it so much – it's definitely not my favourite but I still find myself buying it because it was her little treat.' His chin wobbled. 'Sounds daft, doesn't it? Ten years, it's been, and I still buy her favourite instead of mine.'

Becca studied her cake, reluctant to eat it now it had a whole wreath of symbolism wrapped round it. *Mum on a plate.* She stifled an inappropriate giggle, but it wouldn't stay in and she burst out laughing.

After a moment Frank joined in too. 'We're as nutty as each other, aren't we?'

His words stuffed her laughter back down her throat. She coughed. *He thinks I'm nutty. Still nutty. Will he always see me like that?* Was it a label she'd have for the rest of her life? She took a huge bite of her cake, filling her cheeks with it until she looked like a hamster, but she didn't care. With difficulty, she swallowed it down, taking a big gulp of tea to get rid of the taste. She wasn't keen on lemon drizzle cake either.

Kate arrived in a bustle of shopping bags when Becca was washing up after tea.

'Hiya!' she called from the hallway, and Becca heard the front door bang.

She dried her hands and went to greet her sister, who was beaming in a way Becca hadn't seen for years, her cheeks glowing, eyes sparkling. Becca stepped forwards and gave Kate a hug. 'You look fantastic. Going away obviously suits you.'

As soon as the words were out of her mouth, she regretted them, given the fact she was going to have to go back on her promise of having Frank to stay. 'Come into the kitchen,' she murmured, glancing up the stairs, where Frank and Mia were playing hide and seek in the bedrooms. 'I need to speak to you about something.'

Kate frowned, obviously puzzled. 'That sounds sort of ominous.'

Becca cringed but tried to make her voice light. 'I made a lasagne if you want some. It's in the oven keeping warm.'

'Lovely, but you've got me wondering now… Go on, spit it out.'

Becca closed the kitchen door behind them, glad that Frank's house was still compartmentalised, unlike her open-plan home. Still, she pulled Kate close so their voices wouldn't be heard.

'Bit of a problem. I got home from work to find Dean and Dad having an enormous bust-up. Mia was terrified, poor kid.' She puffed out a frustrated breath. 'Anyway, Dean had a go at me for asking Dad to stay, said he didn't want him in the house.'

Kate's eyes grew wide. 'Oh my God, I didn't think there was a chance of a crossover – you said Dean wouldn't be back until tonight, so there'd be no chance of them bumping into each other.' Kate couldn't keep Becca's gaze, her eyes falling to the floor. 'I thought it would be okay.'

'It would have been if Dean had come back later, like he'd said.'

Kate pulled a face, the sparkle gone from her eyes now. 'Oh, dear.'

Becca nodded. 'That's right. It's messed everything up, really. I know I promised I'd have Dad more often to give you a break, but I'm afraid that can't happen yet. Not until I can persuade Dean to change his mind.' She caught her sister's eye. 'Why did you never tell me that Dean and Mum knew each other?'

Kate's face froze, startled. 'Oh, I… um, I…' She swallowed, sounded defensive. 'Yes, maybe I should have said something, but we thought it was up to Dean, not us.'

Becca gritted her teeth. 'Do you know what they were arguing about on the day she died?'

Kate didn't respond for a moment, then shrugged a shoulder and looked away. 'Oh, I don't think it's anything mysterious. Some people don't like each other.'

Becca huffed, her hands gripping the worktop behind her. 'You know that's not it. I can tell when you're lying because you won't look at me.'

Kate snapped her eyes up from the floor.

'Come on, you know, don't you?'

Kate folded her arms tightly across her chest. She was silent for a moment, her fingers tapping her ribs as if she was playing percussion on them. 'I honestly don't know the full details. I wasn't there. All I know is Dad links that argument with Mum's death, and you know he's still angry that she died, and left him on his own, so he's transferred that anger on to Dean.' She gave another shrug, mouth twisted to one side. 'That's my take on it.'

Becca considered her reply. 'Whenever I've asked Dean why they can't get on, he's always said he thinks Dad's jealous of him and won't accept that I'm married now and have my own family. Dad says Dean is responsible for Mum having a stroke by getting her so upset. That's two very different stories.'

'I know.' Kate sighed. 'Grief doesn't make sense, does it? We all process death differently, and as far as I can see, Dad needs someone to blame. Unfortunately, he's chosen Dean.'

Becca thought about that all the way home.

There was something in Kate's demeanour that made Becca wonder if she was telling her the whole truth.

CHAPTER NINETEEN

It was after eight o'clock by the time Becca was able to drag Mia away from the house. Mia had wanted to go through the whole box of Beanie Babies and show them to Kate, telling her their names and which were the naughty ones, and which were her favourites. She'd had them all laughing, and Becca had realised that it wasn't often that she spent any time with Kate these days. *Got to sort out my work–life balance*, she decided as she arrived home and pulled up the drive behind Dean's car.

Mia had fallen asleep as soon as they'd turned on to the dual carriageway, and Becca carefully lifted her out of her car seat, trying not to wake her, because then it would be a nightmare getting her to settle again.

She popped her head into the lounge, but Dean wasn't there. Quietly, she carried Mia up the stairs and laid her on the bed, taking off her shoes but nothing else, for fear of waking her. She tucked her in, tiptoed out of the room and walked straight into Dean as he came out of the bathroom.

She put a finger to her lips, warning him to be quiet.

His expression was stony, eyes glinting. *He's still angry with me.* Her heart flipped.

'Sorry about Dad,' she whispered. 'And sorry I got all uptight and shouty.' She reached for his hand, but he snatched it away as if she was contagious, making her flinch.

His lips were clamped together. 'I need to show you something,' he said before he turned and walked downstairs, Becca following in his wake.

Her laptop was open on the kitchen worktop. She swallowed, dread swirling in her stomach. This wasn't about Frank. This was about something else entirely.

He brought the sleeping computer to life and she saw her Twitter account. Her conversation with Connor. Her stomach lurched as she remembered everything she'd said to him, her outpouring of all the things that were making her sad and anxious. How she felt about her marriage and Dean and work. Mia's sickness. And the very last message in the conversation was hers, telling Connor that she missed him too. She squeezed her eyes closed, as if that would make the situation disappear.

'I see you've been chatting to Connor,' Dean said in a voice that suggested he didn't mind.

She opened her eyes, and saw that his voice had been lying. He was seething. Properly furious.

'He just popped up on there, and…' She spluttered to a halt. *Pathetic.*

'You didn't have to reply, did you?'

'You've been reading my messages.' It was a pitiful form of attack, given what was in the conversations, and she could feel herself shrivelling up inside, her face aflame.

'Well, it was good to have a read.' His voice was scathing. 'Because at least now I know what you think about me and our marriage. I understand that what I'm doing, busting a gut for you, isn't good enough.' His hands clenched and unclenched by his sides, his face taking on a reddish hue as his voice grew louder. 'And your ex needed to know all our private business, didn't he?'

She bit her lip, tears clouding her vision. There was no excuse. 'I'm sorry. I know it looks bad. I shouldn't be telling someone all those things, but on social media it's like talking to yourself, really. Especially with someone who's in Australia.' She blinked at him. 'I just needed to talk to someone. I'm on my own so much and you're always too busy to talk, or when I do try and discuss things, your mind is somewhere else and you're not really listening.' She swallowed. 'I'm sorry, it was wrong of me. But—'

'But what?' he snapped.

She hesitated, looked at his angry face. 'Can't you see how lonely I am? And I'm worried about Mia, and on Wednesday morning you… you called me Alice.'

He looked stunned.

Furious tears pricked at her eyes. 'And that wasn't the first time you've called me Alice. It's happened a few times now.' She covered her face with her hands as the tears trickled down her cheeks.

He sighed, and a few moments later, she felt his arms around her as he pulled her into a hug. She laid her head on his chest and he stroked her hair, and she remembered all those times when she'd been distraught with grief after her mum had died and when she'd had the miscarriages, and he'd always been there to comfort her. Always. She felt awful now for being disloyal and confiding in Connor.

'Do you…' He hesitated, his voice thick with emotion. 'Be honest with me, Becca. Do you ever regret staying with me instead of going back to him?'

'No, Dean. No.' She leant back to see his face, her eyes scanning his. 'How could I ever regret Mia?'

He shook his head, slowly. 'That wasn't what I meant. Do you regret being with me? Would you rather be with him?'

She pulled away, tears rolling down her cheeks. 'No, sweetheart. Please don't ever think that. I'm just feeling a bit… lost. I miss you. I miss us. Being a couple.' She glanced at the laptop. 'All that chat with Connor… it's me looking through rose-tinted glasses. We'd broken up before I came back. It was over. But, in a way, talking to him… it's helped me to understand how I feel. I love you, Dean. Really, I do.'

He gently wiped away her tears. 'It came as a shock, I have to admit. Seeing everything laid out like that.' His Adam's apple bobbed up and down. 'I know we had a quick chat earlier, but I hadn't understood how my work has put a lot of pressure on you. And you're right that we don't spend enough time together. I'll try and rein things back, how about that?'

She nodded, too choked up to speak.

'Like I said, I'll be able to start delegating more to Alice once we get her an assistant to help, and I'll work more behind the scenes.'

She could see the concern in his eyes.

'Would that be better?'

She nodded.

'You've got to block him, though. Delete all that conversation. He's the past, Becca, and he needs to stay there.'

He dropped his arms and she realised he meant now. Right now. She had to delete Connor from her life, and he was going to watch to make sure she did it. The idea of something so final caught her unawares, making her heart skip. But this felt like a pivotal moment, and she wanted to reset the tone between her and Dean, wanted to feel that their relationship was still strong. If she did as he asked, there was still a chance they could get back to how they'd been at the beginning, when she was Dean's world and she'd felt loved and secure.

Dean tapped the laptop back to life.

Becca swallowed, her hand shaking as she blocked Connor from her Twitter feed and left the conversation, while Dean watched, his hand on her shoulder. 'There, he's gone,' she said, a tremor in her voice.

'Sounds like he still wants you.' She couldn't look at him, didn't want to see the question in his eyes.

'That's not the same as me wanting him, though, is it?'

And she tried to convince herself that was true, while a part of her heart yearned for what might have been.

She closed her laptop. *That's it. Finished.*

CHAPTER TWENTY

They made love that night, for the first time in months. It should have been a moment to rejoice in the reconnection, but Becca couldn't revel in the closeness, her mind too fixed on her worries to allow her to relax.

Mia's cries were an almost welcome disturbance, and she wriggled from her sleepy husband's arms, slipped on her robe and dashed into her daughter's room. It was happening again, the poor child sitting in a pool of vomit. Dean appeared in the doorway a few minutes later, and between them, they once again managed the clean-up operation.

When Mia was finally asleep, Becca put all the soiled clothes and bedding in the wash while Dean made cups of tea for them both.

'Another tummy bug,' Dean said as he sank into a chair at the kitchen table.

'I don't think it's a virus.' She sat opposite him and sensed now was the time to tell him her theory, talk it all through.

Dean blinked, then frowned. 'What? Well, what else can it be?'

'I've been trying to work it out, eliminating all the possibilities, and the only thing I can think of is…' She hesitated. 'I've researched the life out of it, been through it so many times in my head, and the only conclusion I can come to is… someone is poisoning her.'

Dean's jaw dropped.

'I know how it sounds.' She held up a hand as if to protect herself from the disbelief which was surely heading her way. 'But I've ruled out everything else.'

'Oh, come on, Becca,' he scoffed. 'That's ridiculous. Who'd want to poison a child?'

'I don't know. Honestly, I haven't got that far. But her symptoms fit.'

'Is it something in the house that she's getting her hands on, do you think? What about those washing pods? Or the dishwasher things. They look like jelly sweets. Could it be either of those?'

Becca sighed. 'There's nothing in the house within reach. I've checked the whole place, top to bottom. I keep all the cleaning stuff on the top shelf of the cupboards—'

'But you have to take them down to use them. Perhaps that's when it's happened, and you've just nipped to the loo or something. Have you been watching?'

Becca was starting to get annoyed now, frustrated that he didn't believe her. She laid her hands flat on the table, calming her voice. The last thing she wanted was an argument – she just needed him to understand they had a real problem and she had no idea how to deal with it.

'I never leave anything out that could poison her. I always put it back as soon as I've finished using it. After all the problems at the hospital, I'm paranoid about that stuff.'

Dean frowned. Becca cringed, remembering that he didn't know.

'At the hospital? Where you worked all those years ago? You've never mentioned problems. You said you left because you were stressed. Went to Australia to take some time out.'

Becca sighed, her heart sinking. *I'll have to tell him now.* She took a deep breath, her hands finding each other on the table, fingers interlinking, holding tight.

'That's the truth,' she said, carefully, avoiding his gaze. 'But there was more to it than that. The ward I worked on noticed a problem… A number of the patients were having relapses, strange symptoms. They concluded that someone was deliberately altering medication for some of the patients.' She hesitated, knowing how bad it sounded. 'I was suspended while they investigated.'

Dean's expression had changed now. Eyes narrowed. He was listening hard.

Judging.

'It wasn't me,' she said louder than was necessary.

'The investigation found you innocent?'

She swallowed. This wasn't going to sound quite as definitive as she would have liked, but she wanted to be truthful. 'Initially, they did find a correlation between the onset of symptoms and the times when I was on shift. They did all sorts of psychiatric assessments on me – would you believe they thought I had Munchausen's by proxy? I think they call it factitious disorder these days. Usually it's mums harming their kids, but it does crop up in medical settings at times. I suppose because doctors and nurses have the knowledge and the means…' She shook her head, trying to get her thoughts back on track. 'Anyway, new information came to light and the ward manager was arrested.'

He hesitated before speaking. 'So… you were fully exonerated? You didn't do anything wrong, even unknowingly?'

She scowled at him, her hands squeezing each other so tight her knuckles were white. 'I'm telling you, I did nothing wrong.' Anger burnt in her chest. 'You can make statistics say all sorts of things which aren't true. It was just coincidence that I happened to be on duty. That and the fact I was the one who ended up doing CPR on two of the patients.'

'So, you saved the lives of people who'd been intentionally overdosed?'

She nodded. 'I did. Then they decided to point the finger at me. Suggesting I had some sort of attention-seeking mental illness.' She huffed. 'To be fair, there was another investigation in the news at the time, and it had got everyone jumpy. It was close to being a witch-hunt, people coming to ridiculous conclusions.'

'But you were cleared?'

'That's right. I was.' She glared at him. 'Nobody died because of me. Nobody was harmed. But you know what… a lot of procedures were improved because of that investigation, and a number of staff had to be retrained on certain aspects of care. So the end result was positive. Except… the whole thing had a really bad effect on me. Completely shattered my confidence and… well, as you know, I had a bit of a mental health crisis.'

'A breakdown.' It was a statement, rather than a question, and it irked her.

'If you want to call it that.' She cleared her throat. 'I had to move back home. Mum didn't get it at all. She was all stiff upper lip, "just get back on the horse" type of thing. But Dad was great with me. It sort of left things strained between us all. Split loyalties. That's when I went to Australia.' She shook her head, wanting to forget about that dark time in her life. 'Anyway, you know all that.'

He frowned at her. 'No, I didn't know most of that, actually. I knew you had a crisis, but we've never really talked about it. And I definitely didn't know about the hospital investigation.'

She thought for a moment. 'Do you feel differently about me now that you know?'

He looked dazed, her question catching him unawares. But if he could be direct with his questions about Connor, then she could be direct about this. She had a horrible sense of déjà vu about the whole thing. And she was starting to feel she was being undermined, the conversation hinting at something in a way that made her feel distinctly uncomfortable.

It was time to bring everything back to the facts. He couldn't argue with that.

'Look, this is how I see it.' She took a deep breath. 'I know I can catastrophise at times, if I'm feeling stressed. And I know I've bothered the doctors before when I've worried about Mia's health issues. But basically… this is not normal for her. Agreed?'

He rubbed the back of his neck, silent as he considered her question. 'You're right. We've never had anything like this.' His eyes met hers. 'What did the doctor say?'

'She thinks it's a virus.'

His shoulders relaxed. 'Well, then. And have you spoken to anyone else about it?'

'Yes, I spoke to Carol.'

'And what did she say?'

'She thinks... she thinks if I'm worried, I should trust my instincts. I left a sample with her on Saturday, so we should have results from that. I also got blood tests done this morning. Just to make sure there's no underlying condition.'

'Well, then?' He looked at her as if she was being thick. 'Let's assume the doctor knows what she's doing and wait for the test results.'

'But, Dean, I think I'm right. The symptoms fit. And if someone is harming our daughter, I want to find out who it is.'

'Why would someone be poisoning Mia? Honestly, Becca, you need to listen to yourself.'

Her whole body tensed, her voice curt. 'I do. I do listen to myself, and that's why I'm worried.'

'And I'm worried because you sound like you've lost the plot and yet you're in charge of our daughter.'

His words hit her like a blast of shotgun pellets, every one of them leaving a little indentation in her mind, a wound that would take time to heal.

She clamped her jaw shut. *There's no point telling him anything else*, she cautioned herself. *He thinks I'm losing it.*

And she had to stop for a moment and consider. If it had happened before, could it be happening again?

CHAPTER TWENTY-ONE

Becca couldn't sleep, tossing and turning as the past and the present merged together until she no longer knew what was the truth and what might be imagined.

The next morning, she felt robotic as she went through her routine, Dean quiet and wrapped up in his own thoughts. She was too angry to want to talk to him anyway so just let him do his own thing. It was only as she was getting Mia dressed that she remembered she had no childcare organised. The situation with Ruth had been left up in the air, no definite arrangements made, but she was supposed to be at work and couldn't let Carol down.

Quickly, she gave Ruth a ring.

'Hello, Becca.' Ruth's voice was precise and measured. 'I wasn't expecting to hear from you.' There was silence for a moment.

'I… um… I just wanted to apologise. Not just for the upset with Frank and Dean but I'm so sorry about Saturday. I didn't mean to accuse you of anything. I got myself all wound up and I know you wouldn't deliberately harm Mia.'

'No, I wouldn't.' There was a tremor in Ruth's voice and the line went dead. She'd hung up.

Becca stared at the phone, shocked.

She rang Frank, her words tumbling out in a panicky rush. 'Is it okay if I bring Mia over this morning? I've no childcare organised, and Ruth… um, she's not available.'

'No problem, love.' He sounded delighted. 'I'm sure we can manage to entertain each other.'

'Is Kate there?'

'Yes, she's working at home today, so there'll be the both of us.'

Somehow that felt better, and Becca checked her watch and speeded up. Then she called Carol to tell her she'd be half an hour late because she had to get to Bangor and back, but she'd stay as late as was needed to get the round finished.

By the time she got to work, she felt like she'd already done a full day.

'You're still looking peaky,' Carol said when Becca pushed through the office door to get her list of patients for the morning.

She sighed. 'Mia was sick again last night. Same thing.'

Carol pursed her lips, thinking. 'Hmm. Just a thought, but are there any plants in the garden she might be eating?'

Becca shook her head. 'We've just moved into a brand-new house, and the back garden is grass. Just a rectangle of lawn. Same at the front. We haven't got round to doing anything with it yet.'

'Well, that's a mystery, isn't it?' Carol's frown deepened. 'Did you say you had a sample for testing?'

'I gave it to you on Saturday, remember?'

'What? Are you sure?' She clicked on to her screen, frowning as she scanned the record of lab tests. 'It's not on the log.' She looked on her desk, then checked the basket where they kept samples ready for sending off. 'Nothing here.'

Did I give it to her? Becca rummaged in her bag, just in case she'd forgotten, but it wasn't there.

'Let me ring the lab. Just in case I forgot to log it in.'

Becca waited, watching Carol's face, knowing as soon as she put the phone down that it hadn't been sent.

Carol shrugged, a little sheepish. 'It happens, doesn't it? Things going astray, especially after the weekend. Hopefully, it'll turn up, but just get another sample if it happens again.'

I did give it to Carol, didn't I? She couldn't be 100 per cent sure – she was so distracted there was a chance she'd forgotten. Or got it mixed up with samples for her patients. To be honest, her focus hadn't been as sharp as it should have been this past week.

She picked up her patient list and hurried out of the office.

Over the next week, Mia had two more sickness episodes. Two trips to the doctor, with no conclusive results – the blood tests had come back normal and the stool samples were still being processed. It was frustrating, but there was nothing Becca could do. She could feel her stress levels ramping up, a constant headache throbbing at her temples and behind her eyes, as her concerns about her daughter's welfare blotted out everything else.

The third time it happened, Dean was away again, and Becca was so tired and anxious, she took Mia straight to the A & E department at the main hospital, which was half an hour from where they lived.

Typically, by the time she arrived, the worst was over, and Mia was quite chirpy about being somewhere new and interesting. Thankfully, Becca had brought a stool sample with her for testing, and she handed it over to the triage nurse, who sent them back to the waiting room until it was their turn. Eventually, she talked to a doctor, a bald-headed oblong of a man, who listened patiently while she laid out everything that had been happening over the last couple of weeks.

'Please could you do some blood tests?' she asked.

The doctor frowned. 'I noticed on her record that she's just this week had blood tests, and everything was normal.'

Becca suppressed a frustrated sigh, fed up with being told everything was fine when it clearly wasn't. She could feel her eyes stinging, a rising swell of emotion filling her chest and thickening her voice. 'The thing is… well, I'm worried that she's either got some serious illness or is being poisoned.'

The doctor snapped to attention. 'Poisoned? By what?'

Becca sighed. 'That's the thing – I don't know but perhaps a blood test would give us a clue?'

The doctor gave her a kind smile. 'I know this sort of thing is very distressing, but the tests we've already run were very thorough, and I really think we've covered all the possibilities. She seems fine, doesn't she?'

Becca heard Mia giggling as a nurse pretended to be surprised to find her where she was hiding behind a curtain.

'I know she's okay now,' Becca snapped. 'But you didn't see her three hours ago, puking her guts up with a nappy full of liquid shit.'

The doctor's smile stayed in place, although a muscle twitched at the corner of his eye. 'I think we've done what we can for the moment. I've given her a thorough check over. Children pick up all sorts of bugs. It's actually good for them. Strengthens the immune system.'

'I'm a district nurse,' she said, curtly. 'I'm aware of what's normal and this definitely isn't. What if there's an underlying condition that's causing this? Something serious. Life-threatening even?'

'And what sort of condition do you have in mind?' He cocked his head, eyes studying her face, which was now burning.

She gritted her teeth. 'I don't have *anything* in mind. I just want you take me seriously.'

The smile slipped off his face. 'I can assure you that I am taking your concerns seriously.' His voice was calm and measured. 'I've made a note of everything you've told me. We've sent the stool sample for testing, but it can take a while for results to come through, sometimes a couple of weeks, depending on the particular test, as I'm sure you're aware. In the meantime, I'm not going to cause this child distress by taking more blood samples when they've so recently been done.' He glanced over at Mia, who was now pretending to be a lion. 'I honestly don't think there's anything to worry about.'

By the expression on the doctor's face, Becca knew that was the end of the conversation. She called Mia and they left. What did she have to do to get them to listen? *I'll have to take her earlier,* she decided. *When she's covered in sick and shit, let them see for themselves what's happening.*

A few days later, at half past eight in the evening, when Dean was at an event at the local golf club, it happened again. She wasn't going to wait this time. She rang Dean, who said he was just wrapping things up and promised to meet her at the hospital as soon as he could.

An hour later, when Mia had been cleaned up and calmed down and fresh samples taken, Becca once again told her story and voiced her suspicions to a different doctor. This one was younger, with a wonderfully sympathetic manner that left her feeling she might have struck lucky.

'All the tests show everything is functioning normally, so I'm not worried about underlying conditions. Hopefully, that will put your mind at rest?' He cleared his throat. 'I am concerned that she's repeatedly presenting with the same symptoms, though, because it must be distressing for both you and your daughter.'

'It is.' Becca nodded emphatically. 'I just don't know what to do next. You're positive there's no other tests you can do? What about a scan?'

'We're still waiting for some of the stool sample tests to come back, but initial results show nothing abnormal.' He sat back in his chair. 'My best guess is that she's eating something she shouldn't be eating. Or it's an allergic reaction. So my suggestion is that you keep a food diary. Check at home and speak to anyone she's been in contact with to see if they've given her something that might be disagreeing with her.'

Becca sighed, too exhausted to say that she'd done all that.

'Let's hope this is the last of it,' the doctor said, his eyes meeting hers. 'I'll make you an appointment with paediatrics when the final tests are through. But from what I can see, and from the notes colleagues have made previously, your daughter is generally a happy, healthy three-year-old.' The doctor stood, the conversation obviously over in his mind.

'She's being poisoned, I'm sure of it.' Becca was determined that she wasn't going home until she got to the bottom of the situation. She was thoroughly frustrated by voicing her concerns to people who weren't prepared to accept her conclusion – it was time to be more forceful. She was desperate for Dean to arrive and lend his support, another voice to echo hers. *What's taking him so long?*

The doctor sat back down, his face clouded with concern. 'I understand you've made this allegation before.'

'Yes,' she snapped, 'and nobody is taking me seriously.'

'Do you have a suspicion as to who it is?' He was staring at her intently now.

Becca chewed her lip, startled that the doctor was finally taking an interest in her theory. 'No…' She stopped and considered his question for a moment. In all truth, the only people who had access to Mia were members of her family. And Ruth. Was she really accusing one of her nearest and dearest of deliberately doing this to Mia? It was a shocking thing to have to consider. She rubbed her clammy palms on her trousers, unable to reply, not ready to voice names.

'If you honestly think someone is harming your daughter, then I think it's a matter for the police.'

Becca blanched.

His eyes searched her face as he waited for her to say something.

She hadn't thought through the consequences, her mind fixed on getting a definitive answer about Mia's illness. A clear diagnosis being her only focus. But now… she hadn't got as far as what next. Her heart skipped. *The police?*

The doctor must have caught her shocked expression and his mouth tightened, eyes boring into Becca's as if trying to read her mind. His countenance had changed from reassuring to assessing, and Becca squirmed in her seat, suddenly feeling far too hot.

'If someone is deliberately poisoning your child, that's classed as child abuse. They must be identified and stopped.' A nurse popped her head into the cubicle and the doctor glanced at her before standing. 'I wonder if you'd mind taking a seat in the waiting room. I'm just going to talk to a colleague for a second opinion. I'll come and get you when we're ready.'

Becca looked around. 'Leave Mia?'

The doctor nodded. 'Just for a few minutes. It's okay, your husband just arrived, so she's not on her own.'

Becca hesitated, then stood, walking through to the waiting room with fear in her heart. *A second opinion.* Was that a good or a bad thing?

CHAPTER TWENTY-TWO

'Becca.' She turned at her name and saw Dean walking towards her, Mia holding his hand. His face was grim. 'They want to have a chat with you.' He nodded his head towards a doctor and nurse, who stood by the door of a little meeting room that opened off the waiting area.

'Is everything okay? Do they know what's wrong with her?'

A third person came bustling through the double doors. A woman with a stethoscope round her neck, but not in the white coat used by the A & E doctors. *A consultant*, Becca thought, her heart leaping up and down now, hands clammy.

Dean sat down and pulled Mia on to his knee. The three people were standing by the open door of the room, obviously waiting for her.

'Aren't you coming in?' Becca asked him.

He shook his head, an odd expression on his face that she couldn't quite interpret. 'It's just you they want to talk to.'

Mia snuggled into his chest, clearly exhausted.

Three of them? Oh God, no, this is serious.

She took a deep breath and steeled herself for bad news. *I'm a nurse. I've heard bad news before. I can handle this.* Giving them a tight smile, she walked into the meeting room and sat in the chair they indicated. Waited while they introduced themselves, not really hearing anything as her pulse whooshed in her ears.

Silence.

'Have you found out what's wrong with my daughter?'

They glanced at each other and the woman with the stethoscope nodded. 'Yes, we think we have.'

Becca waited.

'We think someone has been deliberately poisoning her.'

Becca swallowed. Her skin prickled as she took in the stern faces, three pairs of eyes fixed on her.

Do they think it's me?

She shook the ridiculous, paranoid thought from her head.

'I knew it.' Becca felt validated, a release of tension allowing a relieved smile. 'I'm a district nurse, you see. So, I've worked through all the possibilities myself, and poison was the only one that made any sense.'

'We have no answer as to what the poison is unfortunately,' said Dr Baddiel, the on-call paediatric consultant. 'Do you have any ideas?'

Becca gave a frustrated sigh. 'I'm completely stumped, to be honest. I've been wracking my brains to try and get to the bottom of it.'

Silence again. Three pairs of eyes staring at her. Becca's hands found each other in her lap, sweat sticking her shirt to her back.

'The question is… why would someone want to poison a three-year-old child?' Dr Baddiel asked.

Becca nodded. 'That's the same question I'd like answering too.'

Dr Baddiel frowned. 'It's quite a dramatic accusation, don't you think? That someone is poisoning your daughter?'

A sneaking suspicion that things were veering on to a familiar path slithered into her head, but before she had time to consider it further, the A & E doctor spoke.

'Mrs Thornton, I have to tell you that we have concerns about the welfare of your child. She has now had eight poisoning episodes, and we have to take that extremely seriously.'

Becca was about to speak and say she'd been trying to get people to take her concerns seriously for the last couple of weeks when the door opened and Dean walked in, carrying the overnight bag he kept in his car.

'Ah, Mr Thornton, thank you for joining us,' Dr Baddiel said. 'Please do sit down.'

Dean looked haggard, and he pulled out the chair next to Becca. She flicked him a grateful glance, glad that he'd been allowed in to support her. He ignored her, though, focusing instead on the doctors in front of him. 'I came back as quickly as I could.'

Becca frowned. 'Came back? You were just outside.'

Dr Baddiel spoke. 'We're keeping Mia in for observation, and your husband will be staying on the ward with her overnight, so he had to go and grab a few things.'

'Where is she?' Becca's frown deepened. 'I'll stay with her. Dean's got work tomorrow, haven't you?'

'She's in the playroom on the paediatric ward, with a nurse.' Dr Baddiel smiled at Dean, something she hadn't done to Becca. 'She'll be very glad to see you.' The consultant looked at Becca then. 'We wanted to talk to both of you together so you understand the situation and what will happen next.'

'What do you mean?' Becca could feel the weight of her fear, like a boulder in the pit of her stomach. Something strange was going on, something she knew nothing about, and she didn't like it at all. She glanced at Dean, who was rubbing a hand over his face; a sure sign that he was stressed.

'We have child safeguarding concerns,' Dr Baddiel said, making Becca's head snap round, her mouth gaping. 'Given the number of times your daughter has presented with the same undiagnosed symptoms, I'm afraid we've had to initiate our safeguarding procedures. Social services have been contacted and we're in the process of gathering up all the information and talking to any health professionals who have been involved in this case to date.'

Becca gasped. 'Hold on a minute. What do you mean, child safeguarding?'

The A & E doctor wouldn't meet her eye, but Dr Baddiel had no such qualms. 'We have to initiate an investigation. And while that is underway, we feel it would be better if your daughter was cared for by your husband.'

'What? But he can't look after her. He's got work. I'm her main care-giver.'

Dr Baddiel nodded. 'And that's exactly why we can't allow her back into your care until the investigation is complete.' She sighed. 'I'm sorry, but given the information we have available to us, we have to consider the possibility that you are harming your daughter, Mrs Thornton. Whether intentionally or by neglect. And we need to understand exactly what is happening before we can let her back into your care.'

Her voice made it sound like it was a perfectly reasonable course of action.

Becca's heart jumped as if she'd had an electric shock. 'No, you can't do that.' She grabbed her husband's arm. 'Dean, tell them how worried I've been. Tell them.'

'I'm sorry, Becca. I think it might be for the best. Just until we get to the bottom of things.' He took her hand and gave it a squeeze. 'Perhaps it'll be good for you to have a break. You've had a lot on your plate while I've been working away. Think of it like a holiday.'

'What do you mean, a holiday? How can it be a holiday if my only child is in hospital?'

'We're only keeping her in overnight,' Dr Baddiel said.

Dean shifted in his chair. 'She can come home then, can't she? If it was me looking after her. That's what you said, wasn't it?'

Dr Baddiel shook her head. 'Not quite. I'm afraid Mrs Thornton would need to leave the family home for that to be a viable option.'

Becca gulped, unable to believe what she was hearing.

'Just until the investigations are completed,' the A & E doctor said, obviously uncomfortable with the whole proceedings. Becca noticed now how young he looked and wondered if this was the first time he'd been in this sort of meeting. *He's the one who flagged it*, she reminded herself and glowered at him.

'You can't do this!' She turned to Dean. 'Tell them, I'm the one who's been trying to get a doctor to listen to me. Why would I do that if I was harming her?'

Becca swallowed back her angry words, aware that she was sounding as frantic as she felt. The implications revealed themselves in her mind, like the unveiling of a statue. The doctors would have checked her medical records. Would have seen the tentative suggestions over ten years ago that she could be suffering from factitious disorder. She knew exactly what they were insinuating – that she was harming Mia so she would get attention. They hadn't said it, but she was pretty sure that's where all this was going. Even though she had been vindicated all those years ago, that would still be there as a question mark in relation to her mental health. Then there'd been the breakdown. Followed by depression over more recent years when she'd had the miscarriages. When you gathered it all together, it didn't present a comforting picture. But it was the opposite of the truth and she had no patience with their theorising.

'This is ridiculous,' she said, getting up. 'I'm going to get my daughter and I'm going home. The social worker can visit us there.'

Dean put a hand on her arm. 'I really think it might be best if we play this by the book. Then it'll get sorted out quicker.'

She glared at him, dumbfounded. 'I can't believe you just said that.' Her voice was a desperate squeak. 'You think they're right?'

'Sweetheart, I know this is tough, but you have been pretty stressed recently.' His voice was full of forced patience, his eyes darting over her face as if he was searching for the bit that had 'unstable' written on it. 'Your moods have been unpredictable, you know, and I do feel your judgement has been a bit off-kilter with some of the things that have been happening.'

Her mouth fell open. 'What things?'

'Well, you've managed to fall out with the childminder, haven't you, by accusing her of poisoning Mia? Even though she's inspected by Ofsted, has all the correct procedures in place and is the most sought after in the area. Then there was the conversation we had about what happened before you went to Australia. Things you'd never told me.'

Becca pulled her arm from his grasp, appalled that he'd brought that up, reinforcing the idea that those false accusations might have had some substance. She'd buried the whole traumatic experience in the past, had told him in confidence, and now he'd mentioned it. If they hadn't already done so, the authorities would definitely be digging it all up again. She unclenched her jaw, her eyes pleading with the doctors as she spoke. 'I was cleared of any wrongdoing.' Her fists clenched. 'You can't do this.'

'On the contrary, Mrs Thornton, it's our duty to do this.' Dr Baddiel had a pained expression on her face as though Becca's behaviour was somehow making her suffer. 'Every NHS trust has very clear child safeguarding protocols, which I'm sure you're aware of. We're just following that, nothing more.'

'This is all wrong,' she said, shaking her head. 'I've been trying to protect her. Why would I go to the doctor's and come here if it was me poisoning her?'

'I think you know the answer to that.' Dr Baddiel was starting to sound impatient.

'Why don't you go and stay at your dad's for a little while until this is sorted,' Dean said, as gently as if he was talking to a frightened kitten that was clinging to the curtains and wouldn't come down.

Becca scanned the faces in the room and understood that she had no choice. She was being separated from her daughter and sent away from her home, all with her husband's consent and the force of the law behind the decision.

And that made her wonder: *Is Dean the one causing Mia's illness?*

CHAPTER TWENTY-THREE

They wouldn't even let Becca go and say goodbye to Mia, and she stumbled out of the hospital feeling shaken to the core, tears streaming down her face. She'd never been away from her daughter, not even for one night, and now she had no idea when she'd see her again.

She rang her dad, and through her sobs she managed to tell him what had happened.

His voice was warm with sympathy. 'Oh, Becca, that's awful. I'm so sorry this is happening again.'

'No, not again, Dad.' She sniffed back her tears, a snap of frustration in her voice. 'It didn't happen the first time, remember?'

'Sorry, love. That came out wrong. I meant you getting on the wrong side of the hospital authorities. Being accused of things.'

She swiped at her tears, her voice unsteady. 'Can I come and stay?'

'Of course you can, love. You come right over. I'll tell Kate what's going on and we'll see you soon.'

They said their goodbyes and Becca drove to Bangor, her body shaking so much she felt she probably shouldn't be driving. When she drew up outside her dad's house, she leant back in her seat, body sagging with relief that she'd finally arrived. She sat for a moment, trying to compose herself. Crying wasn't the answer, but her tears were being stubborn, and it took a few minutes before she was confident she had them under control.

She trudged into the lounge and slumped on to the sofa, too weary to take off her jacket and shoes and leave them in the hall as were the house rules. She registered the shocked expression on her sister's face and closed her eyes, wishing this was not real, that she didn't have to explain herself yet again.

'Becs, what the hell's going on? Dad said you can't go home.' Kate sounded as confused as Becca felt.

She sighed, tears filling her throat, not really up to recounting what had happened. *Maybe it'll make more sense when I tell someone.* She was about to speak when Frank came into the room.

'I thought I heard the door.' Sympathy pulled at the corners of his mouth. 'Tell you what, I'll make us a cuppa then you can tell us what's going on.'

He disappeared into the kitchen, coming back a few minutes later with mugs of tea and a packet of biscuits. He put them on the coffee table and sat on the edge of his chair. Kate sat on the sofa beside her. Becca could see from their expressions, she might as well have had 'guilty' written on her forehead. Kate hadn't believed her the last time she'd been accused of wrongdoing. Only Frank had been sympathetic. *But did he believe me then?* She wasn't sure. Perhaps he was just being protective.

Slowly she told them everything that had happened, stuttering over the details, getting things in the wrong order, having to go back and correct herself. As storytelling went, she made a right mess of it, facts and assumptions all mixed together.

'Let me get this straight,' Kate said when Becca finally ground to a halt. 'They think you're poisoning Mia to get attention, is that it? Is that what this factitious thing is?'

Becca nodded, her voice plaintive. 'How ridiculous is that? Problem is, it's usually mothers who harm their kids in this way, so I suppose I shouldn't be surprised I'm the prime suspect.'

'Oh, love, what a terrible situation,' Frank said. 'Especially after last time. It looks bad, doesn't it, to be accused of the same thing twice?'

Becca gritted her teeth. 'It's not the same thing at all, Dad. Mia is my daughter, my very precious daughter, and I'd never…'

Her voice cracked, and she covered her face with her hands. She hated crying in public, but this was overwhelming.

She heard movement, felt an arm round her shoulders, floral perfume wafting in the air as Kate held her while she cried.

'I suppose there's nothing you can do for the time being,' Kate said, practical as ever. 'You're just going to have to let them go through the process, and then they'll work out it isn't you and you'll be able to go back to normal.'

'How can I ever go back to normal after this?' she sobbed. 'Dean thinks I'm dangerous to have around Mia. He thinks I'd hurt her.' But it was even worse than that. 'He thinks... I'm mentally ill.'

Frank tutted. 'What a mess.'

Becca sat up and angrily swiped at her eyes, determined not to submit to whatever injustice was playing out. She wouldn't be separated from Mia. She had to find a way to be heard.

'This is Dean's doing,' she said quietly. 'If he hadn't told them about...' She pressed her lips together. 'He's set me up for some reason, I'm sure of it.' Now she'd started her train of thought, her words rushed out of her, gathering steam, her voice getting higher, faster. 'And if it's him poisoning Mia, if it's even a possibility, then how come they're letting her live with him, and I have to be banished from my own home? There's nobody to protect her.' Her hands clasped her cheeks, the very thought shooting arrows through her heart.

'Hey, love, don't go getting yourself worked up,' Frank said. 'Let's have a proper think, see if we can sort out what to do.'

Kate rubbed Becca's arm. 'Dad's right. Let's not go jumping to conclusions. Let's be logical about this.'

'Logical! How can I be logical when I've been accused of harming my child and told I can't live with her?' Her finger jabbed at the arm of the sofa. 'And my bloody husband has colluded with the doctors. Nothing about that is logical but it just happened.'

Kate shushed her, pulling her closer, her hand gently squeezing Becca's arm. Finally, Becca stopped resisting and leant into her, welcoming the comfort of her embrace.

'Mia's still in hospital, you say?' Frank got up and started pacing the floor, one hand rubbing his chin. 'So she's safe for now.'

'Yeah. She's safe in hospital. But what if Dean *is* doing this? She won't be safe when she gets home, will she?'

'Come on, Becs,' Kate murmured. 'Why would Dean be hurting Mia? What does he get out of it?'

'Well, he's got me out of the house, hasn't he?'

Kate snorted. 'And why would he want to do that?'

Becca sighed and studied her hands, picking at a fingernail. 'Things haven't been… Well, it's not been great for a little while. He's so busy with work, he's never at home, and sometimes I think he'd rather *not* be at home. And he keeps calling me Alice, so I wonder if there's something going on there.' The picture was becoming clearer in her mind, and she wriggled from Kate's embrace. 'What if he's having an affair with Alice? He's got me out of the house, now he can move her in.'

Kate laughed, picked up her mug and took a big gulp of tea.

'I don't see why that's funny,' Frank said, and Becca silently agreed, startled by her sister's reaction.

'Well, come on, Dad, the whole conspiracy thing is ridiculous. Dean wouldn't hurt a hair on Mia's head. He dotes on that little girl. And anyway, he's not that sort of person, is he?'

'I don't trust him,' Frank replied. 'Not after the way he behaved.'

Kate glared at her father. 'Forgive and forget. We agreed that's all in the past. If I can do it, why can't you?'

Becca didn't really understand what they were talking about, unnerved that the conversation had veered into foreign territory. It was a habit of theirs, though, talking in code, and Becca had no patience. 'I'm going to go home,' she said, standing. 'Nobody can stop me, can they?'

Frank dashed past her and stood in the doorway, blocking her exit. 'Now you don't want to be doing that, love. Not when you've been told to stay away.'

'But nobody's there tonight – they're at the hospital. If I've got to move out, I need clothes, don't I? So I'm going home. Tomorrow, I'm going back to the hospital to see what's going on. Hopefully, by then they'll have test results and they might have found something to explain Mia's illness that doesn't involve me poisoning her.'

'I don't think you're in any fit state to drive,' Kate said, eyes narrowed, assessing her. 'This is what we'll do. I'll take you home so you can pack a bag. Then while we're doing that, Dad can sort out the sofa bed in the office for you. Tomorrow, I'll come to the hospital with you, and hopefully it'll all be down to an overzealous doctor making assumptions that are plain wrong.'

Becca thought for a moment then nodded her agreement. Kate was right – she was far too wound up to be safe on the roads. 'Thanks, Kate. I know it's late and you've got to work so—'

'No problem,' Kate interrupted, ready to get going. 'That's the beauty of being self-employed. I sort out my own hours.' She tapped Becca on the shoulder. 'Right, come on, let's get a move on.'

Becca wandered round her house, picking up the bits and pieces she'd need to take, feeling like she was in some sort of trance, sleepwalking through the nightmare of her life. She couldn't understand how everything had fallen apart so quickly. *It has to be Dean, doesn't it?* He had the most to gain. Calling her Alice. It all smacked of an affair.

He'd deny it. Of course he would. So if things went badly at the hospital and she was banned from her home, and denied contact with Mia, she'd have to work hard to clear her name. Especially with her tarnished past.

Factitious disorder imposed on another was a psychological disorder that was difficult to diagnose. Nothing was precise about the label. It took several sessions of assessments with a psychiatrist, and even then it was subjective. That was the worrying thing. How many people would attest to her odd behaviour, fussing about Mia's symptoms, not seeming to be coping? She cringed. There were quite a few. When you added it all up, as an outsider, it did seem pretty damning. Just like it had when she'd been accused of harming patients at the hospital. Her stomach griped, her head hurt.

I didn't do it.

I didn't.

It wasn't me.

CHAPTER TWENTY-FOUR

Becca couldn't sleep. The sofa bed squeaked every time she turned over, the mattress paper thin, hardly masking the metal springs underneath. Eventually, she decided to get up, have a hot drink and try again. Frank always had hot chocolate in the cupboard, and she had a yearning for some. That's what her mum had made for her whenever she hadn't been able to sleep as a child. They'd sit snuggled up on the sofa, with their steaming mugs, just the two of them. Not even talking. Just being together. Those were some of her favourite memories of her mum, and she embraced them like the hug she really needed as she stood in the doorway to the lounge.

Standing in the quiet, she felt closer to her than she had since she'd died, the disagreements put to one side, allowing the positives of their relationship to make themselves known. As her thoughts stilled, she understood, as a mother herself now, that her mum had argued with her out of love. Just wanting what was best for her, wanting her to let go of troubles instead of worrying at them. Perhaps she'd been right. Something shifted inside her, a wrinkle smoothed out. Perhaps she just needed to get on with things instead of getting herself worked up into a knot of nerves, a tangle of what ifs.

Feeling calmer, she padded into the kitchen. Her handbag sat on the worktop, and while she was waiting for the milk to warm, she got out her phone and started a message to Carol saying she would be off work for a couple of days and would call her to explain. She pressed send, made her hot chocolate and went to sit in the lounge, curling up in her usual spot on the same sofa that had been there since she was a child. It had been re-covered several times, but Frank was one of those people who didn't throw things out if they were still functional.

While her drink cooled, she flicked through her phone to see if she had any messages. If Dean had tried to call. No, he hadn't, and that in itself was confusing. Surely he'd want to talk to her about what was happening? It was hard to comprehend how quickly he'd turned against her, and that added fuel to her suspicions that everything was down to him.

She paused when she saw she had a message on Twitter. From someone called Surferdude. Her heart fluttered. It could only be Connor. She opened it up.

You blocked me! If it was intentional and you really do want to stop talking to me, then that's cool. I understand. But I'm hoping it was a mistake. You hit the wrong button or something? You know I still love you xxx

She reread his message. Her heart skipped. *He still loves me?* She breathed the idea in, allowing it to fill her up, before letting out a sigh. Then she answered.

Dean made me block you. He saw our conversations. Awkward!

She pressed send and sipped her drink, enjoying the warmth of it sliding down her throat. Her thoughts stayed on Connor. The man who said he still loved her. If that was true, surely he'd want to help her? *It would be good to talk to him.*

The thought was as warming as the hot chocolate. He knew everything that had happened to her before she'd gone to Australia and had never for a moment doubted that she was innocent in the hospital incidents. He'd understood. Not like Dean, whose whole demeanour had changed, immediately suspicious of her. Maybe that was why she'd never told him all the details, keeping it vague. Had she always doubted him in her heart?

She tapped out a new message.

Can we talk? I mean FaceTime or on Messenger or something? I can't do phones so well. Prefer to see the person I'm talking to. I have so much to tell you. It's too hard typing it all.

Her finger hovered over the send button for a moment, then she pressed it. He'd been such a friend to her when she'd really needed one, such a good listener, always measured and thoughtful with his responses. She felt a flicker of hope. *Maybe I'm not alone in this.*

She desperately needed someone on her side, someone who could help her find a way out of her impossible predicament. Connor was the only person she could think of. Frank was sympathetic, but after she'd had a go at Ruth, Becca felt he was wondering whether her mental health was all it should be. Kate had laughed at her theories, so she couldn't talk to her. Carol, although a friend, was her boss and would be part of any investigation that the child safeguarding team would instigate, so she was out of bounds. As were the other district nurses she worked with. And Ruth for that matter. Apart from Connor, she had nobody to turn to.

She checked her phone every couple of minutes, but no reply. She sipped her drink. There was no choice but to wait.

Eventually, she trudged back to bed, falling asleep when the grey light of dawn filtered into the room.

Kate woke her at eight o'clock, when she came in and opened the blinds. 'Wakey, wakey,' she said in a sing-song voice.

Becca squeezed her eyes shut, her head throbbing, the light too bright. She'd been in such a deep sleep, it was confusing to suddenly be awake in a strange room and a strange bed. Panic flared in her chest, adrenaline surging through her, making her heart race. Something was very wrong, but she couldn't immediately grasp it. When she saw Kate peering at her, she started to remember and closed her eyes again.

Mia. They think I'm poisoning her. The weight of her problems landed with a thud, pressing her into the mattress; she couldn't move.

Kate started shaking her shoulder. 'Sorry, Becca, but I need you to get up. I've work to do and I'm expecting a conference call in half an hour. We need to get this bed tidied up.'

'Okay, okay,' she mumbled, her mouth so dry it was a struggle to form words. She clambered out of bed and went to get a shower. When she returned, Kate had put the bed and bedding away and handed her the bag of clothes she'd packed the night before.

'Would you mind getting dressed in the bathroom?' Kate asked, all impatient. She looked stressed, her hand rubbing her forehead. 'I really need to get everything sorted for this call.'

Already, Kate was starting to annoy Becca, and she went into the bathroom, as instructed, mumbling curses to herself about bossy sisters. *No wonder Frank gets fed up with her if she treats him like this too.* She stomped downstairs to find her dad in the kitchen making bacon butties.

'Morning, love. I made your favourite. Thought it might cheer you up.'

Becca flopped into a chair, the smell of bacon making her stomach rumble and her mouth water. She mustered a fleeting smile. 'Thanks, Dad.' A mug of coffee appeared in front of her, followed by food, and she ate as Frank talked, not hearing a single thing he was saying, her mind paralysed by the thought of her daughter being taken from her. A group of strangers, passing judgement on a situation they had no understanding of. *Will they even listen to me, or will Dean's views have already poisoned their minds?* It wasn't just Dean, though, was it? Everyone she'd gone to for help with Mia's illness probably thought she'd been making a fuss.

'I'm just nipping out to get some grocery shopping,' Frank said as she sipped her coffee. 'Want to come?'

'That's my idea of torture,' she said, the weekly shop always being something she'd hated with a passion. 'I really didn't sleep well last night, so I'll probably have a snooze on the sofa, if that's okay.'

Frank opened the cupboard under the sink and retrieved his stash of shopping bags. He waved a hand over the mess on the worktop, the remnants of breakfast. 'Don't you worry about that; I'll tidy up when I get back.' With a pat on the shoulder as he walked past, he was gone, whistling as he shut the door behind him. The house settled into quietness.

Her phone was on the table where she'd left it the night before and she picked it up, checked for messages. Carol had replied, asking her to call. Dean had sent her a message to say that the child safeguarding team had started work on their case and he would be talking to them later. He'd be home with Mia by evening at the latest and would call her then. The muscles in her shoulders tightened. A tear rolled down her cheek, then another.

Just pull yourself together, girl. Get on with it. Her mum's voice in her head, making her take a deep breath as she tried to step away from the brink of darkness and find something light to focus on.

Swiping away the tears, she checked Twitter, and her heart leapt when she found a message from Surferdude. A cartoon character blowing heart-shaped kisses, and underneath he'd written:

Glad you connected. Love you, Becca. Can I hope you still feel the same about me? Put me out of my misery, babe. Do you still love me? Because my heart and soul are yours xxx

Becca read the words over and over. It wasn't the message she'd hoped for. He actually sounded quite needy, she thought, which was the opposite of how he'd been when they were together.

It struck her then that maybe he'd got back in touch because he wasn't in a good place himself. The last thing she needed was someone else's troubles to deal with, because she knew she'd find it hard not to get involved, trying to make things better for him regardless of her own situation. It was in her nature. He hadn't responded to her request for a video conversation either.

Connor's not going to be able to help, is he?

She put her phone down, fingers drumming on the table as she thought about the events of the previous night. It had all happened so quickly, the outcome so unexpected. Dean's message said he'd be back home that evening. *Maybe I should be there waiting for him?* The only way to sort this out was face to face. But the evening was hours away.

Mia's face filled her mind, and her heart ached for her absent child. Mia would be missing her, confused, wondering what was going on. Becca stood, her body pulling her towards her daughter, the need to be with her, to hold her, too strong to resist.

The whole situation was so wrong, she couldn't believe it was really happening. Had she misunderstood? Suddenly, she knew the only way to really sort this out was to go to the hospital and make them talk to her, give her an opportunity to change their minds about what was happening. She couldn't wait for Kate. Now. She had to go now.

An hour later, she arrived at the hospital and asked for Dr Baddiel, only to be told she wouldn't be on duty until later. She explained that her daughter was on the paediatric ward, and the receptionist gave her directions. With her heart racing, she dashed down the corridors until she found the right place and pressed the entry buzzer. A voice answered.

'Hello,' Becca said, all cheery. 'I'm Mia Thornton's mum. Just wondered if I could come in and see her please?'

She could hear a muffled conversation, then a voice through the speaker asked, 'Can you just wait there for a moment, please? Someone will be out in two ticks.'

Becca saw a line of seats against the wall and went to sit and wait. Ten minutes later, the door opened, and Dean came out, dark smudges under his eyes, looking as weary as she felt. She tensed, her body ramrod stiff as he came and sat next to her.

This is his fault.

'Is Mia okay?' she asked, the very closeness of him making her skin prickle. 'Can I see her?'

'I'm sorry, sweetheart, but they won't let you.' He was talking to her as if nothing had happened between them. As if he hadn't betrayed her, hadn't doubted her sanity. 'It's been referred to this team who deal with child safeguarding, and they're now responsible for deciding what's best for Mia. There's a whole process they have to go through.'

'That's ridiculous!' She couldn't stop her temper exploding as she bounced to her feet. 'We're her parents. We know what's best for our daughter.' She grunted in frustration, her hands buried in her hair. 'I mean, the stupid thing is, I came here because I wanted help, a proper diagnosis. But instead, I've been accused of intentionally harming my own child. It's… It's…' She pulled at her hair, unable to express how angry and frustrated and helpless she felt. 'Can't you tell them they've got it wrong?'

'But have they?' He gave her a strange look. 'You've not been yourself recently, Becca. You've said as much, and I can see by your conversation with your ex that you're not happy. You're saying you feel neglected, even though I'm always telling you I love you.' He sighed. 'You've got this secret history of mental health issues, and it turns out you've been more or less diagnosed in the past with suspected Munchausen's by proxy, or whatever they call it these days.' His Adam's apple bobbed up and down and he shifted in his seat. 'I honestly don't know what to think, but I can't let this go on.' He was pleading with her, his eyes locked on hers. 'If we just go through the proper process, let the professionals assess everything, then I'm sure you'll be exonerated, and they'll work out where the problem is.'

The tapping of footsteps stopped her reply and she turned to see two people hurrying towards them. A middle-aged man with a shiny, bald head the shape of a rugby ball and a squat woman, who waddled due to the advanced stage of her pregnancy, her stomach huge.

'Mr Thornton,' the man said, looking at Dean, then Becca. 'The ward said your wife had arrived.'

Becca frowned at him as he stuck out his hand. 'Eric Barnsley. I'm here from the child safeguarding team. Social services. I've had a chat with your husband and Mia, so I'm pleased that you've come in. It'll speed things up.'

Becca shook his hand, his skin dry and leathery against her clammy palm.

'This is Angela Jones, part of the hospital's safeguarding team.' Another handshake, Angela's touch light and soft and fleeting, like she'd rather not shake hands at all. A horrible feeling of dread clutched Becca's throat, gripping so tightly she couldn't speak. *They're not going to listen to me.* She knew it before they'd even begun, could see the judgement already there on their faces.

'If we can have a chat, Mrs Thornton, we can explain the situation and take it from there?'

Becca nodded. *Don't make assumptions*, she told herself, firmly. *You might be jumping to all the wrong conclusions. Again.*

Eric took a key from the bunch in his pocket and opened a door, flicked a light switch and led Becca into a small meeting room. 'Mr Thornton, would you join us, please? I won't keep you long, then you can get back to your daughter.'

The small table had four blue plastic chairs round it, a couple more pushed up against the walls. She sat, Dean next to her and the two officials across the table.

'Now, Mrs Thornton, perhaps you can tell us in your own words how you see the situation?'

Relieved to have her say, Becca recounted the events of the last few weeks keeping her voice as calm and controlled as she could.

When she finally finished, the two officials looked at each other.

Dean coughed. 'Becca's been very stressed,' he said. 'Working and having Mia to care for has been a struggle, especially as I've been away a lot, so she's had to cope on her own.' He glanced at her. 'I think it's just been a bit too much.' He looked down at his hands. 'I feel bad that I didn't see the warning signs. I shouldn't have let it get to this stage.'

'Now don't go blaming yourself, Mr Thornton. These situations tend to creep up on people.'

'Excuse me,' Becca said, firmly, determined not to let them talk about her like she wasn't there. 'I think there's a strong possibility that my husband is behind all this.' Dean reeled back, clearly shocked by her accusation. 'I think he's been giving Mia something. He wants me out of the house.'

The officials looked confused. Dean glared at her. 'What the hell are you talking about? How can it be me when this has happened when I've been away?'

He had a point. Becca swallowed. 'I don't know,' she whispered, a surge of heat flooding her body as she understood how unhinged she sounded. 'But it wasn't me.'

CHAPTER TWENTY-FIVE

Becca was closely questioned by the two officials, who carefully picked over her version of events. Then they focused their attention on her: was she on medication, where did she store cleaning materials, where did she keep her nurse's bag, what medication did she carry in there? All sorts of questions asked from different angles, trying to catch her out. After that, she was seen by the on-call psychiatrist, who'd been asked to do an assessment. It was horribly familiar, bringing back memories of the scariest time of her life, when she'd felt so boxed in by accusations of wrongdoing that she could barely breathe.

The psychiatrist was a nondescript middle-aged man, with short brown hair and a very forgettable face. His demeanour was coaxing and unthreatening – all concerned expressions and a gentle, soporific voice, pretending to be on her side while he tried to trick her into admitting she was overwhelmed and that hurting Mia was her way of crying for help.

He went over her past in minute detail, dragging up her previous episode of depression, brought on by the stress of the police investigation at the hospital. He highlighted the similarities between the situation before she went to Australia and now. She could see where it was going but she felt helpless, unable to convince him that she was innocent. By the time he'd finished, she felt like a worn-out rag, wrung out so many times she was tattered and frayed, no substance left in her threadbare fibres.

The psychiatrist left her alone in the meeting room, and twenty minutes later Eric Barnsley came back in. He gave her a smile, which seemed completely inappropriate given the circumstances. 'Well, Mrs Thornton, I have spoken to all my colleagues on the team, and our initial conclusion is that Mia should stay in the family home with Mr Thornton. You will be legally bound to stay away while investigations are ongoing, and we will aim to expedite the work as quickly as possible.'

Stay away from my daughter? Her heart clenched, her mind spinning. 'What investigations exactly? How long is it going to take?'

'We are still awaiting test results. And we are interviewing family, friends and work colleagues to get a picture in the round, as it were. Also, the psychiatrist has suggested further assessments with you before we make our final judgement as to the way forward.'

'What?' Her eyes felt like they were going to pop out of her head. 'No! How can you be allowed to interfere in my life… our lives like this?' Her hands flew through the air as she spoke. 'It's not right! He wasn't listening to me. Your psychiatrist, whatever his name is. He'd already come to a conclusion.'

Eric patted the air in a 'calm down' motion, a spark of fear in his eyes. 'Now, Mrs Thornton, please don't upset yourself. We want an outcome that's best for the family. But you've got to admit that eight incidents of poisoning, which we all agree is what has been happening here, well, it's got to stop. Please… just cooperate with our recommendations – I can assure you that's the quickest way to get life back to normal.'

She sat and seethed for a minute or two while Eric watched her, his eyes scanning her face. A sheen of sweat appeared on his brow.

He's taking notes, she warned herself. *And you're acting like a crazy person.* She clasped her hands in her lap, feeling angry and powerless and trapped. Her heart thundered in her chest, making her body shake with each beat. There was nothing she could do. Nothing at all.

Play the game, go through the motions and have faith in the process, she counselled herself. The last thing she needed to do was behave in a way that confirmed their suspicions. *Quickly. He said it would be done quickly.* She latched on to that thought like a drowning swimmer snatching at a life belt. 'So, what happens next?' she said, eventually. 'What timescales are we talking about?'

'We'll keep regular checks on Mia. And we want you to see the psychiatrist and accept whatever treatment he recommends.' His stare seemed to intensify at this point, and she squirmed, sure that he could sense her resistance to that part of the process. 'There will be an appointment in the post. I believe you're staying at your father's address. Mr Thornton has given us the details.'

'You're making me live apart from my daughter.' It was more of a statement than a question, and just saying the words made her hand reach for her throat as if she was being starved of oxygen.

'For the time being, yes.'

Her eyes locked with his in silent battle, emotion swelling in her chest, making it a struggle to keep her voice even. 'Well, how's that going to be possible when my husband works away half the time? It's not like he can take her with him, is it?'

Eric studied his notes. 'I believe your husband is taking some time off work while he sorts out childcare.'

Becca tried to think of something to say, anything to persuade this man that he didn't fully understand the situation. Nobody did – even she didn't comprehend what was really happening. But she did know they were approaching the search for a solution from completely the wrong direction.

'I'm not the problem,' she said quietly as she got up and left the room, with Eric calling after her that he'd be in touch.

*

Five hours after she'd left Frank's house that morning, she arrived back, slamming the front door behind her as if it was to blame.

Frank popped his head out of the kitchen door, frowning.

'Don't you start,' she snapped before heading into the lounge, unable to face any sort of conversation, let alone lengthy explanations. She wanted to be alone, to curl up in a ball and purge herself of the storm of emotions that whirled inside her. She pressed her lips tight, trying to stop the sobs that were heaving in her chest as she sank on to the sofa.

'Oh, love,' Frank said, coming to sit beside her, wrapping her in a hug. She clung to him, a child again being comforted by her parent, the man who had always tried to smooth away her woes. 'What's going on? Where've you been? I tried ringing you, but it just went to voicemail. I was so worried.'

Encircled in his arms, his kindness was too much, and her sadness flowed out of her in a river of tears. Finally, her sobs hiccupped to a stop and she pulled away. He grabbed a handful of tissues from the box on the coffee table, handing them to her. 'There you go, love. You dry your eyes, then tell me all about it.' He patted her shoulder. 'A problem shared is a problem halved, remember?'

She sighed and sank back on the cushions, wiping her face with frustrated swipes.

'They're still convinced it's me poisoning Mia. I went to the hospital thinking it was the best way to sort everything out. Head on, like you always say.' Frank nodded and she almost crumpled again when she saw the concern in his eyes. 'Well, I'm not sure if I just made it worse. Anyway. I met the social worker who's in charge of safeguarding, and we had a long chat, going through all the details yet again. Then they turned it all on me and what I might be doing wrong. And he made me talk to a psychiatrist who twisted my words and it's all official now.' Her voice cracked. 'Legally, I can't be with my own daughter until they've completed their investigation.'

Frank whistled between his teeth. 'That seems harsh. I thought that's maybe where you'd gone, but I do wish you'd waited for Kate to go with you like you'd arranged. Do you think it would help if I spoke to them? Vouched for you as a mother or something? Because from what I've seen you're a brilliant mum and Mia adores you.'

Becca blew her nose. 'I don't think Mia's feelings come into this at all, I'm afraid. She's only three, so whatever she says won't really count. Not with me and Dean saying opposite things.' She squeezed the soggy ball of tissues in her hand.

'Bloody Dean!' Frank slapped his leg with a smack that made Becca jump. 'I don't trust him as far as I can throw him.'

'Oh, Dad, not that again. I really don't need any more aggravation.' She sighed. 'They'll be talking to you and Kate at some point, so at least you'll get to have your say. Hopefully, they'll listen.'

Frank huffed a couple of times, clearly unable to think of anything constructive to say. He patted her knee before getting up. 'I'll make us some tea. You look like you might be in shock. Pale as a ghost you are.'

He came back a few minutes later with steaming mugs. 'There you go, love. You'll feel better after that.' His lips pursed as he assessed her dishevelled state. 'I bet you haven't eaten either, have you?'

She shook her head and he returned to the kitchen, coming back in with a plate of ham sandwiches. 'These will keep you going until tea's ready.' He took one for himself, passing the rest of them to her. 'I was just making a snack when you came back, but we can share.'

It was peculiar having her dad clucking around, with her once again the child in their relationship, rather than feeling like the adult. Safe and loved. 'Thanks, Dad,' she murmured as she started nibbling, suddenly aware of the hunger gnawing at her belly.

Ten minutes later, the sandwiches eaten, she felt strong enough to talk again. 'It's legally binding. That's the most awful thing. I can't go near her. And I've got to see the psychiatrist again, agree to whatever treatment he recommends once he's made a diagnosis. That's me he's going to diagnose, which means they're convinced I'm mentally ill.' She glanced at Frank. 'How on earth do you go about convincing people your mental health is fine when they've already decided that it's not? To them, I'm in denial.' She threw up her hands in despair, voice wavering. 'How do I win?'

Frank grimaced. 'That's a tricky one, no doubt about it.'

'What's tricky?' Kate asked as she came into the room.

Becca blinked. Frank coughed. 'Life,' he said, with a quick wink at Becca. She winked back, grateful for his cover-up.

Kate cocked her head, frowning. 'What's going on here?' She glanced from one to the other. 'You two are up to something. Come on, spill the beans.'

Frank and Becca looked at each other.

'Oh, it's going to be like that, is it? Two against one?' Kate folded her arms across her chest, annoyance sparking in her eyes. 'She always was your favourite, wasn't she, Dad?'

Frank tutted. 'No, love. No, I've never had favourites.'

Becca thought he could have sounded more convincing and noticed the furrow between Kate's eyebrows. She didn't want trouble, couldn't face an argument. So she took a deep breath and made the only decision that made sense – she told Kate what had happened.

Kate sank on to the arm of the sofa, clearly shocked. 'And it's up to a psychiatrist now?'

Becca shrugged. 'Not completely. There's a team of people from the hospital and social services who decide. But whatever the psychiatrist recommends in terms of treatment, after these further assessments, I have to go along with it.'

Kate pulled a face. 'Oh God. How long's all that going to take?'

Becca sighed, her shoulders slumped. Now she'd laid it all out for her sister, her situation seemed hopeless. 'They're sending me an appointment. But I doubt if it'll just be one session. I've had patients go through psychiatric assessments and it can take weeks.'

Just the thought of all the time away from her daughter caused a new surge of despair, and she buried her head in her hands.

'Oh, dear. You'll be here a while then?'

'Seems like it,' Frank said, answering for her as he came and sat next to her, his hand rubbing her back.

That night, when Becca was setting up the bed, Kate came in, closing the door behind her. 'Let me do that,' she said as she bustled Becca out of the way. 'I can see you're wiped out.' Gratefully, Becca watched as her sister made up the bed, plumping the pillows and making sure it was as comfortable as possible.

'There you are. I won't need you to be up so early tomorrow, you'll be pleased to know. I've got my laptop, so I can get started in my bedroom first thing.'

Becca sank on to the bed, looking longingly at the squishy pillows. 'Thank you. I could do with a proper night's sleep. I hardly slept a wink last night, and as soon as I dropped off, it was time to get up again.'

Kate sat next to her on the bed. 'Actually, there's something I wanted to ask you.'

Becca wasn't sure she was up to answering any more questions, but Kate carried on regardless.

'As you know, I've been here about three years now, and I have to be honest, it's been a struggle. I just wanted to make sure you don't mind if I start taking the occasional time out?'

Becca stopped smoothing out the duvet. 'I'm not sure what you mean?'

Kate gave her a tentative smile. 'I had such a great time last weekend, I've organised another trip. In a couple of weeks. And then I'm thinking about a holiday. A fortnight away. You'll be okay keeping an eye on Dad, won't you?'

Becca had been expecting a ticking off for not listening to Kate and shooting off to the hospital on her own, so this came as a surprise. But there was no reason for Kate to be at the house all the time.

She nodded. 'Yeah, that's fine. No problem. It's not like I'm going anywhere anytime soon, is it?' She saw the flicker of delight on Kate's face. 'I know it's been tricky having to be here for him, and I'm sorry I haven't been much help recently.' She sighed. 'Thing is, we'd just made plans for him to come over more often. He's like a different man when he's with Mia – they have such a lovely time together. All this has ruined it for him.'

'Don't be so hard on yourself.' Kate put an arm round her shoulder and gave her an unexpected hug. 'You haven't ruined it for him at all. There's nothing to say he can't spend time with Mia. It's just you, isn't it?'

Her words registered in Becca's mind and an idea sprang to life. *That's right. Dad can spend all the time he likes with her.* She wondered if that was a way for her to get to see her daughter. Frank could go and pick her up, take her out and 'accidentally' meet Becca. Who would know? Her pulse started to race.

Would Dean allow it, though? That was the problem, given the fact the two men disliked each other. But a flicker of hope ignited in her chest.

'Here's a deal,' she said to Kate, suddenly animated.

Her sister raised an eyebrow, curious.

'You go away as often as you like as long as you ask Dean if you can take Mia out, to give him a break. Then you can bring her back here, and Dad and I can spend some time with her.'

Kate's eyes narrowed and her arm dropped from Becca's shoulders. 'What? I can't do that. Firstly, it's illegal. And secondly, Mia would tell Dean. Then I'd be the bad guy.' She shook her head. 'No, sorry, I could get into all sorts of trouble.'

Becca let her body flop backwards on to the bed. Kate was right.

'You're just going to have to go along with the process and have faith that it'll all get sorted out.' Kate stood and stretched her arms above her head. 'So, you're okay for Dad-minding duties while you stay here?'

Becca couldn't answer, gripped by the fear she might never be allowed to live with her daughter again.

CHAPTER TWENTY-SIX

The next morning, Becca woke to the sound of shouting coming up from the kitchen below. She clambered out of bed, increasingly worried as the volume rose, Frank and Kate both shouting at the same time. She reached the hall in time to see Kate storm out of the kitchen, her face like thunder, and she pushed past Becca as if she was one of the coats hanging on the wall. The door slammed shut behind her as she left the house.

Becca stared at the closed door, stunned for a moment, still not fully awake. She'd had another turbulent night and was even more groggy today than she'd been the day before. The sound of sobbing made her dash into the kitchen, where Frank was sitting at the kitchen table, his head resting on his arms.

'Dad, whatever's the matter?'

He seemed startled by her voice and jumped up, his back towards her, and went over to the kettle, filled it from the tap and switched it on. He coughed, clearing his throat. 'Cup of tea, love?' He sniffed. Coughed again before he started whistling one of his favourite tunes.

'Come on, don't pretend nothing just happened. I heard you two yelling at each other.' Her thoughts screeched to a halt as she reached a horrible conclusion. 'It's not me, is it? I haven't caused trouble between you, have I?'

Frank stopped whistling but still wouldn't look at her. He reached into the cupboard for a couple of mugs and dropped a tea bag into each one.

'So, what was it about? It sounded like you were going to kill each other.'

Frank's shoulders sagged. 'Would you believe I don't really know?'

'It must have been something.'

He sighed and tipped boiling water in the mugs, made the tea and brought it over to the table. Becca pulled out a chair and he sat opposite. 'She's a bit on edge. I don't know if it's work or…' He shrugged. 'Honestly, I'm not really sure but it feels like when your mother had one of her turns and she morphed into a wildcat. She used to fly at me sometimes and I never knew what triggered her. She'd just say it was the final straw and then…' He studied the table, picking up crumbs with his index finger.

Becca remembered her mum's temper, how she would get frustrated with her dad's messiness, and Kate was pretty much a carbon copy of their mother, even down to looks. She'd definitely inherited her short fuse but she wasn't vindictive. Yes, she could be bossy, but she wouldn't have been yelling like that for no reason. 'Tell me it wasn't about tidying up. That's what Mum used to get uptight about, wasn't it?'

'No, it wasn't that. I've learnt my lesson since she's been here, and I daren't leave things out just in case it starts a row.' He blew on his tea and took a sip, both of them quiet. Seconds stretched to minutes. He shuffled in his seat then put his mug down and looked straight at her. 'Okay, I'll be honest. There's no reason why you shouldn't know, and if you're going to be living here for a while…' He sighed. 'She says I behave like I'm helpless when I'm not and I should get a grip and act like an adult instead of her having to baby me all the time.'

Becca's eyes widened, shocked that her sister would say such a thing, even if there was an iota of truth in it. 'She said that to you?'

He nodded, sadness pulling at the corners of his mouth. 'It's not the first time. It seems to be her go-to argument when she's uptight about something.' He shrugged again. 'She has no patience if she's got something on her mind. And she takes it out on me.'

Becca stretched across the table and found her dad's hand, giving it a squeeze. 'I'm here now, Dad. I think that'll take the pressure off.' She sighed. 'I think she's just frustrated at how her life has turned out and she's lashing out. It's probably not personal, you know? More about her than you.'

His hand squeezed hers. 'Thanks, love. I'm glad you're here.' He gave a little laugh. 'The A-Team back together again.'

She laughed with him, remembering the fun they used to have on their adventures when she was a child, pretending they were on a covert operation stalking the bad guys. 'I could use some help from the A-Team to get Mia back.' Her face fell as her predicament forced its way back into her mind, and she groaned, letting go of his hand. 'What am I going to do, Dad? Nobody will listen to me.'

Frank picked up his mug again, took a slurp of tea. 'What do you want to do? What do you think is happening?'

She ran her hands through her hair as she organised her thoughts. 'Right, well, this is where I'm up to…' Frank gave her a nod of encouragement.

'I can't get past the idea that Dean is behind all this. When you think about it, he has the most to gain from me being out of the house.'

Franked frowned but stayed quiet.

Becca took a sip of her tea, readying herself to admit that she'd been putting a gloss on the reality of her life. 'I've messed up big time, Dad.' She hesitated, not sure how complete her disclosure should be. 'You remember Connor? The guy I was with in Australia?' Frank's frown deepened. 'He popped up on social media, so we started chatting and… Oh God, this sounds so bad, but I felt like he was the only person I could talk to, so I told him all my troubles and then Dean found the conversation.'

She cringed.

Frank's eyebrows inched up his forehead.

'Well, he was fuming and I felt I had to explain myself. Then… well, I told him about what happened before I went to Australia. I hadn't told him all the details before because it didn't seem relevant. It was in the past, wasn't it? Anyway, as soon as I told him, his whole attitude changed.' She studied her fingernails, furiously picking at the cuticles. 'I gave him a gift, a piece of information that he then used to get the safeguarding team worried about me. Goodness knows what else he's said.'

Frank put his tea down and blew out a long breath. 'Well, I can see why Dean wouldn't be happy if you'd been talking to your ex. There's only one reason why Connor would get in touch. Some people find it hard to let old loves go. They think they can go back and rekindle things. Really, it's no wonder Dean was jealous.'

'It was only talking, Dad. And I was just venting. It was like talking to myself – Connor's in Australia, on the other side of the world – but Dean saw all the things I was unhappy with and I suppose it really hurt.' Her cheeks burnt with a sudden flush of shame, wondering if her situation would be different if she'd never written down what was on her mind. The weight of her problems made her head feel heavy and she leant her elbows on the table, her chin cupped in her hands. 'Anyway, it's done now. I think this is Dean lashing out, but he doesn't understand the implications of putting doubts in those people's minds. It's a legal process and getting out of it is not going to be easy.'

'You could have spoken to me if you had problems,' Frank said, gently, a note of hurt in his voice. 'You know I've always got your back.'

'I tried telling you, and you more or less said I was fussing, remember? Then when I tried to talk to Ruth about it, to see if she might be giving Mia something she was intolerant to, you got all cross with me and took her side. You definitely thought I was being unreasonable.'

Frank sighed. 'Yes, well, I'm sorry if I didn't come over as sympathetic. And thanks for being honest with me.' He finished his tea and leant across the table to rub her shoulder. 'Let's try and be positive about all this and see what we can do.'

Becca's mind was racing now, making links that she hadn't understood before. Her thoughts led her to a new scenario that brought a chill to her skin.

'Oh my God, Dad. I've not been thinking straight. Mia isn't safe, is she?'

Frank stroked his chin as he thought. 'Hmm. If Dean's responsible, and your theory's right, then she probably is. My bet is this will all stop and that will make you look even more like the guilty party.'

'But if it isn't Dean? Then whoever's doing it might carry on.'

'We can only take things one step at a time, love.' Frank got up. 'Right, I've got jobs to do. Can't have that sister of yours on at me again. There's a pile of stuff she wanted me to take to the tip. I'll only be half an hour. Then we can go for a walk, see if that clears our heads. Maybe find somewhere to go for lunch. How about that?'

'Okay, sounds good.' But she had no intention of going out for lunch. She had more important things to do.

CHAPTER TWENTY-SEVEN

Becca drove to her house but kept going past when she saw Dean's car in the drive, Alice's red Mini, with the white stripe down the middle, parked behind it.

Very cosy, Becca thought, teeth grinding. As far as Becca was aware, Alice had never been to their new house and it seemed quite a coincidence that she should turn up now.

She needed somewhere to watch and wait, maybe get some photos of the two of them together so he couldn't deny it. Their house backed on to the golf course, and she parked in an estate further up the road then walked back. With a pair of birdwatching binoculars in her hands and her phone in her pocket, she was ready to take snaps should the opportunity arise.

At the rear of their property, a metre-wide gap had been left between a bank planted with an evergreen hedge and the garden fence, designed to give the houses more privacy from the golfers. The fence was made of slatted uprights, with narrow gaps between; perfect for spying without being seen. She walked along until she was opposite the bifold doors that spanned the kitchen and dining area and would, she hoped, give her a clear view into most of the downstairs.

Unfortunately, the glare of the sun meant she couldn't see anything – only a fleeting shadow, which was gone before she could work exactly what she'd seen. She cursed under her breath. Even when she changed position and moved further along the fence, then back the other way, there seemed to be no vantage point that would give her a proper view.

It felt unsavoury, lurking behind the fence. Snooping. Her anger grew inside her, a small voice getting louder and louder until she could ignore it no longer. *Why should I creep about? This is my house!* She hurried out of the golf course and back down the road, glad to see both cars still in the driveway. *Perfect*, she thought as she pulled her keys from her pocket. She'd catch them unawares. Then there could be no excuses.

As quietly as she could, she put her key in the lock and let herself into the house, closing the door behind her with the faintest of clicks. She stopped in the hall and listened. Talking. Upstairs.

With her jaw clamped tight, she crept up the stairs, her phone in her hand, ready to take compromising pictures. Surely, there was only one reason they'd be upstairs. She crept along the landing, stopping outside the master bedroom, listening. But that's not where the voices were coming from, and when she carefully pushed the door open and peeped inside, she saw it was empty.

The spare bedroom was next door and now she could tell that's where they were. With her heart hammering in her chest, she inched along the wall until she was next to the door. It wasn't fully closed, and she could hear their conversation.

'There's not enough,' Alice said. 'We need at least ten more.'

'Let me have a look in the garage. I think I put some in there a week or so ago when Becca had me clearing this room out.' Before Becca could move, Dean appeared in the doorway, fully clothed, doing a double take when he saw her, his mouth falling open.

'Becca! What are you doing here?'

She froze, her mind going into freefall, and all she could do was stare back at him, a flush of heat rushing through her body.

Alice appeared in the doorway. She looked at Dean, then Becca. 'Tell you what, I'll take these shirts. You see if you can find any more and call me later, okay? I'm staying over with Ross, so it'll be easy enough to come and pick them up.'

She disappeared back into the bedroom and came out with a cardboard box in her arms. 'We've got a tournament tomorrow,' she said to Becca, her cheeks pink, obviously uncomfortable at being found upstairs in her business partner's house. 'I just needed to pick up some shirts.' She flicked a glance at Dean. 'I hope you two get everything sorted out soon. He's been hopeless recently.'

Then she was gone, feet thumping down the stairs, the front door opening and banging shut behind her.

'Who's Ross?' Becca asked, her body shaking with an overload of adrenaline.

'Her fiancé. But why that's relevant I have no idea.' Dean rubbed the back of his neck. 'I'm really sorry, but you shouldn't be here, Becca. It's not going to help.'

She leant against the wall, her legs threatening to crumple as she realised she'd got it all wrong. There was no affair with Alice. Her theory was crushed along with any motivation Dean might have for getting her out of the house.

'Where's Mia? I need to see her. Just for a moment.' Her eyes pleaded with him and she noticed then that his normally clean-shaven face was darkened with stubble, his hair lank.

'You're not allowed, remember?' He walked towards her, his hand reaching for hers, but she slid away from him, the idea of his touch repugnant.

'Why are you doing this to me? What did you say to those people? You know I wouldn't hurt her. You know that.'

She sounded aggrieved, aggressive, and he held up his hands in surrender, his brow crumpled. 'I'm sure you don't mean to hurt her. I think it's just… you've got to admit, you're not yourself at the moment.' He ran a hand through his hair. 'I don't know what's going on. All I know is she's been fine since she's been apart from you. So I think it's best it stays that way.' His eyes met hers. 'She's so precious – the little girl we thought we could never have – I've got to make her safety my priority.'

Becca thought she might explode. 'And that is exactly my priority as well.' She felt a little dizzy, the pressure of frustration pounding in her head. 'I don't understand how you can believe that I'm poisoning my own daughter.' She jabbed a finger at him. 'You told them a pack of lies, didn't you? You must have done.'

Dean shook his head, sadly. 'I only told them what I know to be true and what you told me yourself. That's all. I've got to protect Mia. Put an end to this madness.' He gave a sigh and pulled his phone from his pocket, swiped and tapped and put the phone to his ear.

Becca's heart skipped a beat. 'Wait, what are you doing?'

'You're breaking the law being here. I can't allow it. I'm calling Eric Barnsley to ask his advice as to what I should do.'

She grabbed his phone and ended the call. 'I'm going,' she hissed. 'Don't worry, I'll stay away. Don't you dare tell anyone I was here.'

With a sob catching in her throat, she ran downstairs and out of the house.

CHAPTER TWENTY-EIGHT

Becca sat in her car for a while, staring through the windscreen, processing what she'd learnt.

Dean wasn't in the clear yet, but if he wasn't having an affair with Alice, then she couldn't for the life of her think why he'd be the one behind it all. He'd appeared genuinely distraught when he'd spoken to her a little while ago.

She drove towards her favourite coffee shop, not wanting to go back to Frank's just yet. As she passed the playground, her eyes glanced to the left and she jammed on her brakes. A little girl was running towards the swings. *Mia!* Quickly, she parked up and hopped over the fence into the playground.

'Mia! Mia!' she called as she ran, and her daughter turned. But before she could reach her, a woman gathered Mia into her arms. It was Ruth. She seemed a little scared, eyes darting around, obviously searching for reinforcements, or a means to call for help.

She backed away, Mia stretching for her mother. 'I'm sorry, Becca, but I've been told you can't come near her.'

Becca forced a smile, her voice as friendly as she could make it in the circumstances, but there was a distinct wavering, an uncertainty that undermined her words. 'Don't be silly, Ruth. One cuddle can't hurt, can it? And who will know?'

'Mummy!' Mia squealed, wriggling for all she was worth, her face going red with the effort, while Ruth held her tight. Mia winced, her face crumpling. 'You're hurting,' she whined, trying to peel Ruth's fingers off her arm. 'Hurting.' She looked at Becca, her eyes filled with tears. 'Mummy cuddle.'

'You need to go right now,' Ruth said, all stern like she was in charge.

'I'm not going anywhere until I get to hold my daughter.' Becca's voice was trembling as much as her body, her heart aching to hold her child.

Ruth shook her head and backed away another step, her eyes scanning the playground. Two mums had just arrived and sat chatting on a nearby bench. 'Help!' she called, to Becca's horror. The women stopped talking and looked over. 'Help!' Ruth called again, louder. 'Can someone please call the police? She's trying to take my child.'

Her child?

Becca's breath caught in her throat as she saw one of the women pull out her phone and start to make a call, her eyes fixed on Becca, concern written all over her face. Her friend went and gathered their two children, holding them to her as if Becca would snatch them away.

Becca knew she had no choice but to leave – if the police got involved, that wouldn't help her case at all; in fact, it would be a disaster. She was going to have to approach this from a different angle. She walked away, tears streaming down her face as her daughter's screams filled her ears. This was torture for both of them.

Confused and upset, she drove away, muttering to herself as she parked on one of the back streets where her car wasn't obvious, just in case the police were actually called and they came searching for her. She wiped her face and darted into a coffee shop – one that she'd never visited before – making her way to a table at the back, out of sight. Ruth wouldn't know where she'd gone, she was sure of it.

Ruth. Could she be the one poisoning Mia?

She thought back to the start of everything. There was Ruth's cancer scare, over before it really began. *Was that real? Or just a means of getting sympathy?* Her sudden friendship with Frank, when she appeared to have no other friends. And of course Dean would ask her to care for Mia now Becca wasn't at home – why wouldn't she be his go-to person when Mia loved her, and Ruth loved Mia and she was the top-rated childminder in town? Becca frowned, remembering how Ruth had said she wanted to leave a legacy to Mia when she died. *Was that the action of a lonely middle-aged woman, or was it weird?*

She sipped her coffee, deep in thought. Ruth was definitely someone who would benefit from Becca being out of the way. She'd have more or less free access to Mia while Dean was working. Oh yes, she could become invaluable to him and usurp Becca as the woman who was closest to Mia, their bond strengthening while Mia's bond with her mother weakened through lack of contact.

The more she thought about it, the angrier she became. As a theory, it made perfect sense.

Her instinct was to go back to her house and wait for Ruth and Mia to return, then confront her, so Dean could see the truth of it.

I can't do that. Dean had threatened to tell the safeguarding team she was breaching the conditions. And Ruth wouldn't hesitate to call the police, if she hadn't already done so. She gave a little shiver, appalled at her recklessness. All she'd managed to do today was make herself appear dangerous in the eyes of the authorities. Someone who would kidnap her daughter. Someone desperate and deranged.

She buried her head in her hands. Her mind was foggy, everything blurring together, indistinct. What she needed was clarity, but it wasn't happening.

Remembering that she'd left Frank's without telling him where she was going, she pulled out her phone to let him know she'd be back soon. A flush of guilt burnt her cheeks as she tapped in her pin – when she saw that she'd missed six calls from him, she felt even worse.

That's when she noticed she had a new message on Twitter from Surferdude.

You haven't answered. Does that mean you don't feel the same? My heart aches for you. What we had was so special, and those feelings are as strong today as they ever were. Leave Dean. He clearly doesn't love you. Come back and be with me. Xxx

She read his words a couple of times, a swirl of unease in the pit of her stomach. It was a bit over the top, she thought, asking her to leave Dean. Ridiculous even. After ten years apart, what made him think she'd just drop everything and dance to his tune? The tone of this message felt different to their early banter. The delicious but harmless flirting. He'd changed, that was for sure, because the Connor she'd known had never put any pressure on her to do anything. Perhaps she'd been right in her assumption that he was contacting her because things in his life weren't going well. Perhaps this was nothing to do with her and everything to do with him.

Still, he was the only friend who wasn't involved in the safe-guarding team's investigation. She needed him, needed to have a proper chat about what was happening.

Like I said, I need to speak to you. Can we FaceTime or speak on Messenger yet? If you can't, call me. It's urgent.

She added her number and pressed send. There, that was pretty clear. She was about to put her phone away when a message appeared.

What's wrong, babe? You sound a bit stressed.

Stressed? Christ, he doesn't know the half of it. She hadn't the energy to tell him everything. That would take several thousand words, and there was something about these messages that was bothering her. It was strange, wasn't it, that Mia's illness had started just after Connor had got back in touch.

You're being paranoid now. He's in bloody Australia.

Then it struck her. Maybe he wasn't.

CHAPTER TWENTY-NINE

She stopped with her coffee cup halfway to her mouth, put it down on the saucer as she thought it through. You couldn't tell from Twitter where people were. Perhaps he was in the UK for some reason. In which case… was he an ally, or could he be the enemy? She thought back to the way they'd parted, her promises to go back to Australia which had come to nothing. The way she'd moved on to be with Dean. How hurtful that would be to him. Hurtful enough to make him bitter? Be intent on revenge? And what sweeter revenge could there be than separating her from the two people who had kept her from going back to be with him?

She finished her coffee, desperate to try out her theory with somebody, and the only person who would understand was Frank. He would be able to sort out what made sense because her brain was completely fuddled now there were three possibilities: Dean, Ruth and Connor.

She'd almost got to her car when her phone rang. *Connor?* Her heart flipped. What was she going to say? Should she confront him or play it cool? Quietly test out his story or challenge him? Nervous, she fumbled her phone out of her pocket and glanced at the screen, but it wasn't Connor, it was an unknown number.

'Hello,' she said, tentatively.

'Is that Mrs Thornton?'

'It is,' she said before she'd thought it might have been better to deny it, say she'd found the phone on a table in a coffee shop and was on her way to hand it in to the police.

'This is the psychiatric unit, Mr Patel's secretary. I have been asked to arrange an emergency appointment for an assessment. Could you come at three thirty today?'

Her brain froze. *Could I? More to the point, should I?*

'Mrs Thornton, are you still there?'

She cleared her throat, still uncertain what to say. *What if he decides I'm a danger and sections me?* It could happen; she'd seen it with patients. In for an assessment then locked up in the secure unit – for their own safety, of course. *Ha!* She wasn't going to fall for that one.

'I'm terribly sorry, I'm not sure I can make it today. Can I come tomorrow instead, please? My father's not well and I really don't want to leave him on his own. But my sister will be back tonight. Will the morning be okay?'

'One moment, please.' Tinny music filled her ear as she was put on hold. A few moments later the secretary came back on. 'Can you make ten thirty tomorrow morning?'

Becca slowly let out the breath she'd been holding. 'Yes, that would be fine, thank you.'

She'd take Frank with her, and then he could argue her case if there was any sign of them not letting her out. Once they decided that mental illness might be an issue, it could start a whole mass hysteria, nobody wanting to say you were fine just in case you weren't.

Her heart was racing, palms sweaty. She had until the morning to try and get some clear evidence as to who was behind all the trouble. She checked her watch. Eleven fifteen. *Better get a move on.*

CHAPTER THIRTY

Frank was sitting in the lounge watching a nature programme on TV when she got back. His demeanour was glum but he brightened when he saw her, a flash of relief in his eyes.

'Becca, I've been so worried. Why weren't you answering? I called God knows how many times. Didn't you see my texts?' He turned off the TV, giving her his full attention.

She felt bad that she'd ignored his many messages until she'd known she was on her way back home. 'I replied. Didn't you see?'

'Only to the last one. I was going frantic before that what with… you know.' He ground to a halt and she knew exactly what he'd been thinking. That she was a risk to herself.

She puffed out an impatient breath, hands folded across her chest. 'Right, Dad, let's get something straight, shall we? I am not mentally ill. Not even slightly. Stressed, maybe. But my mental health is not in question. I will not be doing "something stupid" as you'd like to call it. So no need to worry if I go out for a couple of hours, all right?' She hated how snippy and shrewish she sounded, not like herself at all.

She flopped on to the sofa.

Frank looked taken aback, like she'd tried to bite him. 'No need to snap. You sound just like Kate.'

Becca glanced at the ceiling, unable to meet his eye, disappointed with herself for taking her problems out on Frank when he had his own to deal with. Finally, she spoke. 'Sorry, Dad. I've had a hell of a morning.' She saw the hurt in his eyes and felt even worse about her behaviour. She sighed. 'That's no excuse, is it? Can I make us a cup of tea and then I'll tell you where I'm up to?' She grimaced. 'I've got a deadline now and I really need your help.'

He gave her a wobbly smile. 'That'd be smashing, love. There's a packet of Hobnobs on the worktop if you fancy?'

She went through to the kitchen and got their drinks and biscuits organised, taking a tray back into the lounge, glad to see that Frank was more himself again and obviously eager to hear her news.

'Right, love. Fire away,' he said, taking a biscuit out of the packet and settling back in his chair.

'It's hard to know where to start...' She took a deep breath and off she went, recounting all the events of the morning, while Frank's face darkened as the story progressed.

He finished his biscuit and took a sip of his tea, thoughtful. 'You're not going to like this, but I think your logic may be a little flawed.'

Becca frowned. 'Flawed? What do you mean? Which bit of my logic exactly?' She sounded horribly defensive and told herself to calm down, just listen to what Frank had to say.

'Dean... I think your logic might be wrong there. Just because he's not having an affair with Alice doesn't mean he's not having an affair, does it?'

Becca's eyes widened, the obvious truth of his words thumping her in the chest. 'Oh God, you're right.' She closed her eyes, couldn't believe she'd not thought of that, her brain fixated on Alice – after he'd called Becca by her name a few times, she'd assumed it was because she was the woman at the forefront of his thoughts. Her eyes flicked open as the obvious question popped into her head. 'But if it's not Alice, then who is it?'

Frank held up a hand. 'Steady on. We're just considering possibilities here. I'm trying to make sure you're not jumping to conclusions and getting yourself into deeper trouble.'

She nodded. That was exactly what she wanted. No, needed, given her habit of acting impulsively, and she seemed to be getting worse the more trouble she was in.

'Dean may not be having an affair at all, but we can't rule it out is all I'm saying.'

She took a biscuit from the packet, thinking as she chewed. 'All right. I'll give you that. So, the next person we need to consider is Connor. What do you think about my theory that he might be over here? That he might be the person behind it all?'

Frank sipped his tea, looking at her over the rim of his mug. 'Now *that* seems like a strange coincidence. The moment he pops up on your social media, things start going wrong for you.'

Becca finished her biscuit, wiping the crumbs from the corner of her mouth with a finger, her eyes focused on her parents' wedding photo that hung on the wall. 'I think I treated him really badly, you know, Dad. We were having a break, but we'd still been talking, and when he took me to the airport, I promised I'd be back.' She sighed. 'Then I stayed here. He deserved a proper explanation, but it never happened, and that was wrong. He's such a lovely bloke, I think you would have got on well with him.'

As she was speaking, she understood what was wrong with this theory of Connor being to blame.

She shook her head. 'You know what? He wouldn't do it. Honestly, there's nothing nasty in Connor. No malice. Revenge isn't in his make-up, not his thing at all.'

Frank gazed at her, his mouth moving as if he wanted to speak but wasn't quite sure. He picked up another biscuit and nibbled at the edge, his eyes unfocused, staring at the wall.

She blew out a frustrated breath. 'I have no idea what's going on, but the real problem is the psychiatrist wants to do an assessment of me tomorrow and I'm really scared after my stupid behaviour. What if Dean and Ruth have told the team what happened today? I'm not even sure if the woman at the playground rang the police, but she was talking to somebody. Maybe that's why they gave me an emergency appointment. What if they won't let me out again? How do you prove you're not mad when people close to you have decided that you are?'

Articulating her worst fear brought goose bumps to her skin, her body prickling with the horror of it.

'I'll come with you,' Frank said, all stern and determined. 'I'll insist that I be your advocate.'

'Advocate for what?' Kate said, doing her stealth entrance once again.

Becca and Frank spun their heads towards the doorway.

'Christ, I wish you'd stop doing that,' Becca snapped. 'Just sneaking into rooms and butting into private conversations.'

Kate raised an eyebrow. 'Keep your hair on. Silly me for thinking I was part of the family and might be able to help.'

Becca squeezed her eyes shut for a moment, lips pressed together, knowing that she was in the wrong. 'Sorry, I shouldn't have bitten your head off like that. I'm just having... It's just something to do with the safeguarding team.' She had no intention of going into details and got up to tidy away their mugs. Kate followed her into the kitchen, shutting the door, so the two of them were alone.

'I need a quick word,' she whispered, coming to stand next to Becca.

'Okay.' Becca felt a twist of nerves, wondering if she was going to get a telling off for being so tetchy.

Kate leant back against the worktop, her arms crossed over her chest. 'The thing is... Well, I wasn't quite truthful about London.' She pulled an apologetic face. 'I did go and visit friends, but I also went for a job interview.'

Becca stopped unloading the tray. That was the last thing she'd expected to hear.

Kate beamed at her. 'They just rang to say I got the job!'

'But I thought you like being self-employed? Didn't you say…' Becca stopped, understanding from Kate's sudden frown that she wanted a different reaction. She forced a bright smile. 'Well, that's… well done.'

'Thank you,' Kate said, a note of sarcasm in her voice. 'Lovely that you're so pleased for me.'

'I am. Honestly, I am. It's just there's such a lot going on at the moment.'

'It's always about you, isn't it?' Kate said, eyes narrowed, arms tightening across her chest. 'Anyway, they want me to start as soon as possible. I'm going at the weekend.'

'So soon? What about accommodation? Won't that take a while? And what about your clients – you can't just drop them, can you?'

Kate glared at her, a scowl twisting her mouth. 'You're so bloody negative. I have the rest of the week to make arrangements. I think I can manage. Personally, I'm excited to have a new start and get out of this… this prison.' She gave a curt nod of the head. 'You're on Dad duty now. Let's see how you like it.'

She stormed out of the kitchen and thumped up the stairs, banging the office door behind her.

'What's got into her?' Frank said, popping his head round the door, looking worried.

Becca was still staring at the empty space where her sister had been. 'She's got a job in London.' She blinked, still processing Kate's parting shot.

Frank's eyebrows shot up his forehead.

'She's going at the weekend.'

'Moving out?' His voice was a squeak.

'That's right.'

Frank's hands clasped his cheeks, his face saying he couldn't quite believe it. 'That's… Flipping heck.' He whistled between his teeth. 'That's sudden, isn't it? But…' He grinned. 'Good for her. She's been threatening to go for a while. Well, well, well.' He grabbed the back of a chair as if to steady himself before he sat down, clearly as stunned by the news as Becca.

It was an opportunistic move by Kate, that was for sure, but even if the whole situation with Mia hadn't blown up, Becca thought the outcome would probably have been the same. Kate had obviously reached the limit of her patience and needed her freedom. Hadn't she admitted herself that she didn't like the person she'd become while she'd been back at home? Worried about her ability to cope with Frank's neediness?

Becca leant against the worktop. Once again, someone else seemed to be deciding her future, making her a pawn in a game that she didn't understand.

CHAPTER THIRTY-ONE

Becca was making sandwiches for lunch, Frank having a lie down upstairs – he'd gone all wobbly and lightheaded after Kate's surprise announcement. With a professional eye, she'd done a covert assessment and thought his blood pressure might be a little high. The last thing she wanted was for him to have another heart attack or a stroke, and he'd meekly gone to have a rest when she'd suggested it, admitting he did feel peculiar.

Her plan was to have a picnic in his bedroom, a reminder of all their happy days out when she was younger, while Kate worked in her office next door. *She can sort out her own lunch.* Having had time to think about it, she was annoyed at the way her sister had taken advantage of Becca's misfortune to free herself of her responsibilities. Not that Becca minded keeping an eye on her dad. The truth was she needed somebody to nurture. Without her daughter, husband and patients to care for, she felt at a loss. But that wasn't the point. Kate could have asked, couldn't she?

The minute she'd got the tray ready with food and drinks to take upstairs, her phone rang, and she snatched it from her pocket. *Connor?*

But it wasn't; it was Carol.

'Phew! Glad I caught you,' her boss said, sounding unusually flustered.

'Carol, I'm so sorry, I meant to call and give you an update, but—'

'It doesn't matter.' Her sigh sent a blast of static down the phone. 'Look… I just have to… I want you to know this isn't easy for me.' She stopped and sighed again, setting off a whirlpool of unease in Becca's belly. 'Thing is, the child safeguarding team have been into the practice to speak to us about your… your case, as it were.' She stopped and there was a moment's silence before she carried on. 'Oh, love, this is the most horrible thing I've had to do, but given the accusations against you, the practice team have had a meeting and… I'm so sorry, but we've no choice but to suspend you from duty pending investigations.'

Becca couldn't quite believe what she'd been told. 'What? I'm not sure I understand. Surely you don't think I'd be hurting Mia?'

Carol gave another big sigh. 'I did fight your corner. Honestly, I did. But they're really nervous about safeguarding – you know what it's like. All belt and braces to prove they've done the right thing.' She was quiet for a moment. 'To be honest, I am a little worried about you, and I don't think having some time off while all this is sorted will be a bad thing. How can you concentrate on patients with all of that going on in the background? No, it would be too easy to get distracted, and you'd never forgive yourself if you messed up someone's medication, would you?'

'You don't believe these accusations, do you?'

'No, of course I don't, but I'm afraid other people don't know you so well, and with your history…' She tailed off.

'Thank you for letting me know,' Becca said quietly before disconnecting. The situation she found herself in was horribly familiar – suspended pending an investigation. *An unlikely coincidence*, that's what they'd be thinking, wondering if she *had* been guilty of wrongdoing all those years ago. It seemed you couldn't get away from an accusation like that. It was there like a stain on her character that wouldn't come out. Her chest tightened as she wondered if her career had just come to a sudden end.

She trudged up the stairs, deciding she wouldn't tell Frank because he didn't need the stress at the moment. At least she had a home here for as long as she needed. But what about the future? She couldn't see one, couldn't see her way out of the predicament she found herself in, and the prospect of not being able to live with her daughter filled her heart with terror.

Her hands gripped the tray a little tighter. *I've got to find out who's doing this.* And as she reached the top of the stairs, she decided that her assumptions about Connor could be misplaced and perhaps he *was* the person she needed to investigate a little more closely.

Frank was lying on his side and his eyes blinked open when he heard her come in. 'I must have nodded off,' he said, pushing himself into a sitting position on the edge of the bed.

She went and sat next to him, putting the tray between them. 'I thought we could eat in here, then you can have a quiet afternoon.'

'That's a nice idea, love.' He picked up a sandwich.

'Ham and coleslaw,' she said, giving him a nudge. 'Just like we used to take on our walks.'

He chuckled and took a bite. 'Your mum used to make them for us when we went on our adventures, didn't she? Always ham and coleslaw. But so miserly with the coleslaw. And the ham. Remember we used to take them apart to see if there was actually anything in them.'

Becca laughed. It had been a running joke of theirs, guessing as they'd walked what might be in their sandwiches, coming up with the most ludicrous combinations they could think of.

He nodded appreciatively as he chewed. 'You've got the proportions perfect. That's a proper sandwich.' He laughed again. 'Don't be offended, but I've not eaten ham and coleslaw since she died. Couldn't face it.'

Becca stopped chewing, unsure now if she'd done the right thing. 'Sorry, Dad. I thought it might make you laugh.'

He patted her arm. 'It did. It has.' He picked up another sandwich. 'They're lovely and I really appreciate the thought.' They ate in silence for a few moments before he spoke again. 'We had some good times when you were young, didn't we? You and me off exploring. My, we covered some ground. We must have walked hundreds of miles if you add it all up. And we saw some things.'

Becca smiled. 'Lots of lovely memories. My favourite was when we saw that vulture. Remember it escaped from a zoo or a private collection or something and it was hanging around Snowdon for a while? And we saw it! I was so chuffed.' She could still see it in her mind's eye, looping lazy circles as it rode the thermals, up and up, a huge wingspan and prehistoric appearance, like a pterodactyl. As a ten-year-old that had been something pretty special.

Frank grinned at her, eyes shining. 'That was fantastic, wasn't it? So many great memories. You and me, kid.' He gave her arm a gentle punch. 'It's not over, though, is it? Lots of adventures ahead of us yet.'

'That's right. Plenty more adventures.'

She choked up all of a sudden, remembering how close they'd been when she was a child and how their relationship had fallen apart at the very point when Frank had needed her most – when her mum had died. *All because of my stupid, thoughtless behaviour.* It was hard to forgive herself, and even though they'd patched up their argument and got along fine these days, that special closeness had been lost. But maybe that was the silver lining to all her troubles. Maybe now she could make amends. *Well, there'll be plenty of time for that, won't there?* said a snarky voice in her head. *He's all you've got now.*

She took a big bite of her sandwich and shoved the thoughts away, not wanting to listen. Instead she chatted about walks they could do, places they'd loved that they could visit again. It wasn't the future she'd dreamt of but maybe it was the one she deserved.

I need to be home with my family.

The truth silenced her, and she stood, picking up the tray with their empty plates, craving some time on her own to work out how to get back to where she should be. Where she needed to be – with Mia and Dean. Her normal little family, with a normal busy life.

Psychiatric assessment tomorrow, she reminded herself, putting new urgency into her movements. 'Just got a couple of things to sort out for work, Dad. Why don't you have a rest and then maybe we'll go out for a walk later. Get some evening air?'

He yawned. 'I can't understand why I'm so tired today.'

'It's been a stressful time, lots of emotion. If your body wants to rest, then I think you should let it.' She picked up the tray. 'I'll come and wake you in a couple of hours, shall I?'

Downstairs, on her own, she pulled her phone out of her pocket and checked for messages. Still nothing from Dean. She wondered if the safeguarding team had told him not to make contact but rang him anyway. It went to voicemail, so she left a message apologising for barging in earlier. Told him she was having an assessment the following day. He probably knew, but it was as well to keep him up-to-date, so he'd think she was cooperating.

She flicked to Twitter. A new message from Surferdude made her heart skip before she opened it.

Are you ignoring me now? Let me come and take care of you, babe. You do still love me, don't you? xxx

He was doing it again, being needy. She frowned, determined now to talk to him. If they had a proper conversation, then she'd know how she really felt about him, wouldn't she? Typed conversations just didn't work the same. If he wouldn't ring her, then she'd find his number and ring him. He had a distinctive surname, Polish, from his father's family who had arrived in Australia a generation before. Connor Hubert Cywinski. He had to be the only one with that combination of names.

It took almost an hour, but she eventually tracked him down via a LinkedIn profile. A profile that said he had a degree in environmental conservation and was living in Darwin. *Darwin?* That was right up in the north of Australia, over 2,000 miles from Sydney, where he'd said he was working. *Perhaps it's out of date?* she thought. Her own LinkedIn profile hadn't been updated for years. Maybe he worked for an environmental organisation in Sydney – a consultancy or something like that.

She saved his details and took a deep breath before she tapped out the number and heard it connect.

After a couple of rings, his voice answered. 'Hey, this is Connor, I'm not here. Leave a message and I'll get back to you.' Short and to the point, but friendly and warm in tone, the voice that she remembered. *It's him! It really is him.* She disconnected, too tongue-tied to speak.

It dawned on her then that it was still night-time in Australia. She'd have to wait a few hours. Her head buzzed with the idea she might be speaking to him soon. *What will I say?*

She took a couple of deep breaths and made herself calm down and focus on the problem. It was a mobile number she was ringing. Which meant he could be anywhere in the world. In fact, he could be here in North Wales, watching her. She shivered and glanced out of the window into the back garden, as if she might catch him hiding in the bushes, or sneaking out of the back gate, or staring at her through the glass.

She frowned and told herself to get a grip. *What's his logic, if he's behind all this?*

He kept telling her that he still loved her. That he wanted to be with her. Was this his way of driving a wedge between her and Dean, separating her from her family, so she'd run to him for comfort? It seemed an extreme way of doing things. *The Connor I know wouldn't do that*, she thought. But then, how well did anyone really know another person? Bitterness could have twisted him out of shape. It happened.

Her mind took her back as she tried to remember him as accurately as she could, not filtering things through the rosy haze of what might have been. They'd spent the best part of six months together – he'd invited her on a surfing trip down to the south coast of Victoria and she'd accepted and never gone back to her job. They'd picked up casual work when they needed money, surfed for a while and then travelled from Victoria right up to Cape Tribulation in the north. It had been the best time of her life. But now her mind had short-circuited. The very idea of talking to him was as daunting as doing a bungee jump off a very high bridge.

Why did he contact me after all this time? That was the puzzle. So that would have to be her first question. *Why now?* A second question appeared: *What does he actually want?* Was he genuine, or was this just a cover while he exacted revenge for leaving him, so she would know what it felt like to have the future she anticipated ripped from under her, like an undercurrent on a beach in paradise?

CHAPTER THIRTY-TWO

Frank came down while she was making tea – just for something to do as she was practically awash with all the liquid she'd already drunk. He persuaded her to go out for a walk instead and they drove to Aber Falls, a local beauty spot with a spectacular waterfall thundering from the mountains over a rocky crag. The path was quiet at this time of day and in the afternoon sun, it was a glorious place to be. It felt good to stretch her legs, get some fresh air and clear her head.

They walked in companionable silence for a while until her newest problem forced its way back into her head. 'I didn't tell you… I've been suspended from work.'

Frank stopped, eyebrows shooting up his forehead. 'They sacked you?'

Her mouth twisted from side to side while anger, sadness and regret all mixed together, forming a blockage in her throat. She swallowed. 'I think that'll happen, to be honest. You can't have someone who is potentially mentally ill and poisoning her daughter dealing with patients, can you?' Trying to make a joke of it didn't help, the feeling of loss weighing heavy in her heart. She looked away, kicked a stone off the path. 'For the moment it's a suspension pending the results of the investigation.'

'Is that how they see it? You're a danger to patients?' Frank sounded incredulous.

She nodded. 'I think so. Carol didn't say it in so many words but, you know…' She scuffed at the path with the toe of her trainers. 'I think it's inevitable they'll let me go, whatever the outcome.' She caught her dad's eye. 'They won't trust me, will they? Especially since it's the second time I've had this sort of accusation levelled against me.'

He rubbed her shoulder, and she rested her cheek on top of his hand, drawn to the comfort of his touch. 'I'm so sorry to hear that, love.'

Now she'd said it, she had to acknowledge the reality of her situation. It seemed to be getting more hopeless by the day, someone carefully taking her life apart, piece by piece.

She started walking again, blinking away a rush of tears, Frank hurrying to catch up.

'It was stressful for you, though, wasn't it, that job of yours?'

She considered that and had to admit he was right. But then, didn't every job involve an element of stress? 'Juggling childcare and doing the job was tricky at times, but I had Ruth, so that worked well. It was only a problem if Ruth wasn't available for some reason. Carol was pretty flexible but I do think I tried her patience at times.' She sighed. 'It's not easy being a working mum.'

'You didn't have to do it, though. Dean's earning good money, isn't he?'

She bristled. 'That's not the point, Dad. I need to do a certain number of hours a year to keep my nursing licence. Once you've lost it, you have to go through a load of retraining to get it back and it can take ages.'

He gave one of his little grunts and it was clear he didn't understand.

'I love nursing. I love caring for people and helping them get better or supporting them in later life. It's not just a job. It's like a… a vocation. Something that I need to do.' She sighed. 'After Rosie died, I promised myself that I'd always know what to do in a health emergency. Nobody would die because of my ignorance ever again. I suppose that's where it all started.'

'Oh, love. Rosie dying wasn't your fault. Nobody could have saved her. She had a brain haemorrhage. That's what she died of.'

'But…' The facts adjusted themselves in her head and she frowned, having no recollection of a brain haemorrhage ever being mentioned. Her assumption had always been that an epileptic fit had been the cause of Rosie's death. 'But if I'd made her go home like her mum wanted, then—'

'It's likely she still would have died.' Frank shook his head. 'Just one of those sad things. You shouldn't be blaming yourself.'

'That's not what her mum said.'

'She was grieving, didn't know what she was saying. I'm sure she didn't mean it.'

Becca was pretty sure that she'd meant every word, could clearly remember the expression on her face when she'd told Becca it was her fault.

Frank nudged her with his elbow as they walked side by side. 'Well, you've got me now. So you can make do with that while we sort out all this stuff with Mia. Surely they'll drop this nonsense now she's okay.'

Becca huffed. 'If only. Mia being okay will be used as evidence that it was me all along. Surely you can see that? I'm in a lose-lose situation.'

'Oh, well… do you know, I hadn't thought of it like that.'

'It gets complicated once the safeguarding team gets involved. There's national procedures to follow. Protocols. They can't just drop it. And deliberately poisoning a child is a criminal act. They mentioned the police getting involved.' She hadn't let herself think further than the psychiatric assessment, but now she was talking through the process, a spike of fear shot through her.

'Crikey. That serious?' Frank sounded worried now.

She nodded, biting her lip.

Frank grabbed her arm and pulled her to a halt. 'Why don't we go round and see Dean? Talk to him together, see if we can come to some sort of agreement.'

'He won't speak to me. Not after this morning.' She heaved a big sigh, remembering the accusations she'd fired at him earlier in the day. All she'd done was confirm his suspicions that she'd completely lost the plot. She gave a defeated shrug. 'I've rung him, but he didn't answer so I left a message. He hasn't rung back yet.'

Frank's clasp tightened on her arm. 'I've had an idea. Why don't I ring the psychiatrist tomorrow and say you're not well and see if we can postpone it?'

She wrinkled her nose. 'I'm not sure. I've done that once already. I don't think they'll want a further delay. It sort of makes me look guilty, doesn't it? And it'll make them more likely to take me in. Keep me in-house while they investigate, just in case I do a runner.'

Frank tutted, a deep frown wrinkling his forehead. 'I'll go and talk to Dean on my own, then. How about that? See if I can find out what the process is now and what you have to do to be able to see Mia.'

Becca huffed. 'I don't think that's a good idea. You two will end up arguing like you always do.'

'I'll be on my best behaviour, honest. It's worth a go, isn't it?'

She knew he was trying his best to help and didn't have the heart to knock his suggestion back again. 'Okay, we've got to try everything, I suppose.' She nodded her assent. 'At least then we'll know where we stand.'

After their walk, they went and got themselves some fish and chips, eating them out of the paper because neither of them had the energy to cook or deal with washing up. Kate had gone out, leaving a message to say she'd be back late, and Becca was relieved not to have to face her, see the pity in her eyes. She knew Kate saw her as a weak, neurotic failure, and she didn't need to have her shortcomings rubbed in her face.

'Right, I'm going to get off and nip over to see Dean now,' Frank said as he balled up his fish and chips paper and threw it in the bin. 'He's bound to be in this evening. The little one'll be in bed, so I reckon it's the perfect time for a sensible conversation.'

'Good luck,' she said, nerves curdling the contents of her stomach. 'Play nice.'

Frank gave her a quick hug and kissed the top of her head. 'Best behaviour, love. Don't you worry.'

Once Frank had left, Becca sat for a while, in the silence, so weighed down by her predicament she hadn't the energy to move. Everything marched in front of her eyes; her suspicions, all her theories which had been proved wrong. Then a face appeared in her thoughts and stayed there. *Connor.* His possible involvement was something she still needed to explore.

She pulled her phone out of her pocket and checked the time. It would be morning in Sydney now. Heart racing, she found his number and rang.

'Hey,' a man's voice said. Sleepy, as if he'd been woken up.

'Is that Connor Cywinski?'

'Yep.'

Her words dried up as her heart raced. It was really him. After all this time, she was speaking to him.

'Can I just ask where you are?'

Silence for a moment. 'Darwin.' Another beat of silence before he spoke again. 'Wait a minute… who is this?'

'It's Becca. Becca… Pritchard.'

'Oh my God, Becca. Really? Christ! How are you? Bloody hell.' She could hear rustling and wondered if he was still in bed. 'Is everything okay?'

The sound of his voice made her crumple, her chest heaving, and she disconnected, her whole body tensing as she tried to stop her emotions from tumbling out. She stood, walking up and down the kitchen, hands pulling at her hair. He was in Darwin.

It couldn't be him that had been poisoning Mia. It was just a coincidence, nothing more.

Hold on a minute. She had another thought and rang his number again.

'Hey, is that you? Becca?'

'Yeah, sorry, I... um somehow got cut off.'

'Phew. I'm so glad you called back.'

'This is going to sound really odd, but... are you Surferdude on Twitter?'

He laughed. 'Twitter? Nah, don't ever go on there. I don't do social media, not after all that stuff on Facebook. You know that.'

She nodded to herself. He was right. She did know that. They'd had long conversations about it, and he'd told her how he'd deleted all his accounts after a bit of cyberbullying had tested his patience. But Twitter hadn't been a big deal when they'd been together – so it had seemed possible that he'd be on there.

'So, you're in Darwin now. Not Sydney?'

Another laugh. 'Come on, Becca. You know me and cities don't go together. I live in a wooden... well, you'd probably call it a shack, on a forty-acre plot just outside Darwin. No surfing for me any more though.' He sighed. 'I had a wipeout and smashed up my ankle. I can't do it now. Anyway... I'm a regular working guy, you'll be pleased to know, with a piece of rainforest to call my own.'

'Well, that's um... that's great to hear.'

Silence, only the sound of her pulse whooshing in her ears. The messages had been fake, the profile made up. Her brain felt numb, her assumptions wiped out like a huge wave clearing pebbles from the beach. For a moment there was no thought, just a mental picture of Connor's face, hers next to it, the broadest of grins, happiness sparkling in their eyes.

'What's going on, Becca? This is really weird.'

'I'm sorry, Connor.' Her voice was little more than a whisper. 'I'm sorry I left you like that.'

Silence.

He cleared his throat. 'Is that why you rang? After all this time… to say sorry?'

'No, but I just need to say this first. I should have tried harder to contact you at the time. I know I should, but Mum had just died, and I was so angry and upset and confused I did this really stupid thing and then…' She sighed, her face burning. 'Then I was too ashamed.'

'It's okay. I sort of understand.' He gave a quick laugh. 'You know I poured out my heart and soul in that letter, and I waited and waited for you to reply, and then when you never did, I knew you weren't coming back.'

She frowned. 'Letter? What letter?'

'I wrote it at the airport. It broke my heart to see you going back on your own when I should have been going with you. I hated myself for being such a self-centred prick. It was a bit of a defining moment, if I'm honest. A turning point.' He was quiet, just his breath in her ear. 'I'm not gonna lie, Becca, not getting an answer broke my heart at the time, but I can't say I blamed you. It's not like I was good husband material just floating around, picking up jobs here and there. What could I offer you? Certainly wasn't the stability you wanted.' He gave a quiet laugh. 'In a way, you leaving was good for me. Gave me a kick up the arse and made me get my shit together.' His sigh rattled down the line. 'I know you're married. I know you have a child.'

A worm of suspicion wriggled into her mind, adrenaline speeding up her heartbeat. 'How do you know if you're not on social media?'

'I keep in touch with Tina. She told me.'

Tina! She hadn't thought to ask her friend, because she hadn't thought Connor would stay in touch. Now she had a way to double-check.

She took a deep breath, confused. 'I honestly didn't get your letter. As far as I was aware, you just went quiet on me after you'd said you'd be in touch. That's how we left it. I thought... well, I thought you didn't care.'

She heard him blow his nose. 'Yeah, well, I did lose my phone, lost all my contacts, but I'd put Mum's address on the letter and kept checking with her to see if anything had arrived. It never occurred to me that my letter wouldn't get to you. Bloody hell.' Silence for a moment. 'Anyway, I bumped into Tina and she told me you'd met someone and were having a baby and I knew you'd found what you wanted. It just hurt that it wasn't me.' He sighed again. 'I thought I should leave it there, not bother you. Life moves on, doesn't it?'

'I suppose it does,' she said, unwilling to acknowledge the feeling of disappointment that had settled in her chest, heavy as lead. *What had happened to Connor's letter?* If she'd received it, would it have changed her behaviour, her choices? Would her life have turned out differently? Her head felt like it was being squeezed by a large hand, fingers digging into her neck, her temples. There was so much she didn't understand.

'So now,' he said, 'you've got to tell me why you rang.'

CHAPTER THIRTY-THREE

'I don't want to make you late for work,' she said. *Does he need to know?* He was her past and there was no need to burden him with the troubles of her present.

'I've got a while before I start.' She could hear the sound of a kettle boiling, the clink of a teaspoon, the slam of a fridge door. 'Come on, Becca. There's obviously something bothering you. Maybe I can help? Sometimes just talking things through sorts it out in your mind, doesn't it?'

She cleared her throat, decided she had nothing to lose, and the whole story came pouring out. Suddenly, the time had gone, and he was cursing because he was going to be late. He made her promise to call him the following day after she'd had the psychiatric assessment, and she rang off, feeling better for having told her version of events to somebody who didn't doubt her.

Talking to him had clarified things in her mind and she was certain now that someone was deliberately trying to break up her marriage and separate her from her family.

She opened her Twitter app and scrolled through the messages, and by the time she'd finished reading, it was starting to make sense. The neediness, trying to push her to say she still loved him. Someone trying to get evidence that could be used against her to break up her relationship with Dean, or encourage her to leave him? It seemed to be both of those things.

And it had worked. If Dean hadn't seen the messages, she doubted that he would have been so willing to accuse her of hurting Mia. That was him lashing out. *Or… was it him engineering things?*

She'd gone back round the same circle and ended up with Dean as the culprit again. But he'd been away when Mia was ill the second time and a couple of the other times after that. It couldn't be him unless… unless he'd left something for Mia, a secret treat that Becca knew nothing about. Alternatively, it could be someone he was close to. She nodded to herself. He didn't have to actually physically be there, so she shouldn't discount him yet.

Frank's comment came barging into her thoughts: just because Dean wasn't having an affair with Alice didn't mean he wasn't having an affair. Given the number of people he came into contact with through his work events, the potential for meeting someone else was endless. Like-minded people at that.

Becca stared at the pictures on the mantelpiece, not really seeing them as she inspected her relationship with Dean. If she was being completely honest with herself, when it came to interests, they'd never had much in common. He loved socialising and golf and could be quite competitive. She was all about the outdoors, the mountains and beaches, enjoying nature. Her job was sociable enough, and afterwards, she liked some time to herself.

The desire to have children was the glue that had stuck them together originally and had kept them together through all the emotional agony of miscarriages. But now they had a child, their differences were becoming more apparent, their lives travelling in different directions. His focus was on making his business a success, increasing his profits every year. That was the challenge he got out of bed for. Becca didn't really care about money. Or golf, for that matter.

Are we even compatible?

Maybe not on a shared-interest level, but Dean was a kind bloke, decent and honest. She couldn't imagine him being able to think up a twisted scheme like this to get rid of her, let alone able to harm his daughter. Yes, they had drifted apart, but she'd taken it for granted they still loved each other, even if it wasn't that mad, just-fallen-in-love passion any more.

How well do you know the ones you love? Now that was a tricky question and the answer seemed to be not at all – Dean's willingness to separate her from Mia being the biggest shock of her life. He'd always been on her side. Always.

The front door opened and banged shut, shaking her from her thoughts. Frank appeared in the lounge, red-faced and flustered.

Becca frowned. 'How did it go?'

Frank shrugged off his jacket and went back into the hall to hang it up and take off his shoes. He came back in, puffing out his cheeks and shaking his head. 'He wouldn't let me in.'

Her heart sank. 'A wasted journey, then?'

'He said to tell you he wants a divorce and don't even try for custody because you haven't a hope in hell.' Frank's chin started to wobble and she thought he might burst into tears.

Becca gasped, her hands flying to her mouth, her brain fixed on the word 'divorce'. She was shaking and sank back in her seat, too dazed to speak.

He came and sat beside her, looking contrite. 'I'm sorry, love. I probably should have found a better way to say that.'

'A divorce,' she murmured, hardly able to comprehend how quickly her marriage had fallen apart. After everything they'd been through, surely their union was stronger than this? The news ran on a loop in her mind and she was unable to think or move or do anything apart from repeat the words 'he wants a divorce', her unseeing eyes staring at the wall.

She didn't notice Frank leave the room, but he came back in a few moments later and pushed a hot mug into her hand. 'I've put lots of sugar in for the shock. You've gone awful pale.'

Divorce. No discussion, no attempts to salvage their relationship, refocus and get back on track – that's what people did; they didn't just suddenly throw everything away. Especially when there was a child involved.

She sipped at her tea as her thoughts zig-zagged backwards and forwards through recent events.

'I found something out,' she said eventually, and the words didn't seem to be coming from her, distant and weak. 'Connor and that Surferdude Twitter profile were fakes. Just somebody trying to cause trouble for me. Can you believe that?'

Frank blinked, the conversation taking a turn from what he'd expected, and it took him a minute to catch up with her. 'What? Are you sure?'

'I rang him. I found his number and I rang Connor. The real one.' She told her dad about her awkward conversation, how he was in Australia and didn't use social media. How he couldn't possibly be involved. 'It's all part of a set-up. This whole thing has been staged to make me appear mentally ill, a criminal, in fact, and put doubts in Dean's mind about my commitment to him and our marriage. It's all about getting me out of the house, making sure I stay out and then having evidence to use against me.'

Frank whistled between his teeth. 'That's some theory you've got there.'

'And it's completely stupid,' Kate said, stepping into the room.

Neither Becca nor Frank had heard her return, and they both jumped at the sound of her voice. She sat on the arm of the sofa.

'I wish you'd stop doing that,' Becca snapped, wondering how long she'd been listening, how much she'd heard. 'I was talking to Dad.'

'It doesn't really matter who you were talking to. That is the most ridiculous conspiracy theory I've ever heard. You need help, sis.' Her voice was soft, cajoling, sympathy in her eyes. 'You've been under a lot of stress, going back to work and looking after Mia when Dean's not there to help, and it's manifested itself in harmful behaviour.' She gave a slow shake of the head. 'It's understandable. It's also a repeat of what happened before. Even if you did get away with it that time.'

Becca's mouth gaped in horror. 'What are you talking about? I didn't get away with anything. I was innocent. That was just my boss causing trouble for me.'

Kate rubbed Becca's shoulder. 'Bit of a coincidence, don't you think?'

Becca slapped her hand away and Kate stood, putting some distance between them.

'Now, Kate. I think that's unfair.' Frank could have sounded more convincing, and Becca scowled at him, wondering if Kate had spoken her father's thoughts.

'Dad, you've got to stop encouraging her.' Kate's voice was firm, like she was ticking off a naughty child. 'It's all nonsense. What she needs to do is accept the help that's being offered. Go and see the psychiatrist, use their professional support and treatment. Then she'll start to feel better, and in time, things will go back to normal.' She gave a shrug. 'Somebody has to tell it how it is, and I'm just thinking about what's best for you, Becca.'

'No, you're not. You're thinking what's best for you. And that's for me to be here to keep an eye on Dad while you go and take up your fancy job in London.'

Kate folded her arms across her chest, glaring at her sister. 'Okay, let's be honest. I'm sure he'd much prefer to have you here anyway.' She threw an angry glance at Frank then stood and left the room.

Frank sighed, waiting until they'd heard her footsteps pound up the stairs and her bedroom door slam shut. 'I'm glad she's going. It pains me to say it, but I think we need a break from each other.' He looked at his fingers, knotted together in his lap. 'I've always tried to be fair. And she's got a short memory when it suits her. I remember when she found out that you and Dean were an item and I spent a lot of time giving her a shoulder to cry on.'

Becca frowned, confused. 'Why would that bother her? I know you were both mad at me for leaving the funeral tea early, but what's Dean got to do with it?'

Frank pursed his lips, hesitated. 'They were together for a while before you came home from Australia.'

Becca's eyes widened. 'Dean and Kate?' She couldn't imagine it. In terms of personalities they would be niggling at each other the whole time. It would be like sleeping on a bed of nails.

Frank nodded. 'It was an on–off kind of relationship. Volatile, I suppose you'd call it. They had a bust-up just before your mum died. Poor Kate didn't take to being dumped very well.' He gazed out of the window, remembering. 'She was really cut up about it, wasn't eating or sleeping properly. And she just lashed out at everyone. Next minute you turn up with him.'

'I can't believe I didn't know that,' Becca said, incredulous that it had been kept a secret. Anger flared in her chest. 'Why the hell did nobody tell me?'

Frank turned his wedding ring round and round his finger. 'I didn't think it was my place to say anything. It was up to Kate and Dean to tell you. Anyway, they'd been broken up for a month or so when you came home. It was over between them and that was that as far as I knew.'

Kate and Dean? Shock rattled her brain, shaking up her memories, resetting all those assumptions which had obviously been wrong. She thought back to the times when they'd had family get-togethers, wondering if she should have noticed anything. But all she'd sensed was indifference. Two people sliding past each other, not engaging. Separate. *It was all an act.* She'd always thought it was a shame that Frank and Kate hadn't seemed to like Dean, but this new revelation gave her a different perspective. Her stomach churned.

'And Dean ended it?'

'Apparently, he wanted to settle down and start a family, and Kate wasn't sure if she even wanted children. She had career ambitions, you know what she's like.'

A shiver of unease ran down Becca's spine, her mind busy reinterpreting her past, spewing out a whole new stream of questions. 'Do you think Kate hoped they'd get back together?'

Frank thought for a moment. 'I think so. But then you were pregnant and Dean was out of her reach.'

'You should have told me!' Becca thumped the arm of the sofa. 'Honestly, Dad. How could you keep that secret?'

'Just a minute, you don't need to go all shirty on me.' Frank wagged a finger at her. 'How am I supposed to know what Dean and Kate have told you, eh? Like I said, it wasn't for me to say. Not after the way he reacted when your mum tried to reason with him about Kate. No, I was done with him. Hoped he'd left our lives forever and—' He stopped what he was about to say, gave an impatient huff.

Becca glared at him, but his words took root in her mind and she knew it wasn't his fault. Dean should have told her. *So why didn't he?*

Perhaps Dean never really wanted *her* at all. Perhaps it was more about wanting a family. Becca thought about the timings for a moment. 'Is that why Kate moved to Manchester?'

Frank sighed. 'I think she found it easier to be further away. She's always been the jealous type, hasn't she? And competitive with you. I suppose she didn't tell you because she felt bad about being rejected and Dean choosing you over her.' He shrugged. 'Who knows what goes on in that head of hers?'

They heard footsteps clumping down the stairs, the thump of something heavy on the floor. Becca jumped up, an idea taking shape in her mind. Kate was the common denominator in all her problems.

'What if it's her, Dad?' she whispered, not wanting her sister to hear. 'What if it's Kate doing this to me?'

Before he had time to reply, Becca stormed out of the lounge, certain she was right.

Kate was in the hall, shrugging on her coat, a large suitcase and a couple of bags at her feet.

'Going somewhere?' Becca asked, furious now that she'd worked everything out.

'I'm off to London. I thought I might as well go now, then I've got a few days to find a place. I'll be back for the rest of my stuff when I'm settled.'

'It's you, isn't it?' She poked her sister in the chest.

Kate's eyes narrowed and she took a step back. 'What are you ranting about now?'

'You're the one who's been causing all this trouble for me. You've been pretending to be Connor.' The logic clicked into place. 'It would have been easy enough to have a read of my journals when you cleared out my desk. That's what gave you the idea, isn't it?'

'Don't be ridiculous.' Kate had a wild look in her eyes and Becca knew it was the truth.

'You're just jealous Dean wanted to be with me, aren't you? I've got the man you thought you should have.' She knew she was on the right track when she saw the flicker of surprise in Kate's eyes – surprise that she'd worked it out. 'You've done all this to break up my marriage.'

Kate continued fastening up her coat. 'You're being ridiculous.' She gave Becca a hard stare. 'But let's face it, you trapped him by getting pregnant. He's a genuinely good guy – of course he stood by you, but that doesn't mean he wanted to.'

The words hit Becca like a slap in the face. 'We were happy enough until all this started. If our marriage is in trouble, then it's your doing. This weird vendetta you've got going.' Her hands bunched into fists by her sides as she struggled to resist the impulse to lash out.

'Oh, I haven't got the energy for this nonsense.' Kate gave a dismissive flap of her hand. 'More of your hysterics.' She picked up a holdall and lifted it on to her shoulder, leaving her hands free for the suitcase and the other bag. 'I am so glad to be out of here. You won't listen to the voice of reason, either of you.' She flicked a glance towards the lounge. 'You're welcome to each other.'

Becca stood in front of the door. 'You're not going anywhere.'

Kate walked right up to her, their noses almost touching, annoyance flashing in her eyes. 'Stop being so childish. Get out of the way.'

Becca had no intention of moving. 'I'm right, aren't I? You've been giving Mia something to make her poorly, so the suspicion falls on me. You're putting doubts in everyone's mind about my sanity. All out of spite.'

Kate hissed through her teeth. 'I'm not even going to respond to that.' She stepped back, silent for a moment as if the force of her stare would remove Becca from her place in front of the door. 'I'm off anyway. I doubt I'll be back for a while. So if it's me causing the problems, that's the end of it, isn't it?'

Becca stilled. *Is that a confession?*

Kate pulled at Becca's shoulder, trying to get her to move from the door and let her through. 'Come on, out of the way.'

Becca slapped her hand away and stayed where she was, her jaw clamped tight.

Kate flung her bags on the floor, grabbed Becca's shoulders and shoved her with such force that she stumbled and had to grab at a coat hanging on the rack to stop herself from falling. 'I really do not care what you think in that fuddled little brain of yours. It's my turn,' she snarled, her face looming over Becca's. 'I'm not going to wait until it's too late for me to have the life I deserve. I've only ever done the right thing. It was me who came back and put my life on hold to look after Dad. Where were you?' Rage flared in her eyes. 'Now it's your turn to look after him.'

She pushed Becca with both hands, sending her sprawling to the floor, leaving her too shocked by the sudden fall to move.

Kate picked up her bags and opened the door. 'Good luck,' she called over her shoulder.

The door banged shut behind her.

CHAPTER THIRTY-FOUR

Becca clambered to her feet and staggered back into the lounge. 'Thanks for the support, Dad,' she said in a voice loaded with sarcasm.

Frank winced. 'I'm sorry, love, but I can't get involved in fights with Kate. I always lose. There's no point. I thought she might listen if it was just you and her.'

'Well, she didn't.' Becca went to the window and watched Kate's car drive off down the road.

'The good news is that she's gone.' Frank gave a relieved sigh. 'We can relax now.'

'But Dad, you're missing the point. I need her to own up to what she's been doing, otherwise I can't be with Mia.' Becca's frustration was mounting, her voice getting shrill as she tried to make Frank understand the seriousness of her situation. 'I'll always have this hanging over me until I can prove that I've done nothing wrong. And if Dean's going to file for divorce, there's a strong chance I won't get access to my own daughter.'

Frank blanched. 'Yes, yes, I see what you mean. I'm sorry, I wasn't thinking straight.' His voice cracked. 'She's been horrible to me recently, Becs. It wasn't so bad when she first moved in, but now she's got me frightened to disagree with her. Everything has to be done her way. Honestly, she can be so harsh and critical and… just plain mean.' He glanced at Becca, and guilt squeezed at her heart.

She went and sat on the arm of the chair, leaning her head on his shoulder. 'Different regime now, I promise. But my priority has to be getting Mia back, and if Kate's gone…' She sighed, exhausted now. 'I don't know how I'm going to do it.'

They were silent for a while until Frank kissed her head and eased her off his shoulder. He opened the door of the cabinet next to his chair. 'I need a bit of fortification after that,' he said as he pulled out a bottle of whisky and a couple of glasses. 'I think you could do with one too.'

Becca watched him pour a very generous measure into each glass but shook her head when he passed one to her. 'I can't do whisky. Honestly, it turns my stomach, but don't let me stop you.'

Frank downed his drink in a couple of gulps, smacking his lips as he put the empty glass on the mantelpiece along with the one he'd poured for Becca. 'I'll save that for later, then.'

He turned to her, a sparkle of mischief in his eyes. 'Tell you what… let's go and have a nosy. If your theory is right and it is Kate behind everything, she might have left something you can use as evidence.'

Becca snorted. 'Yeah, like she's going to be that careless.' She sighed as she watched her father's face fall and was sorry she'd been so dismissive. He was only trying to be positive and helpful. She flashed him a smile. 'Sorry. There's no harm in looking, I suppose.'

'I'll make us a cup of tea, shall I?'

Becca wondered why people of her dad's generation seemed to think that tea was the answer to everything, but she nodded. 'Lovely. I think I'll start in the office. I know she will have taken her laptop, but I might be able to get into her desktop computer. If she was the fake Surferdude, then I should be able to find the account on there.'

Ten minutes later, Frank came upstairs with tea and put a mug on the desk next to her. He peered over her shoulder. 'Any luck?'

'I can't get into the damned thing. Any idea what she might use as a password?'

Frank pursed his lips and thought for a moment before coming out with a stream of suggestions that Becca had already tried. She smacked the desk in annoyance, making Frank jump. 'Sorry, Dad. It's just so bloody frustrating.'

'I know, love.' He scanned the room. 'Shall I leave you to have a look in here and I'll check her bedroom?'

'Okay, good idea.'

Becca left the computer, deciding that she was never going to guess the password and her time would be better spent searching through the drawers and filing cabinet. If Kate had been using Becca's journal entries to shape Surferdude's 'memories', perhaps she'd copied some of the pages. She pulled open the top drawer of the desk and had a rifle through. It was meticulously tidy, everything organised in a little tray with sections for pens and paperclips, staples and other bits of office equipment. The next drawer held stationery. The next had rails for hanging files that were organised by client name. Nothing remotely interesting.

The only thing left to check was the filing cabinet. She pulled at the top drawer but it wouldn't budge. Neither would any of the others. *Locked.* She grunted and kicked at it, needing to lash out at something. With a clatter, a plastic box fell on to the floor, a Tupperware container, which had been stuffed in the gap between the cabinet and the wall.

She bent to pick it up, and put it on the desk, pulling off the lid. Inside were little packets of jelly Haribos – Mia's favourite. Next to them a syringe and a bottle of clear liquid. Her eyes widened, hands covering her mouth.

'Dad! Dad, you need to come here. I've found something.'

Frank dashed into the room, his hand on her shoulder as he peered into the box.

'Oh my God! She's been doctoring sweets.' He pulled the chair out from the desk and sank into it, the strength seeming to have gone from his legs. His complexion was grey. In fact, he didn't look well at all. 'I can't believe she'd do this. I sort of agreed with her when she said your conspiracy theory sounded outrageous. But… well, I've got to admit you were right.'

Becca put the lid on the desk. 'Don't touch this, Dad. I've got to tell the police. What she's done is criminal, and she can't be allowed to just waltz off to London. Anyway, the safeguarding team won't listen to me unless I can prove what I'm saying is fact.' She leant against the filing cabinet, their discovery so shocking it seemed to have stolen the words from their mouths.

Although it proved her theory, Becca was struggling to come to terms with the evidence. Would Kate really go to those lengths to break up her marriage?

Their relationship had been frosty for a while, after their mother's funeral, but more recently she'd felt they'd reconnected. She was good with Mia and seemed to enjoy being an aunt, or at least Becca had thought that was the case. Now she recognised that friendship had been false, a means to an end, getting close to her so she could enact some horrible revenge for stealing a man she'd thought was hers.

Twisted. There was no other word for it. And although Kate had a bossy streak to her personality, always thinking she was right, underneath there had often been a kindness too. She was a contradiction. Unfathomable.

'Do you know where she's staying in London?' Becca turned to see a tears trickling down Frank's cheek. 'Oh, Dad, come on, it's not your fault this has happened.'

He sniffed and swiped at his face. 'How could I have produced a daughter capable of this? It sickens me. It really does.'

Becca put an arm round his shoulders and kissed his head, pulling him to her. 'No point getting yourself upset about it.

What we need to do is find out where she is and tell the police. She's not getting away with this. No way.'

She rubbed Frank's back, staying silent as her mind searched for a way through the tangled mess of her life. *How do I get Mia back?* That was her priority, but it wasn't going to be easy.

Dean was the answer. He was the one who had brought up her past with the health professionals. He was the one who had sown the seeds of doubt, made them suspect she had mental health problems, and she supposed, from his point of view, it had been made to appear that way. That was the goal of the whole exercise. Kate wanting to punish both of them for their betrayal, as she saw it. It made perfect sense now she had all the pieces of the puzzle and could see the full picture.

'I'm going round to see Dean,' she said, clear now that this was the best way forward. 'If I can show him the evidence and get him onside, he can help me stop the investigation. I'm sure of it.'

Frank put a hand on her arm. 'Hold on, love. You're not going on your own. I'm coming with you.'

She wondered for a moment if it was a good idea, the way Dean and Frank were around each other, but she also knew she'd feel stronger with Frank there beside her, backing her up. He'd seen the evidence. He believed her now.

She looked at the Tupperware box on the desk. 'I'll just take some photos, so I can show Dean, then we'll leave that and the police can do whatever they need to do.'

She pulled her phone out of her pocket and snapped from different angles, still unable to believe her sister would do such a thing. The enormity of her betrayal hit her then, and a trembling started in her stomach, working its way through her body. She clung to the filing cabinet to stop herself from sinking to the floor.

'I'll drive,' Frank said. 'Come on, the sooner we go, the sooner this will be sorted.'

CHAPTER THIRTY-FIVE

They arrived at Becca's house to find all the lights off and the doors locked. There was no sign of Dean's car on the drive or parked on the road outside.

'That's odd.' Becca squinted at the property, searching for signs of life. 'He didn't say he was working away. In fact, I'm pretty sure he said he was taking a week off to be with Mia.'

'Perhaps they've just popped out to the shops. Or gone to get something to eat.' Frank shrugged.

Becca checked her watch and frowned. Almost eight o'clock. 'Yeah, you're right. He could be back soon.' She thought for a moment, her heart sinking as she realised there *was* something else she could do. 'I suppose I could check with Alice, just in case. She'll know what his plans are.' Alice was the last person she wanted to talk to, but she was the only person who could help so Becca pulled her phone out of her pocket and made the call.

'Oh, hi, Becca. He's… um… yeah, he has taken a week off and he did leave me a message to say he might be going away.'

Becca's body went rigid. *He's taken Mia away?* That definitely hadn't been discussed. Her heart started to race, uneasy at this new development. *What if he doesn't come back?*

Alice sounded cagey and Becca was sure there was something she wasn't telling her.

'Do you know where he's gone? Did he say?'

'No, sorry. I didn't ask.' She was getting a little snippy.

Becca thought for a moment. 'Has he gone with someone, do you know?'

Alice sighed, impatient. 'That's his business. I'm sorry, Becca, I'm in the middle of something here, I've got to go.'

The line went dead. She'd clearly felt compromised, which suggested that Dean was doing something Becca wouldn't be happy with. She felt empty, hollowed out by the knowledge she wouldn't be seeing her daughter, a sense of panic growing inside her. Frank sat silent beside her, deep in thought.

She got her keys out of her pocket. 'I can get some things while I'm here. I'll only be a few minutes. Then I'll try giving him a call, though he's not been answering me the last few times. Straight to voicemail.'

'I'll come in with you,' Frank said, getting out of the car. 'You never know, he might have left something lying around that'll give us a clue as to where he's gone.'

Becca didn't reply, thinking it was very unlikely. Everything was done online these days – no handy brochures or leaflets to signal a possible destination.

'You know there's apps you can get to find your phone if it's missing,' Frank said when they were inside. 'There was a discussion on local radio recently. I remember thinking it was a good idea. Perhaps we can get one of those downloaded? Then we'd know exactly where he is. Stop us wasting time.'

'Hmm. Not a bad idea, Dad. Not a bad idea at all.' She flashed him a smile and gave him her phone. 'You see if you can find one while I nip upstairs and grab some clothes.'

Dad is full of surprises these days, she thought as she hurriedly stuffed underwear and clean clothes into a small suitcase. It was easy to assume older people hadn't a clue about technology, but he had time on his hands and was probably more up-to-date on some things than she was.

She went to the bedside cabinet to get her book. A glint of something caught her eye and she bent down to get a better look. There on the carpet lay an earring. Emerald green. Dangly. And definitely not hers.

She picked it up, held it in the palm of her hand, a symbol of her husband's infidelity. Although she'd had her suspicions, in her heart she hadn't wanted to believe he'd be unfaithful, but now she had the evidence and there was no denying it. Tears stung her eyes as she studied the earring. It was familiar, and she wracked her brains for an image, a match. *Who wears jewellery like this?* But she couldn't quite grasp the fleeting image that came to mind, gone before she could properly focus.

She felt like an intruder in her own bedroom and knew she'd be in deeper trouble if she was found to have come here, and broken the rules set by the safeguarding team. *I've got to get out quick.* She slipped the earring into her pocket, zipped up her bag and was about to go downstairs when she stopped and turned, making her way to Mia's room instead. It was like a magnet – the need to have something of her daughter's too strong to resist. *I'll be quick*, she told herself. *Just a cuddly toy.*

She stood in the doorway. It was in a state of disarray, the bed unmade, toys all over the floor, drawers opened and clothes strewn on top of the dresser. *Panic packing*, she thought, which was unlike Dean. He was meticulous when going on trips – always ready early rather than running late. She frowned as she stooped to pick up the unicorn, Mia's latest 'must have' toy. It was a firm favourite now, and went everywhere with them. In fact, Mia wouldn't go to bed without it. Dean knew that, which made her wonder if someone else had done the packing. Dean's lover, possibly? Her hand tightened round the unicorn. Someone who didn't know Mia very well.

Her mind took her back to her conversation with Alice. *Could it be her?* It was Dean who had persuaded Becca that Alice wasn't interested in him and had mentioned a fiancé. *But he could have been lying.* And she'd been so uncomfortable talking to Becca on the phone. *Guilty?* Becca tried to remember if she'd ever seen Alice with a partner, and her mind was a blank. She'd never mentioned anyone, and Becca was certain she'd never seen her with a boyfriend.

Her hand brushed against the earring in her pocket, evidence that he'd moved on to someone else. No wonder he'd been so quick to instigate divorce proceedings, seizing the opportunity like a starving person tearing into fresh bread. In that respect, the whole situation with Mia had been an absolute blessing for him, really. Allowing him to make a move he'd perhaps been reluctant to make before. It had swept away any problems about custody of Mia, and who would live in the house. Such an easy solution. *Too easy.* Her heart skipped. *Is Dean involved too?*

She went to find Frank, who was sitting in the lounge, studying her phone. He looked up when he heard her come in.

'He's on the A55,' he said before she could speak. 'I've got this app working and it's brilliant. I can watch him.' He held up the screen to show her. 'Look, he's that little dot.'

Becca squinted at the screen, trying to work out what she was seeing 'Whereabouts on the A55?'

Frank took the phone back to check. 'Just coming up to Deeside.'

Becca pictured the route, calculated the distance. 'He's not been gone that long then. An hour at most, probably.' She frowned. 'I wonder where he's going?'

Frank glanced up from the screen. 'We can keep checking in and find out.'

Becca opened her hand and dangled the earring in front of Frank's face. 'Is this familiar?'

Frank stared at it. 'I think…' He scrunched up his nose. 'You know me. I'm not good at noticing things like that.'

Becca could see the blush creeping up his neck. *He knows.* And now she could make a good guess. 'It's Kate's, isn't it?'

He nodded. 'I think… it might be.'

It was obvious, now. Of course Kate was the other woman. She was taking back everything she thought Becca had stolen from her all those years ago. Doing a life swap.

She sank on to the sofa next to Frank, dazed for a moment. Her husband and her sister. They were in this together. Rage burnt through her chest, firing up her resolve. They couldn't take her daughter and ruin her life like this. She wouldn't let them.

Her jaw tightened. 'I know where they're going,' she said, everything slotting together in her mind. 'They're going to London. I think Kate's with him.'

She stood and went out to the garage, opened the door, and there was Kate's car. Dean was driving her sister to London.

Is he going to move there with her?

The thought sent waves of panic through her body and she had to lean against the wall while she took a few deep breaths to calm herself down. She slid to the ground. Dean held a lot of events in the south of England, and he could run his business from anywhere. Alice could deal with things locally. It would be an easy thing for him to relocate. And wouldn't life be simpler if he made a new start far away from neurotic, mad Becca?

He was going to take her daughter away, make sure Becca couldn't be part of her life. She hadn't known he had such cruelty in him. But maybe he wasn't the one making the decisions. Maybe that was Kate.

CHAPTER THIRTY-SIX

'Becca, you all right, love?' Frank crouched beside her, his face creased with concern. 'Here, let's get you up. We're going home.'

Becca's limbs felt like they belonged to someone else. She couldn't move and Frank had to heave her to her feet and practically drag her to the car. Words wouldn't come, her brain so shocked that Dean and Kate would do this to her.

Frank chattered all the way back to Bangor, talking to himself as much as to her, going over recent events in the light of their new knowledge, seeing how a fresh interpretation could be given to seemingly innocent things.

Finally, she found her voice. 'That first weekend Mia was ill. Do you remember? Both Kate and Dean were away. He was supposed to be in Scotland. Said there was patchy reception. I think he switched his phone off. I bet he went to London with Kate instead.'

Frank grimaced. 'You could be right, you know. I suppose he must have given Mia some sweets before he left. Told her not to tell you? Or Kate could have done. She was home, wasn't she, when you called round?'

'It makes so much sense now. Easier for the two of them to be working together on this. Although…' She shook her head. 'How could Dean allow his daughter to be harmed? He saw how ill she was, how distressed.'

'Love is a strange thing,' Frank said. 'Makes people blind to their actions and the consequences. I suppose he knew it wouldn't kill her, whatever they used. Just a temporary bout of sickness and diarrhoea that would pass. No long-term harm.'

'I think he was pretty horrified, though, when she was ill that time he was home.' Becca huffed. 'Made sure he wasn't around the next few times, though.' Her hands clenched round the toy unicorn in her lap. 'How could he? And then pin it on me. Not only has he taken my daughter away from me, he's taken my career too. I'll never get nursing work again. Then I've got to go through this psychiatric assessment, and I'll have to do what they recommend, or they won't give me access. He must know they won't let me near Mia.'

'Handy, that,' Frank said as they turned into the drive of his house.

'Oh, Dad. What are we going to do? I can't be without Mia. I can't. I'm her mum and she needs me.' Becca burst into tears, clutching Mia's unicorn to her chest, her heart breaking.

They sat in the car in silence, the engine ticking as it cooled, neither of them having an answer.

'Let's have a cup of tea,' Frank said eventually as he opened the car door.

They'd talked round and round the problem for almost an hour when the phone rang. It was the landline, which lived on top of the cupboard, next to Frank's chair. He leant over and picked up the receiver, Becca watching his face as it went from a frown to wide-eyed shock.

'Just a minute,' he said to the person on the phone. 'I'm going to pass you to my daughter, if you wouldn't mind giving her the details. I'm not… I can't take it in.'

Becca grabbed the phone and introduced herself to the caller.

'I'm afraid there's been an accident,' a woman said. 'A collision on the M6. I'm calling from the hospital. Birmingham City

Hospital. Just to inform you that Kate Pritchard is in our intensive care unit.'

Becca gulped.

'The driver has minor injuries and is being treated for shock.'

'My daughter! What about my daughter?' Becca screeched. 'She was in the car too.'

'The little girl is fine, I believe.'

Becca gabbled her thanks, told the caller they were on their way and put the phone down. 'Come on, Dad. Let's go.' The colour had drained from Frank's face and he was shaking, but she bundled him into the hallway, collecting jackets on the way out of the door.

The thought of any of her family being injured was horrific, and for a moment, she forgot what Dean and Kate had done to her, forgot why they were on the motorway in the first place. All she could think about was Mia and the need to comfort her after what must have been the most terrifying incident of her short life.

'We'll take your car, Dad. It's blocking mine in the drive and we haven't time to shift them around. Anyway, yours is faster.' He rummaged in his pocket and pulled out the keys, passing them to her.

'Intensive care, that's what they said, wasn't it?' Frank said, after a few minutes.

'Let's stay positive. She's in good hands.'

Two and a half hours later, they arrived at the hospital and were directed to the ICU, where a nurse let them into the waiting room. It was bright and cheerful with Impressionist prints hung on the walls, the mood at odds with the doleful faces of the current occupants. Everyone was sitting quietly, staring at the floor or the walls, some nursing paper coffee cups, waiting for news of loved ones.

Becca had expected to see Dean and Mia, but they weren't there. Adrenaline was still pumping round her body, after their dash from North Wales, her heart racing.

'I'll tell the doctor you're here,' the nurse said and left before Becca could ask where her family were.

Frank slumped into a chair, elbows on his knees, head hanging between his shoulders. Becca perched on the one next to him, her leg bouncing up and down. His hand found hers and she gripped tightly, impatient for the nurse to return. Unable to settle, she got up. 'I'll just see if I can talk to someone, find out where Dean and Mia are.' But before she could do that, a doctor swept into the room.

'Mr Pritchard?'

Frank nodded, Becca grabbed hold of his hand again and they followed the doctor down the corridor a short way to a small meeting room.

'I'm afraid Ms Pritchard… your daughter has sustained serious head injuries. There was a side impact, which shunted the car across the carriageway and down an embankment. She also has chest injuries. Unfortunately, the airbag didn't inflate properly.'

Becca stared at the doctor, open-mouthed. Frank didn't say anything, and she wondered if he was in shock. She squeezed his hand, but he didn't respond.

The doctor carried on. 'We've had to sedate her to give the swelling on her brain time to subside. It's very much a waiting game with this type of injury, I'm afraid.'

'Will… will she fully recover?' Frank said, his voice wavering as if he hardly dared ask.

'It's early days. I can't promise anything, but rest assured we are doing everything we can to make sure the prognosis is positive.'

Becca clasped Frank's hand a little tighter. 'I think Dad might be in shock,' she said to the doctor, who looked over at the nurse.

'Let's get you a cup of tea,' the nurse said. 'Lots of sugar. See if that helps.' She led them out of the room and Becca thanked the doctor before following them back to the waiting room, where the nurse organised tea for them both, saying she'd be back to check on Frank.

There was still no sign of Dean and Mia.

'I don't suppose…' Becca started, as the nurse was about to leave. She turned. 'My sister was travelling with my husband and three-year-old daughter. I don't know where they are.'

The nurse frowned. 'Perhaps they're still in A & E? I haven't seen them, but I've just come on shift. Let me go and ask for you.'

'Oh, thank you. I don't want to be any trouble, but I just…' Becca's voice cracked. 'I need to see my daughter. Make sure she's okay.'

The nurse put a comforting hand on her shoulder. 'Of course you do. Have a seat, keep an eye on your dad and I'll go and see what I can find out.'

Frank sipped at his tea, obviously lost in his own thoughts. Becca fidgeted with the car keys, which were still in her hand. She stuffed them in her handbag, and when she could wait no longer, she got up and paced the corridor. It was better than sitting still.

Finally, the nurse reappeared. 'Sorry I took so long. Got waylaid. Apparently, your husband is waiting for stitches in his hand. Still in A & E. Your daughter is just being checked over now. I've told them you're here and will be coming down.'

'Thank you so much.' Becca's heart was skipping with relief. 'Where's A & E?'

The nurse gave her directions and promised to monitor Frank while she ran down corridors, desperate to be with her daughter.

Ten minutes later, she found Mia with a nurse, who was obviously waiting for Becca to appear as her face lit up with relief when she arrived. 'Here's Mummy.'

Mia's face was tear-stained, a bruise on her cheek, her lips puckered as she gulped down her sobs. She squealed when she saw Becca, eyes round with delight.

'Is she okay?' Becca asked, scooping her daughter into her arms, stroking her hair as Mia snuggled her head into Becca's neck. She could feel her hot breath on her skin, her little fingers tangling in her hair as if she was trying to anchor herself. Becca's breath hiccupped in her throat as she tried not to cry; the relief at being with her daughter again almost overwhelming. She held her tighter, kissing her cheek, tasting the salty tears.

The nurse smiled. 'She's just a bit shaken, a few bumps and bruises, but apart from that, she's fine. I'll get the doctor to come and have a word in a minute, if you like?'

'Lovely,' Becca said, nervously scanning the curtained cubicles, unsure if Dean was in one of them, listening. 'Um… I believe her dad… my husband is in here, somewhere.'

'Yes, that's right. He's just seen the doctor. There's a nasty gash on his hand and there might be broken bones, so he's just gone down to X-ray. If you'd like to go through to the waiting room, I'll give you a shout when he's back, shall I?'

Becca's mind was racing as she clung on to her daughter, hardly able to believe she was back in her arms. 'That would be great, thanks.'

'There's a toy box in the corner and a few books to keep her amused,' the nurse added before showing them through the double doors and out of the department.

This is my chance.

As soon as the nurse had gone, Becca walked out of the waiting room and out of the hospital. Nobody was going to take Mia away from her now she had her back. Nobody.

Kate was critically ill. Dean was injured and incapable of driving. Frank appeared to be in shock, so wouldn't be able to help her. None of them were going anywhere anytime soon, giving her time to make her escape and get a head start before anyone would miss her and Mia.

She hurried to Frank's car, her eyes scanning the car park, expecting to see somebody running after her, but it was quiet at this time of night. Her heart thundered in her chest, making her feel lightheaded as she clasped her daughter tight.

'Everything's going to be fine,' she murmured as she speed-walked across the car park while her mind tried to catch up.

What's the plan? She had nowhere she could go. Nobody who could help. She was on her own.

CHAPTER THIRTY-SEVEN

Mia started screaming as soon as she saw the car and understood she was supposed to get in it.

'Not going in there, Mummy. Not going!' She squirmed and wriggled like a live eel, shrieking and crying, creating the sort of noise that would make anyone believe she was being murdered.

Becca had to put her down but kept a firm hold of her hand, glancing around to make sure nobody was paying attention. Fortunately, the car park was empty, and she put a hand to her chest, her heart pounding at a rate that was surely unnatural. She cursed herself for not realising her daughter would be petrified of cars after the accident. She hadn't been a fan before but now it was going to be nigh on impossible to get her to cooperate. Then she remembered her secret weapon: the unicorn.

'Look who I've got here,' she cooed as she fumbled the toy out of her bag. 'Peppa came with me. She missed you.'

Mia was silenced immediately, as if Becca had pushed an on–off button, staring at her toy with big round eyes, still troubled but curious. She sniffed and held out a hand and Becca pretended to make the unicorn jump into her arms, snuggling against Mia's chest. Delighted, the little girl swung to and fro, squishing the toy against her while she covered its face with kisses.

Becca leant against the car, stuck for ideas as to what to do next. If she couldn't use Frank's car, she'd have to get herself to the station. It would be simple enough to get a train back to Llandudno, if that's where she wanted to go. Or Bangor. But those were obvious destinations and she'd be found immediately, accused of kidnapping, and everything would be ten times worse. She sighed and ruled it out as an option. Really, though, they could go wherever they wanted, have an adventure. She didn't have to go anywhere near North Wales.

Her mind raced on, jumbling a plan together. She was sure Mia wouldn't get in a taxi, so if she was going anywhere, she'd have to get a bus to the station. A glance at her watch told her it was coming up to midnight. There'd be no buses until the morning now. Realistically, she couldn't expect Mia to walk any distance after the trauma of the crash, and Becca's arms were already aching from holding her. Reality hit home, making her eyes sting. *I'm not going anywhere.*

She scanned the deserted car park, searching for inspiration, but she couldn't focus. And although she was desperate to get away with her daughter, the fact that her sister was in intensive care kept forcing itself to the front of her mind. It was a puzzle as to why she'd suddenly turned vindictive now, when Becca and Dean had been together for so many years. Perhaps when she'd come back from Manchester and was closer to him again, that had reminded her of the relationship she'd lost. Becca wanted justice, but there was no way she wanted her sister dead. In fact, Kate dying would make everything worse – any evidence that Becca had of Kate's involvement was circumstantial at best, and what she really needed was a confession. Without that, the authorities would still think she was the one harming Mia and was conveniently blaming it on her dead sister. Then she'd be forever branded as unfit to be a parent to her child.

She looked back at the hospital. That's where the solution to her problems lay, with Kate and Dean. Running away wouldn't solve anything, it would make her troubles worse. The answer was to confront Dean with what she knew. If he wasn't involved, he'd be appalled that Kate would do such a thing, and there was a chance he would help Becca to prove her innocence. If he *was* involved… well, at least if she confronted him face to face, she might be able to tell from his body language whether he was lying.

Even if Dean hadn't been spending as much time with Mia as Becca would have liked, he was a caring father, and she'd always thought he'd lay down his life to protect their child. She nodded to herself, sure that this had to be Kate acting on her own. Her objective was very clear, a double whammy: Becca to be disgraced and ejected from the family so Kate could take her place. Then Becca would have nowhere to go but back to live with Frank, and she would take over caring duties.

'Hungry, Mummy,' Mia said, and Becca was jolted from her thoughts and back to the question of what to do now. She hadn't eaten since lunchtime and she had no idea when Mia had last eaten either.

One step at a time. That's the way to do this.

Mia was shivering and Becca wondered if there was something in the car she could use to keep her warm. She had a root around in the back and found a fleece of Frank's. It was enormous on Mia, but with the sleeves rolled up, it would keep her warm. Becca was about to lock the car when she spotted Frank's iPad stuffed into the pocket behind the passenger seat. It would be handy to keep Mia distracted, she thought, and put it in her bag.

'Let's go and find something to eat, shall we?' she said to Mia as she picked her up again and swung her on to her hip. She was pale and the bruise on the side of her head was darkening, but the promise of food brought a smile to her face before she laid her head on Becca's shoulder and latched her fingers into her hair once more.

The hard way is the easy way. It was a quote Becca had read on one of Kate's motivational posters, and it had struck her as being the truth. The people she needed to speak to were here in the hospital, and the only way to sort out this whole nightmare situation was to confront it.

The café run by the volunteers was shut, although the dining area remained open. There was a vending machine full of snacks and she bought sandwiches and some drinks, which she took to a table in the corner of the L-shaped room. A couple of the other tables were occupied by exhausted-looking people, who gave Mia wan smiles. Hospitals were strange places at night, she'd always thought, hushed and serious. Often sad. When all was said and done, there weren't many reasons why you'd choose to be here in the middle of the night. Births and deaths, two ends of the spectrum of life.

Dean will be trying to find us, she thought as she chewed her food. *What if he calls the police?* Quickly, she took her phone out of her bag to message him, cursing when she found the battery was flat.

Then she remembered Frank's iPad in her bag. She could use that instead. He'd told her his passcode as she'd used it recently to download programmes for Mia to watch last time they'd been in his car.

She tapped in the number, relieved when it sprang to life. It opened on a Twitter account. She blinked, not understanding for a moment what she was seeing. But there really was no mistaking it – Surferdude's account was staring right at her.

CHAPTER THIRTY-EIGHT

Her brain froze as her eyes scanned the page. With shaking hands, she went to messages, and there they were, all their conversations. It had been Frank she'd been talking to, pretending to be Connor.

Mia saw the iPad open and clambered on to her knee. 'Peppa Pig, Mummy. Let's watch Peppa.'

On autopilot, Becca found an episode and let it play, sound down, while Mia snuggled in to watch, the ear of the unicorn in her mouth, always a precursor to sleep. Becca rocked gently from side to side, stroking Mia's hair while she watched the animated figures on the screen, not seeing them, as her mind wrestled with her new discovery.

After a few minutes, when she was sure Mia was settled, Becca went back to Twitter and soon found the fake Connor Cywinski account that she'd blocked originally. There was no mistaking it now, no way she could argue his innocence. It had been her dad all along.

The revelation brought a heaviness to her body, a weariness to her brain. The man she'd trusted most had been secretly undermining her marriage, smashing her life apart. The more she thought about it, the more clearly she could see that Frank had as much to gain as Kate from the breakdown of her marriage. It was something that would suit them both in equal measure. Frank wanted Kate gone and Becca to take her place.

Her thoughts took another step, reaching a conclusion that shocked her to the core. The only way he could be sure of that was if he created a situation where Becca wouldn't be allowed to live at home. By making her appear to be an unfit mother.

Were Kate and Dad in it together? Were those rows a sham? A way to make me feel sorry for him? And what about Dean?

Her head ached but she knew she couldn't stop now. She was getting close to the truth and wanted to gather as much evidence as she could to substantiate her theory before she went to the police. The internet search history on the iPad showed a whole list of articles on how to make people sick without being found out. Epsom salts was the answer, apparently, but not too much or you could damage the stomach lining and kill people. She closed her eyes for a moment, shocked that anyone would take that risk, but she would bet that once the liquid in the syringe was tested, that's what it would be. She'd even seen the bag of Epsom salts in the bathroom at her dad's house, had listened to him telling her how it made for a nice relaxing bath. She gritted her teeth and made herself read on. There were numerous articles on factitious disorder. The hairs stood up on the back of her neck.

It was chilling to see how carefully her dad had done his research and planned everything out. He knew Becca's weakness, knew that having been under suspicion in the past, it would be straightforward enough to make people doubt her again. Fury built inside her as she scrolled down the entries until she could look no more and flicked the case back over the screen.

She thought she knew the truth now. The problem was… would anyone believe her?

CHAPTER THIRTY-NINE

She sat for a long time, letting her mind drift over the problem, studying it from different angles. Frank wasn't the only person who used the iPad, that was the issue – so he could easily deny all knowledge and point the finger back at Kate. She came back to the idea that the two of them were working together. Or maybe it was Kate all along, cleverly doing the research and running the Twitter account on Frank's device to shift any blame. The box she'd found upstairs couldn't be classed as hard evidence as it could have been planted by any one of them.

Then it struck her like a hammer blow, leaving the thought ringing in her head. *The blame could be put back on me.* She had access to the iPad. Her fingerprints were all over the Tupperware box with the syringe of liquid and the sweets in it.

She tugged at her hair, frustrated by the cleverness of the trap.

With Kate in intensive care, it was a difficult time to pursue the truth. What if Kate was innocent? How would Becca feel if her sister died, and in her last living moments, Becca had hated her for something she hadn't done? She'd learnt from her mother's death that someone dying when there was bad feeling tainted memories, left you wishing you'd done things differently, moved to resolve issues when you'd had the chance.

She needed to talk to someone outside the loop, someone who could give her a fresh perspective, who wasn't involved in the investigation. The only person she could think of was Connor.

She pulled her phone out of her bag then remembered when the screen wouldn't come to life that it was dead.

'Bloody stupid thing,' she muttered, throwing it on the table.

Her limbs were leaden with exhaustion, the day having stretched for what seemed like a week. Unsure what to do for the best, she rested her head on top of Mia's. The silky softness of her child's hair against Becca's cheek was such a precious sensation, she closed her eyes for a moment, thinking that she would do whatever it may take to keep Mia by her side.

She was woken by a hand shaking her shoulder. Not gently, but a rough tug, making her teeth rattle.

'Becca! What are you doing? Give her to me. Right now. Give her to me.'

Before she was fully awake, Mia had been wrenched from her arms, leaving a cold, baffling emptiness. Becca blinked, disorientated and confused.

Dean was glaring at her, Mia on his hip. She was obviously as perturbed as Becca, not sure what was happening, and her bottom lip wobbled. His left hand was bandaged and in a splint, his face bruised and swollen from where the airbag had hit him. He was in a sorry state, but his eyes sparked. This was Dean the Protector, doing whatever was needed to keep his daughter safe.

Becca's anger ignited, her whole body infused with a sudden burst of energy. Fight or flight, that was the choice, and this time she knew she had to stay. She was in the right; she had the moral high ground. He was the one having an affair, who'd been running off to London with his lover. She glared at him, forcing her words from between clenched teeth.

'You were being treated in A & E. Mia was restless and the nurse had other things to do. We were hungry, so we came here.' Her eyes narrowed, her voice getting louder as the rage blazed inside her. 'I've done nothing wrong. You, on the other hand… well, you've got a lot of explaining to do.'

'Don't you come near us,' Dean hissed. 'You're bloody deluded. I can't trust you after the things you've done.'

Becca's eye widened and she reeled back in her chair. 'And what exactly have I done? Because there's a hell of a lot of wrong assumptions being made here. Two and two making five.'

He seemed taken aback. 'I don't have to spell it out. You shouldn't be here, and you know it. I'll have to tell the safeguarding team that you've contravened the rules. Again. It won't look good.'

They stared at each other, gladiators circling, considering the best place to strike.

'You and Kate,' she snarled. 'How long's that been going on behind my back?'

His right eye twitched and she noticed his Adam's apple bob up and down.

'When were you going to tell me? What was the plan, eh? Move to London with her and then send me a change of address?'

Mia started to cry, upset by the tone of their voices, the vitriol that infused the air between them. The other two people in the café were watching them. She swallowed back the torrent of angry words and gave her daughter a reassuring smile, hoping she wouldn't know that she was seething inside, the curve of her lips a pretence. Dean shushed Mia and kissed his daughter's head, wincing as he knocked his damaged hand.

The strength seemed to go from him then and he sank into a chair on the opposite side of the table. She could see his jaw working, could tell from his pinched expression that he was in pain. They were silent while they waited for Mia to settle again. Finally, when her eyelids drooped and her body relaxed against Dean's, it was time for round two.

'Let me show you something,' Becca said, her voice a murmur, so as not to wake Mia. She opened the iPad and found the Twitter account, then turned the screen so he could see. 'This is Dad's iPad.

Looks like he put up the fake account, pretending to be Connor. He was trying to trick me into saying I still loved him. Trying to get evidence to break up our marriage.' She gave a derisive snort. 'He didn't need to go to all the trouble, did he? If he'd been patient, you would have broken us up anyway.'

Dean was silent, staring at the screen.

Fuelled by injustice, she decided she might as well throw the full story at him. See how he felt about his shiny new life then.

'I think Dad is the one who was poisoning Mia as well. Or it could be Kate. Maybe the two of them. When she left today, I found a box in her office with sweets and a syringe and this clear liquid, which I think from the research history on here is Epsom salts. Thing is, he could have planted it there.'

Dean was listening intently now.

'So either this is all Dad or it's Kate and Dad, working together to get what they both want. Kate wants you. Dad wants me to look after him. And if that's what's happened, neither of them gives a toss about Mia.'

Dean swallowed, his face screwed up in anger. 'Our daughter, used in some sick plan? Is that what you're saying?'

She nodded, and he glanced away, eyes focused on the wall behind her. She could almost see his thoughts whirring and decided to give him time to process what she'd just said.

'It's my fault,' he said, eventually. 'I caused the accident.' He glanced at her, blinking back tears. 'What you've just told me about sweets being doctored, it makes sense. The whole thing had been puzzling me and I was trying to talk it through with Kate when we were on the motorway but she was being so horrible about you and I said she wasn't being fair and then we got into this big row and Mia was screaming and I didn't see the car in front pulling in until it was too late.' He paused for breath, his voice cracking when he continued. 'I swerved at the last minute, lost control and we went down the embankment.' His face crumpled and his shoulders shook. 'It's all my fault.'

There was nothing Becca could say.

'And you're wrong. Me and Kate… we're not together.'

CHAPTER FORTY

Becca scanned his face for signs that he was lying, but all she could see was regret deepening the grooves at the side of his mouth.

He sighed. 'Worst decision of my life. I said I'd give her a lift to London because I had to go and visit a client anyway. She said she'd keep an eye on Mia for me if I helped her find an apartment. She had a few lined up to view. It was a win-win for both of us.'

She narrowed her eyes. 'I don't think Kate saw it like that. I think she probably saw it as the beginning of something.' Her hand went to her pocket and she pulled out the earring. 'I found this next to our bed. Dad seemed to think it's Kate's.'

He ran his tongue round his lips, his gaze dipping. 'I've no idea how that got there.'

She huffed, satisfied now that she'd been right. 'Oh, I think you do.' She leant towards him. 'Don't you think it's time to stop playing games?'

She watched the blush colour his cheeks. 'Okay, okay.' He sighed. 'You're right. She came round to see how I was doing. We got drunk and started talking about old times and...'

'Yeah, like that's an excuse,' Becca hissed. 'I know the history between you two. Dad said your relationship was on–off. "Volatile" I think was the word he used.' She could hardly speak through her anger. 'It would have been good to know about that before we got married. How come I never knew you two had even been an item? Why didn't you tell me?'

He still couldn't meet her eye, and when he finally spoke, his voice was so quiet she could hardly hear him. 'I didn't want you to think I was marrying you just because you were pregnant.'

'But you were,' she said, the truth obvious to her now. 'That's exactly what you were doing, wasn't it?'

He stroked Mia's hair. 'It's complicated. I wanted to do the right thing.' He blew out a long breath, clearly struggling to admit the truth. 'I desperately wanted a family. Kate had never been keen – that's what our fights were about. That's why I ended it with her. I was ready to settle down; she wasn't.'

There was a familiarity about his story that struck Becca hard. *Isn't that just the same as me and Connor?* One wanted to settle; the other wasn't ready. The question was what to do about those unresolved feelings. All she'd done was talk to Connor, whereas Dean had broken the bond of trust by sleeping with Kate.

'Our relationship was never about me, was it? It was always about having a baby.' She shook her head. 'You never really loved me. That's the truth, isn't it? It's always been Kate.'

'Of course I loved you. Honestly, Becca, you've got to believe me. But… well, me and Kate…' He pressed his lips together, obviously debating with himself how much to say.

Loved. Past tense. The hurt stabbed through her heart. 'You might as well be honest with me now, Dean. Don't pretend there's nothing going on.'

He looked at her then. 'You want the truth? You and me, well, we don't have a great deal in common any more, do we?' He glanced down at his sleeping daughter. 'We have Mia, but over the last year, I've come to see that's not enough. I'm sorry, Becca. I really thought we could make it work, but…'

He blinked, adjusting Mia's position on his knee.

'A year?' Her voice was louder than necessary, but she couldn't contain her fury. 'You and Kate have been seeing each other for a year?'

'I don't know,' he mumbled. 'It may be that long.'

Her jaw clamped shut. This was not the place to let loose with the rage that was burning her throat. Mia had been upset enough, and she wasn't going to disturb her peace. This was, however, an opportunity to take control.

When she finally spoke, her words were crystal-clear, her demeanour ice-cold. 'So, this is what's going to happen. I'm taking my daughter and going home to our house. You can't look after her with a broken hand, and I'm sure you want to stay with Kate, given you're the one who put her here.' She handed him the keys to Frank's car. 'You can tell that scheming father of mine that I don't want to see him again. We are over. Done. And after this, we'll see what the authorities have to say about access.'

She picked up her things and gathered Mia from Dean's arms without any resistance. His shoulders were hunched, his head hung low, but she couldn't feel sorry for him, not when their life together had been built on a lie. When he'd almost destroyed her.

Bastard, bastard, bastard. It was the only thought in her head as she found her way to the reception area.

She checked Google Maps on the iPad and headed out of the hospital towards New Street station. She'd get a train home. Mia liked trains; she'd be excited rather than scared once she woke up and understood what was happening. The station was two miles or so. Forty minutes to walk. She hitched the dead weight of her daughter a little higher and told herself it didn't matter how tired she was – she could do it. If that was what it took to make her way to freedom, she could definitely do it.

And then what? the voice in her head asked.

She had to get away from her toxic family. Start again.

But what about the safeguarding team? They'd never let her be with Mia. She had to get to the police. Give them the evidence. Then they'd have to believe her.

'Becca! Becca!'

She turned at the sound of her name, astounded to see Ruth running towards her from the direction of the hospital. 'Thank goodness I caught you.' Ruth was blowing hard after her dash to catch up and she put a hand on her chest, taking a minute to get her breath.

Becca stared at her, thoroughly confused by her sudden appearance.

'Frank called and told me about Kate's accident,' Ruth said, still breathless. 'He sounded in a bad way, so upset. And when he said Mia had been in the car too, well, wild horses wouldn't have stopped me from coming. I had to make sure my little girl was okay, and Frank said he'd like me to come because you'd disappeared, and he hadn't a clue what was going on.'

'Wow, that's above and beyond the call of duty. I didn't know you two were so close.'

Ruth's brow crinkled. 'I had to make sure Mia was all right. Poor mite must have been terrified.' She put a hand out to stroke Mia's cheek, but Becca moved away before she could touch her. If Ruth was in Frank's corner, could she be involved in some way?

Ruth's face fell, and she seemed genuinely distressed by Becca's action. Guilt poked at Becca's heart as their eyes met. She'd always relied on Ruth, had trusted her completely with Mia. *Can I trust her now?* She wasn't sure and held Mia a little tighter, as if Ruth was going to snatch her from her arms.

'Kids are amazingly resilient, aren't they?' Becca said and kissed her daughter's head, glad she was asleep – if she'd been awake, she would have wanted a cuddle with Ruth, and then things could have become very difficult. They definitely had a strong bond, and when Mia wanted something, she could be incredibly determined.

Ruth didn't reply, her mind fixed on her own agenda and her eyes fixed on Mia. 'Frank was asking for you. I've been searching all over the place, then Dean turned up in the ICU and said you might have left.' Ruth frowned, disapproval written all over her face. 'I can't believe you're walking out on your poor dad and sister.'

Becca's jaw clenched, hating the way she was being judged. 'You really don't know who you're dealing with, Ruth. It's Kate and Dad who've been poisoning Mia. I've got evidence. I can't speak to him. Not now.'

Ruth gasped, her hands flying to her mouth. 'No. I don't believe it.'

Becca turned to walk away, but Ruth grabbed her arm.

'You can't just throw that at me and not explain.' She softened her voice. 'Come back inside. Let's go and get a drink in the warm and you can tell me. Perhaps I can help.'

Becca wrenched her arm from Ruth's grasp, but the tussle had disturbed Mia, whose eyes flickered open, and as soon as she spotted Ruth, Becca knew that her choices were limited to one. The chance of a quick escape had gone.

Doesn't matter, she reassured herself. The trains wouldn't be running yet. And maybe Ruth *could* help. Reluctantly, she followed her inside, Mia wriggling to get down and give Ruth a hug. They walked with the little girl between them, each holding her hand. For a moment, Becca imagined a different version of reality, where instead of Ruth walking beside her, it was her mum, and they'd been able to enjoy her child together. It reminded her that, in terms of support, Ruth was all she had, and she obviously loved Mia with all her heart. *She wouldn't harm Mia, would she?*

It was impossible to know what or who to believe. *Watch and listen*, she cautioned herself. Then she could decide. But being on permanent high alert was exhausting, and after a day that refused to end, she was tired to the bone.

Back in the café, Ruth bustled around getting coffee from the machine and a drink for Mia. Becca observed as she interacted with her daughter, noticed the gentle patience.

'I want those sweets,' Mia said, pointing to some jelly bears.

'No, I'm sorry, I'm not buying those. Remember what I keep telling you? Sweets are bad for your teeth? I will never buy you sweets, so there really is no point asking.'

'Please,' Mia wheedled. 'Dandad gives me them.'

Becca's eyes widened as her daughter confirmed what had only been suspicion up to now. But who would believe a three-year-old child? She couldn't be counted on as a reliable witness.

'How about these cheesy biscuits,' Ruth said, already putting the money in the machine and pressing the buttons. 'You like those, don't you?'

Mia clapped her hands as the machine whirred and the packet was magically delivered to her. She held it up for Becca to see like she'd won a prize, and Becca gave her the thumbs up as she came running back.

Something else about the exchange lodged in Becca's brain. Ruth's insistence on something savoury, the refusal to buy sweets. In her heart, she couldn't believe Ruth would harm Mia. And looking back, there'd been no problems with her daughter's health while she'd been in Ruth's care.

I've got to trust somebody.

When Ruth came back to the table, and Mia was busy feeding her biscuits to her toy unicorn before popping them into her own mouth, Becca told Ruth everything she knew, her voice a frantic whisper as if she couldn't rid herself of the words fast enough.

Ruth's expression hardened as she listened, and she punctuated Becca's narrative with little intakes of breath and tuts, completely focused on what she was saying.

'Well, he's not getting away with it,' she said when Becca had finished, her face flushed with anger, clearly horrified by what she'd just heard. She pulled her phone from her bag.

Becca frowned, a surge of panic wiping out her weariness and putting her on alert again. 'Wait… what are you doing?'

'I'm calling the police.'

Becca's breath caught in her throat. 'No, you can't. Please. I don't actually have any proper evidence. It's all circumstantial and could be explained away.' Her fear at the consequences was making her heart race. 'It could even be made to point the blame back at me, and that would make everything a whole lot worse.' Her thoughts galloped on towards the inevitable consequences, her breath coming faster, as if she was running. 'They'll find out about the safeguarding order and take Mia off me. Then social services will be crawling all over us and I might never get her back.'

Ruth stopped what she was doing and leant across the table, patted Becca's arm. 'That's not going to happen,' she said, firmly. 'Mia is not going back to your husband. He's in no fit state with a broken hand, is he? I know they won't let you have her until they've followed their investigation through to the end. But I can take care of her while all this gets sorted out. I am her childminder after all, and my house is geared towards young children. Perfectly safe.' She nodded as if confirming it to herself. 'Continuity of care, that's what they'll be after.'

The seconds ticked by as Ruth googled the number for the local police on her phone. Becca's heart was doing palpitations again and her hand went to her chest. Had she made a terrible misjudgement? Was she about to lose everything?

'Nobody would notice if you came to stay with me as well,' Ruth said, flapping an impatient hand, and Becca knew then that she'd got it right. Ruth was on her side. Her only ally. Her shoulders sagged with relief as Ruth carried on talking. 'Details. These are details we can sort out.'

Ruth leant across the table, speaking in a conspiratorial whisper. 'The thing is, I'm a witness. I saw Frank giving Mia sweets.'

Becca's mouth fell open. She had a witness, a proper adult witness, and that was exactly what she needed.

'That's right,' Ruth continued. 'I saw him. He sort of did it on the sly. I don't think he knew I spotted what he was up to. Obviously, I didn't approve because I don't ever give the children sweets. But he's her grandad and I don't know him that well, so I thought you must have said it was okay.'

Becca let out the biggest sigh, her heart dancing a strange jig as she watched Ruth make the call to the police.

It's going to be okay, she told herself, hardly able to believe this might be the end of her troubles. She pulled Mia on to her knee, holding her child close.

EPILOGUE

Exactly one year after the accident and Frank's subsequent arrest, Becca woke feeling excited. She could hear the murmur of voices out on the veranda – Mia chattering and Connor answering, laughing at something she'd said. They were staying with his mum, Jackie, who ran a bed and breakfast not far from Connor's property outside Darwin. She'd insisted they stay with her, even though it was the middle of the dry season and she was busy with visitors. Connor was basically camping on his plot of land while he slowly built his house, which was definitely still a work in progress and not yet fit for guests. Jackie had been a wonderful hostess, warm and friendly and completely smitten with Mia, making the whole trip so much easier than she'd thought it might be.

Becca had a quick shower and got dressed in her T-shirt and shorts, a warm breeze filtering through the house, silky soft against her skin. The guest house, like many in the area, was built of wood and perched on stilts, designed to catch a breeze and stay cool in the humid conditions. It was basically a block of bedrooms in the middle, with a wide, covered veranda on four sides providing the living space. It was set in verdant gardens with all manner of wildlife scampering around and fluttering in the canopy. Mia was bewitched by the place, especially the colourful birds and butterflies, and Becca thought she'd have trouble when it was time to go home.

'G'day, mate,' Connor said as she appeared at the breakfast table, a greeting that always made her feel warm and fuzzy because it was true – they were definitely mates. She sat down and took the glass of orange juice he'd poured for her. 'Mia says she wants to go and see the crocodiles today.'

Becca looked over at her daughter, who was flipping through a picture book full of Australian wildlife, her favourite book of the moment. 'Really?'

'I thought we could go to Kakadu National Park.'

It was a place Becca had yearned to see, teeming with wildlife, but getting Mia there could be an issue. 'That's quite a drive, isn't it? You've seen what she's like in the hire car.' She'd made the decision to have her own transport while they were in Australia, just in case things got awkward and she wanted to strike out on her own. Even a year after the accident, Mia still hated getting in the car, and Becca had tried to keep their adventures local as much as possible to prevent unnecessary upset.

He grinned at her. 'She says she'd like to go in the truck.' Connor had a massive four-by-four vehicle that would get him through any sort of terrain, and Becca supposed it didn't really seem like a car when you were in there. More like a tractor and definitely safe. 'I said I'd have to ask because little girls aren't normally allowed in trucks but she says she's a big girl so it will be okay.'

She smiled. He always knew how to tip situations on their head to get the better of Mia's contrary nature. 'Well, I'm definitely up for it. We've only got another few days, so it'll be good to make the most of it.'

The excitement dimmed in his eyes and he pulled a face. 'I hate this talk about you going.' He reached across the table and held her hand. 'These three weeks have gone in a flash, haven't they? I can't tell you how much I've loved having you both here.'

She swallowed and studied the garden, not trusting her voice.

Her reason for coming to Australia had been very specific, and although they hadn't talked about it, she knew they were both in the same situation. Having been in touch with him again, and having talked to him for a year now over video chats, she had to know how she really felt – and that could only be confirmed face to face. Had it been true love, or had it been a wonderful interlude that she was now romanticising and should be relegated to the past?

The previous evening, they'd stayed up late, talking about the future, but there was still a subject that had been skirted around. Months ago, she'd written to her father about the missing letter from Connor, and he'd eventually admitted that he'd burnt it, worried that Becca would go back to Australia if she read the contents. He'd told her that it was an apology and a proposal. All those years ago, Connor had asked her to marry him, and she'd never known and never been able to reply. Just another example of how Frank had been trying to manipulate her life choices for years.

In all honesty, her heart and her head were having a ferocious battle because life was complicated enough without Connor in the mix. But she'd had to come – because what if she'd never known, what if she'd spent the rest of her life wondering about what could have been? Ending her life with regrets. It was only a year until Mia started school, so if she was going to go away for any length of time, it had to be now. Plus, she had some money from the divorce settlement, and she wasn't yet committed to permanent work. The timing had been perfect, and without letting herself think too hard about whether it was a good idea, she'd gone ahead and booked the flights.

Now, as she let her eyes drift over the lush rainforest, her mind took her back to a year ago and everything that had brought her to this point in time.

Mia had stayed with Ruth in the beginning, while all the allegations were being investigated and the proper protocols were followed. Becca had found an apartment to rent nearby, which suited her just fine. It had taken a few weeks for everyone to be convinced that Becca didn't have mental health problems and wasn't the one poisoning her daughter. But in the end, she was fully exonerated. After a few months off to rest and recuperate, she had taken on some agency work as a home carer. The work was less stressful and fit better round Mia's needs and was perfect for now.

Dean had kept the house, having bought Becca out, and Kate was living with him now, their relationship out in the open. She was still in a wheelchair, but her coordination was slowly improving, and she was determined to become fully mobile again. Obviously, she hadn't been able to take up her job in London, but she was helping Dean with his business.

It had taken a few months, but Ruth had persuaded Becca that she should talk to Kate and clear the air. It had been difficult at first, the sense of betrayal dominating Becca's thoughts – all she could focus on was the fact that Kate had been having an affair with her husband. However, having lost her mum with bad feelings still between them, she couldn't let the same happen with Kate. Yes, she was bossy, and they didn't always see eye to eye, but she was her sister, and Becca was trying to be adult and rational about everything. Although Dean felt guilty about the crash, and that might have brought them even closer together, in her heart, Becca thought the two of them actually made a good couple.

Becca's relationship with Dean had been built on the wrong foundations, shaky from the start, with both of them on the rebound, and she was sure that neither of them would find what they needed with each other. Thankfully, they had managed to keep things civilised and had agreed shared access to Mia. With Dean's work, though, that meant she only went to stay with him a couple of weekends a month, and Becca was happy to keep things flexible.

Kate had denied any involvement with Frank's scheme, and Becca believed her. Apparently, she'd told him several times that she couldn't carry on living with him. She knew she'd behaved badly around him, but she'd found his behaviour so passive-aggressive and manipulative, she couldn't cope. Every time she'd said she was leaving, though, he'd had a health scare, or some little accident round the house, and she'd ended up staying because he couldn't be trusted to live on his own, and Becca was too busy with her family and work to help.

Poor Kate. She'd had as difficult a time as Becca in a way, and talking everything through with her, and then Ruth, had allowed Becca to see things from a different perspective. Gradually, they were rebuilding their relationship and although they would never be best friends, they would always be sisters.

Frank had been convicted of child abuse, although there had been a lot of wrangling about the diagnosis of factitious disorder imposed on another and whether he was actually suffering from it or whether it was a convenient label to hide behind to avoid prison. Eventually, after several psychiatric assessments and a failed suicide attempt while on remand, the decision had been made to hold him in a secure hospital unit, rather than prison. He had written to Becca and apologised, explained that he wasn't himself and was still suffering from grief after losing her mum.

Becca had done a lot of research about the disorder. Her own feeling was that Frank had always been a hypochondriac, an attention-seeker, and his problem was, as one psychiatrist had suggested, a narcissistic personality disorder. He'd had problems adjusting to life on his own and had a sense of entitlement, thinking his daughters should look after him the way his wife always used to. His sense of reality had become blurred, but he'd known what he was doing. He had basically been using Becca's past against her to engineer a situation where he would, once again, be the centre of attention.

Becca was glad she'd found a support organisation, Fiightback, to help her, and had been shocked to find how prevalent wrong accusations of factitious disorder, or fabricated illnesses, had become. She wasn't the only one who had suffered false accusations and been separated from loved ones, and talking to others in a similar situation had helped her to come to terms with her ordeal and start to move on.

One thing Becca was sure of was that Frank couldn't be trusted to be near her daughter now or ever. She had to make sure there was a distance between them. It was sad, but her relationship with her father was never going to be as close as it had once been. In reality, though, nothing about their relationship had been what she'd thought it was. It had been an illusion, and that was another thing she had to come to terms with.

Connor's hand squeezed hers and brought her back to the breakfast table and the sound of the kookaburras calling in the trees. 'You were miles away,' he said.

'Oh, I was just thinking about everything that's happened.'

'Don't go.' His eyes met hers. 'Not yet.'

She sighed. 'I can't afford to stay.' She watched a flock of parakeets arguing in the trees, then, in a flash of rainbow colours, they were gone. It really was a magical place, so vibrant and full of life. 'I've already spent a big chunk of my capital by having time off and coming here.'

'Ah, about that… Mum's had an idea.'

He had a big grin on his face. 'She wondered if you'd like to help out in the guest house for the rest of the holiday season. She couldn't pay you much, but you could live in and get all your meals. Then we'd have a few more months.' His eyes sparkled. 'What do you think?'

Her heart leapt with excitement. Could he be part of their lives for a little while longer? There was no doubt it was tempting, and Mia loved being here. But could she separate Mia from her father?

Dean's last words to her before she'd left pushed themselves into her thoughts. It was when he'd dropped them at the airport, and she'd been about to head off to departures. He'd grabbed her arm and swung her round to face him. 'I know I've behaved badly,' he'd said. 'I can't tell you how sorry I am. Look, you take all the time you need. I'm happy to chat to Mia on FaceTime. And it's my busiest time of the year – I probably won't get much chance to be with Mia over the next few months, given our events schedule.' He'd registered the surprise on her face. 'I mean it, Becca. You do what's right for you.'

She'd mulled it over on the plane, understanding that although Dean loved his daughter, he loved his business almost as much. By giving Becca permission to stay away longer, he was giving himself permission to dedicate less time to parenting and more time to his work.

Now, she understood that it was a situation that suited them both, and from Mia's perspective, she would get to spend more time with Connor, a man who delighted in playing with her and understood how to parent Mia in a way Dean didn't seem to grasp.

'Do you know what?' she said, stroking the back of his hand with her thumb, a grin spreading across her face. 'I think I might just do that.'

Connor whooped and jumped up from his chair, punching the air like he'd just won a gold medal. He picked her up and swung her round, making her laugh until tears were streaming down her face.

His expression was suddenly serious. 'The way I feel about you, Becca… Even after all these years, nothing's changed for me. I'm still in love with you.'

'And I love you too,' she said, knowing that it was the truth.

Her heart fluttered, like a newly emerged butterfly, spreading its wings. She was free from all those bad decisions, free from a manipulative parent. Free from an ill-conceived loyalty to a marriage based on the wrong emotions. Now she could turn back the clock and start again. For the first time in years, she was in charge of her own destiny, and being here with Connor felt like the perfect new beginning.

A LETTER FROM RONA

I want to say a huge thank you for choosing to read *The Ex-Boyfriend*. If you did enjoy it, and want to keep up-to-date with all my latest releases, just sign up at the following link. Your email address will never be shared and you can unsubscribe at any time.

www.bookouture.com/rona-halsall

The idea for this story came from a news article covering concerns that there was an increasing number of families who had been wrongly accused of inventing or causing illnesses in their children. Fabricated or induced illness (FII) is a form of abuse where parents exaggerate or cause their child's medical condition, and the report identified that families and charities were seeing a wave of false allegations. After reading a few case studies, I was appalled at how easily a genuine concern could be misconstrued, leaving one or both parents separated from their families. It's an unthinkable situation and seemed like the perfect subject matter for a psychological thriller as a way to highlight the issue. There is a support organisation called Fiightback which offers guidance to affected families, and in my story, Becca turns to them for help with the aftermath of the false allegations.

I put my main character through the most horrendous ordeal, which I could relate to so much as a mother myself. Aren't we all anxious about our children's health? Haven't we all overreacted – I know I have! – on at least one occasion? Thankfully, my heroine manages to find a way through, as I wanted to show that even the darkest of times come to an end. That happiness can be found again.

Wrapped around this false allegation is the idea of past love and whether it can be forgotten if the loose ends have not been properly tidied up. I like to think that it's never too late to search out true love, even if it does mean revisiting the past.

I hope you loved *The Ex-Boyfriend*, and if you did, I would be very grateful if you could write a review. I'd love to hear what you think, and it makes such a difference helping new readers to discover one of my books for the first time.

I love hearing from my readers – you can get in touch on my website, Facebook page, through Twitter, Goodreads or Instagram.

Thanks,
Rona

RonaHalsallAuthor

@RonaHalsallAuth

www.ronahalsall.com

@ronahalsall

18051355.Rona_Halsall

ACKNOWLEDGEMENTS

Firstly, I would like to thank you, the reader, for choosing my book – I hope you managed to get lost in the pages for a while and enjoyed the journey!

Every book is a team effort, and Team Rona includes some pretty amazing and talented people.

Thanks to my agent, Hayley Steed of Madeleine Milburn Literary, TV and Film Agency, whose endless enthusiasm and wise words make her a joy to work with.

I'd like to thank everyone at Bookouture – so many people working behind the scenes making sure everything is just right. Specifically, I would like to thank my brilliant editor, Isobel Akenhead, who gently prods my stories into shape with tact and kindness and is awesome to work with. I would also like to thank Alex Holmes for sourcing the best copy editors and proofreaders – DeAndra Lupu and Jon Appleton, I'm talking about you! – to make sure the details are right. Thanks also to Kim Nash and Noelle Holten – the Batman and Robin of PR – who are incredibly speedy at sorting out problems and so effective when it comes to making sure the word is spread far and wide about my books. A mention too for Alex Crow and the marketing team for their wizardry.

It's always tricky to know if your story is working, so a massive thanks to my little team of beta readers for your early feedback and general cheerleading activities: Kerry-Ann Mitchell, Gill Mitchell, Sandra Henderson, Wendy Clarke, Chloe Jordan, Mark Fearn and Dee Groocock – you guys are the best!

For all the encouragement, thanks to my friends and family, especially my children – John, Amy and Oscar – who manage to never look bored when I'm prattling on about my books.

Finally, thanks to my husband David, for being there, believing in me and sharing this amazing rollercoaster ride.

Made in the USA
Monee, IL
16 March 2021

62985956R00163